Grandchildren of the Ghetto

Grandchildren of the Ghetto

Israel Zangwill

MINT EDITIONS

Grandchildren of the Ghetto was first published in 1892.

This edition published by Mint Editions 2021.

ISBN 9781513216461 | E-ISBN 9781513214467

Published by Mint Editions®

 MINT
EDITIONS

minteditionbooks.com

Publishing Director: Jennifer Newens
Design & Production: Rachel Lopez Metzger
Project Manager: Micaela Clark
Typesetting: Westchester Publishing Services

Contents

I

The Christmas Dinner

Daintily embroidered napery, beautiful porcelain, Queen Anne silver, exotic flowers, glittering glass, soft rosy light, creamy expanses of shirt-front, elegant low-necked dresses—all the conventional accompaniments of Occidental gastronomy.

It was not a large party. Mrs. Henry Goldsmith professed to collect guests on artistic principles—as she did bric-à-brac—and with an eye to general conversation. The elements of the social salad were sufficiently incongruous tonight, yet all the ingredients were Jewish.

For the history of the Grandchildren of the Ghetto, which is mainly a history of the middle-classes, is mainly a history of isolation. "The Upper Ten" is a literal phrase in Judah, whose aristocracy just about suffices for a synagogue quorum. Great majestic luminaries, each with its satellites, they swim serenely in the golden heavens. And the middle-classes look up in worship and the lower-classes in supplication. "The Upper Ten" have no spirit of exclusiveness; they are willing to entertain royalty, rank and the arts with a catholic hospitality that is only Eastern in its magnificence, while some of them only remain Jews for fear of being considered snobs by society. But the middle-class Jew has been more jealous of his caste, and for caste reasons. To exchange hospitalities with the Christian when you cannot eat his dinners were to get the worse of the bargain; to invite his sons to your house when they cannot marry your daughters were to solicit awkward complications. In business, in civic affairs, in politics, the Jew has mixed freely with his fellow-citizens, but indiscriminate social relations only become possible through a religious decadence, which they in turn accelerate. A Christian in a company of middle-class Jews is like a lion in a den of Daniels. They show him deference and their prophetic side.

Mrs. Henry Goldsmith was of the upper middle-classes, and her husband was the financial representative of the Kensington Synagogue at the United Council, but her swan-like neck was still bowed beneath the yoke of North London, not to say provincial, Judaism. So tonight there were none of those external indications of Christmas which are so frequent at "good" Jewish houses; no plum-pudding, snapdragon, mistletoe, not even a Christmas tree. For Mrs. Henry Goldsmith did not countenance these coquettings with Christianity. She would have told you that the incidence of her dinner on Christmas Eve was merely an accident, though a lucky accident, in so far as Christmas found Jews perforce at leisure for social gatherings. What she was celebrating was the feast of Chanukah—of the re-dedication of the Temple after the pollutions of Antiochus Epiphanes—and the memory of the national hero, Judas Maccabaeus. Christmas crackers would have been incompatible with the Chanukah candles which the housekeeper, Mary O'Reilly, forced her master to light, and would have shocked that devout old dame. For Mary O'Reilly, as good a soul as she was a Catholic, had lived all her life with Jews, assisting while yet a girl in the kitchen of Henry Goldsmith's father, who was a pattern of ancient piety and a prop of the Great Synagogue. When the father died, Mary, with all the other family belongings, passed into the hands of the son, who came up to London from a provincial town, and with a grateful recollection of her motherliness domiciled her in his own establishment. Mary knew all the ritual laws and ceremonies far better than her new mistress, who although a native of the provincial town in which Mr. Henry Goldsmith had established a thriving business, had received her education at a Brussels boarding-school. Mary knew exactly how long to keep the meat in salt and the heinousness of frying steaks in butter. She knew that the fire must not be poked on the Sabbath, nor the gas lit or extinguished, and that her master must not smoke till three stars appeared in the sky. She knew when the family must fast, and when and how it must feast. She knew all the Hebrew and jargon expressions which her employers studiously boycotted, and she was the only member of the household who used them habitually in her intercourse with the other members. Too late the Henry Goldsmiths awoke to the consciousness of her tyranny which did not permit them to be irreligious even in private. In the fierce light which beats upon a provincial town with only one synagogue, they had been compelled to conform outwardly with many galling restrictions, and they had sub-consciously looked forward to emancipation in the mighty metropolis. But Mary had such implicit faith in their piety, and was so zealous in the practice of her own faith, that they had not the courage to confess that they scarcely cared a pin about a good deal of that for which she was so solicitous. They hesitated to admit that they did not respect their religion (or what she thought was their religion) as much as she did hers. It would have equally lowered them in her eyes to admit that their religion was not so good as hers, besides being disrespectful to the cherished memory of her ancient master. At first they had deferred to Mary's Jewish prejudices out of good nature and carelessness, but everyday strengthened her hold upon them; every act of obedience to the ritual law was a tacit acknowledgment of its sanctity, which made it more and more difficult to disavow its obligation. The dread of shocking Mary came to dominate their lives, and the fashionable house near Kensington Gardens was still a veritable centre of true Jewish orthodoxy, with little or nothing to make old Aaron Goldsmith turn in his grave. It is probable, though, that Mrs. Henry Goldsmith would have kept a *kosher* table, even if Mary had never been born. Many of their acquaintances and relatives were of an orthodox turn. A *kosher* dinner could be eaten even by the heterodox; whereas a *tripha* dinner choked off the orthodox. Thus it came about that even the Rabbinate might safely stoke its spiritual fires at Mrs. Henry Goldsmith's.

Hence, too, the prevalent craving for a certain author's blood could not be gratified at Mrs. Henry Goldsmith's Chanukah dinner. Besides, nobody knew where to lay hands upon Edward Armitage, the author in question, whose opprobrious production, *Mordecai Josephs*, had scandalized West End Judaism.

"Why didn't he describe our circles?" asked the hostess, an angry fire in her beautiful eyes. "It would have, at least, corrected the picture. As it is, the public will fancy that we are all daubed with the same brush: that we have no thought in life beyond dress, money, and solo whist."

"He probably painted the life he knew," said Sidney Graham, in defence.

"Then I am sorry for him," retorted Mrs. Goldsmith. "It's a great pity he had such detestable acquaintances. Of course, he has cut himself off from the possibility of any better now."

The wavering flush on her lovely face darkened with disinterested indignation, and her beautiful bosom heaved with judicial grief.

"I should hope so," put in Miss Cissy Levine, sharply. She was a pale, bent woman, with spectacles, who believed in the mission of Israel, and wrote domestic novels to prove that she had no sense of humor. "No one has a right to foul his own nest. Are there not plenty of subjects for the Jew's pen without his attacking his own people? The calumniator of his race should be ostracized from decent society."

"As according to him there is none," laughed Graham, "I cannot see where the punishment comes in."

"Oh, he may say so in that book," said Mrs. Montagu Samuels, an amiable, loose-thinking lady of florid complexion, who dabbled exasperatingly in her husband's philanthropic concerns from the vain idea that the wife of a committee-man is a committee-woman. "But he knows better."

"Yes, indeed," said Mr. Montagu Samuels. "The rascal has only written this to make money. He knows it's all exaggeration and distortion; but anything spicy pays now-a-days."

"As a West Indian merchant he ought to know," murmured Sidney Graham to his charming cousin, Adelaide Leon. The girl's soft eyes twinkled, as she surveyed the serious little city magnate with his placid spouse. Montagu Samuels was narrow-minded and narrow-chested, and managed to be pompous on a meagre allowance of body. He was earnest and charitable (except in religious wrangles, when he was earnest and uncharitable), and knew himself a pillar of the community, an exemplar to the drones and sluggards who shirked their share of public burdens and were callous to the dazzlement of communal honors.

"Of course it was written for money, Monty," his brother, Percy Saville, the stockbroker, reminded him. "What else do authors write for? It's the way they earn their living."

Strangers found difficulty in understanding the fraternal relation of Percy Saville and Montagu Samuels; and did not readily grasp that Percy Saville was an Anglican version of Pizer Samuels, more in tune with the handsome well-dressed personality it denoted. Montagu had stuck loyally to his colors, but Pizer had drooped under the burden of carrying his patronymic through the theatrical and artistic circles he favored after business hours. Of such is the brotherhood of Israel.

"The whole book's written with gall," went on Percy Saville, emphatically. "I suppose the man couldn't get into good Jewish houses, and he's revenged himself by slandering them."

"Then he ought to have got into good Jewish houses," said Sidney. "The man has talent, nobody can deny that, and if he couldn't get into good Jewish society because he didn't have money enough, isn't that proof enough his picture is true?"

"I don't deny that there are people among us who make money the one open sesame to their houses," said Mrs. Henry Goldsmith, magnanimously.

"Deny it, indeed? Money is the open sesame to everything," rejoined Sidney Graham, delightedly scenting an opening for a screed. He liked to talk bomb-shells, and did not often get pillars of the community to shatter. "Money manages the schools and the charities, and the synagogues, and indirectly controls the press. A small body of persons—always the same—sits on all councils, on all boards! Why? Because they pay the piper."

"Well, sir, and is not that a good reason?" asked Montagu Samuels. "The community is to be congratulated on having a few public-spirited men left in days when there are wealthy German Jews in our midst who not only disavow Judaism, but refuse to support its institutions. But, Mr. Graham, I would join issue with you. The men you allude to are elected not because they are rich, but because they are good men of business and most of the work to be done is financial."

"Exactly," said Sidney Graham, in sinister agreement. "I have always maintained that the United Synagogue could be run as a joint-stock company for the sake of a dividend, and that there wouldn't be an atom of difference in the discussions if the councillors were directors. I do believe the pillars of the community figure the Millenium as a time when every Jew shall have enough to eat, a place to worship in, and a place to be buried in. Their State Church is simply a financial system, to which the doctrines of Judaism happen to be tacked on. How many of the councillors believe in their Established Religion? Why, the very beadles of their synagogues are prone to surreptitious shrimps and unobtrusive oysters! Then take that institution for supplying *kosher* meat. I am sure there are lots of its Committee who never inquire into the necrologies of their own chops and steaks, and who regard kitchen Judaism as obsolete. But, all the same, they look after the finances with almost fanatical zeal. Finance fascinates them. Long after Judaism has ceased to exist, excellent gentlemen will be found regulating its finances."

There was that smile on the faces of the graver members of the party which arises from reluctance to take a dangerous speaker seriously.

Sidney Graham was one of those favorites of society who are allowed Touchstone's license. He had just as little wish to reform, and just as much wish to abuse society as society has to be reformed and abused. He was a dark, bright-eyed young artist with a silky moustache. He had lived much in Paris, where he studied impressionism and perfected his natural talent for *causerie* and his inborn preference for the hedonistic view of life. Fortunately he had plenty of money, for he was a cousin of Raphael Leon on the mother's side, and the remotest twigs of the Leon genealogical tree bear apples of gold. His real name was Abrahams, which is a shade too Semitic. Sidney was the black sheep of the family; good-natured to the core and artistic to the finger-tips, he was an avowed infidel in a world where avowal is the unpardonable sin. He did not even pretend to fast on the Day of Atonement. Still Sidney Graham was a good deal talked of in artistic circles, his name was often in the newspapers, and so more orthodox people than Mrs. Henry Goldsmith were not averse from having him at their table, though they would have shrunk from being seen at his. Even cousin Addie, who had a charming religious cast of mind, liked to be with him, though she ascribed this to family piety. For there is a wonderful solidarity about many Jewish families, the richer members of which assemble loyally at one another's births, marriages, funerals, and card-parties, often to the entire exclusion of outsiders. An ordinary well-regulated family (so prolific is the stream of life), will include in its bosom ample elements for every occasion.

"Really, Mr. Graham, I think you are wrong about the *kosher* meat," said Mr. Henry Goldsmith. "Our statistics show no falling-off in the number of bullocks killed, while there is a rise of two percent, in the sheep slaughtered. No, Judaism is in a far more healthy condition than pessimists imagine. So far from sacrificing our ancient faith we are learning to see how tuberculosis lurks in the lungs of unexamined carcasses and is communicated to the consumer. As for the members of the *Shechitah* Board not eating *kosher*, look at me."

The only person who looked at the host was the hostess. Her look was one of approval. It could not be of aesthetic approval, like the look Percy Saville devoted to herself, for her husband was a cadaverous little man with prominent ears and teeth.

"And if Mr. Graham should ever join us on the Council of the United Synagogue," added Montagu Samuels, addressing the table generally, "he will discover that there is no communal problem with which we do not loyally grapple."

"No, thank you," said Sidney, with a shudder. "When I visit Raphael, I sometimes pick up a Jewish paper and amuse myself by reading the debates of your public bodies. I understand most of your verbiage is edited away." He looked Montagu Samuels full in the face with audacious *naïveté*. "But there is enough left to show that our monotonous group of public men consists of narrow-minded mediocrities. The chief public work they appear to do outside finance is when public exams, fall on Sabbaths or holidays, getting special dates for Jewish candidates to whom these examinations are the avenues to atheism. They never see the joke. How can they? Why, they take even themselves seriously."

"Oh, come!" said Miss Cissy Levine indignantly. "You often see 'laughter' in the reports."

"That must mean the speaker was laughing," explained Sidney, "for you never see anything to make the audience laugh. I appeal to Mr. Montagu Samuels."

"It is useless discussing a subject with a man who admittedly speaks without knowledge," replied that gentleman with dignity.

"Well, how do you expect me to get the knowledge?" grumbled Sidney. "You exclude the public from your gatherings. I suppose to prevent their rubbing shoulders with the swells, the privilege of being snubbed by whom is the reward of public service. Wonderfully practical idea that—to utilize snobbery as a communal force. The United Synagogue is founded on it. Your community coheres through it."

"There you are scarcely fair," said the hostess with a charming smile of reproof. "Of course there are snobs amongst us, but is it not the same in all sects?"

"Emphatically not," said Sidney. "If one of our swells sticks to a shred of Judaism, people seem to think the God of Judah should be thankful, and if he goes to synagogue once or twice a year, it is regarded as a particular condescension to the Creator."

"The mental attitude you caricature is not so snobbish as it seems," said Raphael Leon, breaking into the conversation for the first time. "The temptations to the wealthy and the honored to desert their struggling brethren are manifold, and sad experience has made our race accustomed to the loss of its brightest sons."

"Thanks for the compliment, fair coz," said Sidney, not without a complacent cynical pleasure in the knowledge that Raphael spoke truly, that he owed his own immunity from the obligations of the faith to his artistic success, and that the outside world was disposed to accord him a larger charter of morality on the same grounds. "But if you can only deny nasty facts by accounting for them, I dare say Mr. Armitage's book will afford you ample opportunities for explanation. Or have Jews the brazenness to assert it is all invention?"

"No, no one would do that," said Percy Saville, who had just done it. "Certainly there is a good deal of truth in the sketch of the ostentatious, over-dressed Johnsons who, as everybody knows, are meant for the Jonases."

"Oh, yes," said Mrs. Henry Goldsmith. "And it is quite evident that the stockbroker who drops half his h's and all his poor acquaintances and believes in one Lord, is no other than Joel Friedman."

"And the house where people drive up in broughams for supper and solo whist after the theatre is the Davises' in Maida Vale," said Miss Cissy Levine.

"Yes, the book's true enough," began Mrs. Montagu Samuels. She stopped suddenly, catching her husband's eye, and the color heightened on her florid cheek. "What I say is," she concluded awkwardly, "he ought to have come among us, and shown the world a picture of the cultured Jews."

"Quite so, quite so," said the hostess. Then turning to the tall thoughtful-looking young man who had hitherto contributed but one sentence to the conversation, she said, half in sly malice, half to draw him out: "Now you, Mr. Leon, whose culture is certified by our leading university, what do you think of this latest portrait of the Jew?"

"I don't know, I haven't read it!" replied Raphael apologetically.

"No more have I," murmured the table generally.

"I wouldn't touch it with a pitchfork," said Miss Cissy Levine.

"I think it's a shame they circulate it at the libraries," said Mrs. Montagu Samuels. "I just glanced over it at Mrs. Hugh Marston's house. It's vile. There are actually jargon words in it. Such vulgarity!"

"Shameful!" murmured Percy Saville; "Mr. Lazarus was telling me about it. It's plain treachery and disloyalty, this putting of weapons into the hands of our enemies. Of course we have our faults, but we should be told of them privately or from the pulpit."

"That would be just as efficacious," said Sidney admiringly.

"More efficacious," said Percy Saville, unsuspiciously. "A preacher speaks with authority, but this penny-a-liner—"

"With truth?" queried Sidney.

Saville stopped, disgusted, and the hostess answered Sidney half-coaxingly.

"Oh, I am sure you can't think that. The book is so one-sided. Not a word about our generosity, our hospitality, our domesticity, the thousand-and-one good traits all the world allows us."

"Of course not; since all the world allows them, it was unnecessary," said Sidney.

"I wonder the Chief Rabbi doesn't stop it," said Mrs. Montagu Samuels.

"My dear, how can he?" inquired her husband. "He has no control over the publishing trade."

"He ought to talk to the man," persisted Mrs. Samuels.

"But we don't even know who he is," said Percy Saville, "probably Edward Armitage is only a *nom-de-plume*. You'd be surprised to learn the real names of some of the literary celebrities I meet about."

"Oh, if he's a Jew you may be sure it isn't his real name," laughed Sidney. It was characteristic of him that he never spared a shot even when himself hurt by the kick of the gun. Percy colored slightly, unmollified by being in the same boat with the satirist.

"I have never seen the name in the subscription lists," said the hostess with ready tact.

"There is an Armitage who subscribes two guineas a year to the Board of Guardians," said Mrs. Montagu Samuels. "But his Christian name is George."

"'Christian' name is distinctly good for 'George,'" murmured Sidney.

"There was an Armitage who sent a cheque to the Russian Fund," said Mr. Henry Goldsmith, "but that can't be an author—it was quite a large cheque!"

"I am sure I have seen Armitage among the Births, Marriages and Deaths," said Miss Cissy Levine.

"How well-read they all are in the national literature," Sidney murmured to Addie.

Indeed the sectarian advertisements served to knit the race together, counteracting the unravelling induced by the fashionable dispersion of Israel and waxing the more important as the other links—the old traditional jokes, by-words, ceremonies, card-games, prejudices and tunes, which are more important than laws and more cementatory than ideals—were disappearing before the over-zealousness of a *parvenu* refinement that had not yet attained to self-confidence. The Anglo-Saxon stolidity of the West-End Synagogue service, on week days entirely given over to paid praying-men, was a typical expression of the universal tendency to exchange the picturesque primitiveness of the Orient for the sobrieties of fashionable civilization. When Jeshurun waxed fat he did not always kick, but he yearned to approximate as much as possible to John Bull without merging in him; to sink himself and yet not be absorbed, not to be and yet to be. The attempt to realize the asymptote in human mathematics was not quite successful, too near an approach to John Bull generally assimilating Jeshurun away. For such is the nature of Jeshurun. Enfranchise him, give him his own way and you make a new man of him; persecute him and he is himself again.

"But if nobody has read the man's book," Raphael Leon ventured to interrupt at last, "is it quite fair to assume his book isn't fit to read?"

The shy dark little girl he had taken down to dinner darted an appreciative glance at her neighbor. It was in accordance with Raphael's usual anxiety to give the devil his due, that he should be unwilling to condemn even the writer of an anti-Semitic novel unheard. But then it was an open secret in the family that Raphael was mad. They did their best to hush it up, but among themselves they pitied him behind his back. Even Sidney considered his cousin Raphael pushed a dubious virtue too far in treating people's very prejudices with the deference due to earnest reasoned opinions.

"But we know enough of the book to know we are badly treated," protested the hostess.

"We have always been badly treated in literature," said Raphael. "We are made either angels or devils. On the one hand, Lessing and George Eliot, on the other, the stock dramatist and novelist with their low-comedy villain."

"Oh," said Mrs. Goldsmith, doubtfully, for she could not quite think Raphael had become infected by his cousin's propensity for paradox. "Do you think George Eliot and Lessing didn't understand the Jewish character?"

"They are the only writers who have ever understood it," affirmed Miss Cissy Levine, emphatically.

A little scornful smile played for a second about the mouth of the dark little girl.

"Stop a moment," said Sidney. "I've been so busy doing justice to this delicious asparagus, that I have allowed Raphael to imagine nobody here has read *Mordecai Josephs*. I have, and I say there is more actuality in it than in *Daniel Deronda* and *Nathan der Weise* put together. It is a crude production, all the same; the writer's artistic gift seems handicapped by a dead-weight of moral platitudes and highfalutin, and even mysticism. He not only presents his characters but moralizes over them—actually cares whether they are good or bad, and has yearnings after the indefinable—it is all very young. Instead of being satisfied that Judaea gives him characters that are interesting, he actually laments their lack of culture. Still, what he has done is good enough to make one hope his artistic instinct will shake off his moral."

"Oh, Sidney, what are you saying?" murmured Addie.

"It's all right, little girl. You don't understand Greek."

"It's not Greek," put in Raphael. "In Greek art, beauty of soul and beauty of form are one. It's French you are talking, though the ignorant *ateliers* where you picked it up flatter themselves it's Greek."

"It's Greek to Addie, anyhow," laughed Sidney. "But that's what makes the anti-Semitic chapters so unsatisfactory."

"We all felt their unsatisfactoriness, if we could not analyze it so cleverly," said the hostess.

"We all felt it," said Mrs. Montagu Samuels.

"Yes, that's it," said Sidney, blandly. "I could have forgiven the rose-color of the picture if it had been more artistically painted."

"Rose-color!" gasped Mrs. Henry Goldsmith, "rose-color, indeed!" Not even Sidney's authority could persuade the table into that.

Poor rich Jews! The upper middle-classes had every excuse for being angry. They knew they were excellent persons, well-educated and well-travelled, interested in charities (both Jewish and Christian), people's concerts, district-visiting, new novels, magazines, reading-circles, operas, symphonies, politics, volunteer regiments, Show-Sunday and Corporation banquets; that they had sons at Rugby and Oxford, and daughters who played and painted and sang, and homes that were bright oases of optimism in a jaded society; that they were good Liberals and Tories, supplementing their duties as Englishmen with a solicitude for the best interests of Judaism; that they left no stone unturned to emancipate themselves from the secular thraldom of prejudice; and they felt it very hard that a little vulgar section should always be chosen by their own novelists, and their efforts to raise the tone of Jewish society passed by.

Sidney, whose conversation always had the air of aloofness from the race, so that his own foibles often came under the lash of his sarcasm, proceeded to justify his assertion of the rose-color picture in *Mordecai Josephs*. He denied that modern English Jews had any religion whatever; claiming that their faith consisted of forms that had to be kept up in public, but which they were too shrewd and cute to believe in or to practise in private, though everyone might believe everyone else did; that they looked upon due payment of their synagogue bills as discharging all their obligations to Heaven; that the preachers secretly despised the old formulas, and that the Rabbinate declared its intention of dying for Judaism only as a way of living by it; that the body politic was dead and rotten with hypocrisy, though the augurs said it was alive and well. He admitted that the same was true of Christianity. Raphael reminded him that a number of Jews had drifted quite openly from the traditional teaching, that thousands of well-ordered households found inspiration and spiritual satisfaction in every form of it, and that hypocrisy was too crude a word for the complex motives of those who obeyed it without inner conviction.

"For instance," said he, "a gentleman said to me the other day—I was much touched by the expression—'I believe with my father's heart.'"

"It is a good epigram," said Sidney, impressed. "But what is to be said of a rich community which recruits its clergy from the lower classes? The method of election by competitive performance, common as it is among poor Dissenters, emphasizes the subjection of the shepherd to his flock. You catch your ministers young, when they are saturated with suppressed scepticism, and bribe them with small salaries that seem affluence to the sons of poor immigrants. That the ministry is not an honorable profession may be seen from the anxiety of the minister to raise his children in the social scale by bringing them up to some other line of business."

"That is true," said Raphael, gravely. "Our wealthy families must be induced to devote a son each to the Synagogue."

"I wish they would," said Sidney. "At present, every second man is a lawyer. We ought to have more officers and doctors, too. I like those old Jews who smote the Philistines hip and thigh; it is not good for a race to run all to brain: I suppose, though, we had to develop cunning to survive at all. There was an enlightened minister whose Friday evenings I used to go to when a youth—delightful talk we had there, too; you know whom I mean. Well, one of his sons is a solicitor, and the other a stockbroker. The rich men he preached to helped to place his sons. He was a charming man, but imagine him preaching to them the truths in *Mordecai Josephs*, as Mr. Saville suggested."

"*Our* minister lets us have it hot enough, though," said Mr. Henry Goldsmith with a guffaw.

His wife hastened to obliterate the unrefined expression.

"Mr. Strelitski is a wonderfully eloquent young man, so quiet and reserved in society, but like an ancient prophet in the pulpit."

"Yes, we were very lucky to get him," said Mr. Henry Goldsmith.

The little dark girl shuddered.

ISRAEL ZANGWILL

"What is the matter?" asked Raphael softly.

"I don't know. I don't like the Rev. Joseph Strelitski. He is eloquent, but his dogmatism irritates me. I don't believe he is sincere. He doesn't like me, either."

"Oh, you're both wrong," he said in concern.

"Strelitski is a draw, I admit," said Mr. Montagu Samuels, who was the President of a rival synagogue. "But Rosenbaum is a good pull-down on the other side, eh?"

Mr. Henry Goldsmith groaned. The second minister of the Kensington synagogue was the scandal of the community. He wasn't expected to preach, and he didn't practise.

"I've heard of that man," said Sidney laughing. "He's a bit of a gambler and a spendthrift, isn't he? Why do you keep him on?"

"He has a fine voice, you see," said Mr. Goldsmith. "That makes a Rosenbaum faction at once. Then he has a wife and family. That makes another."

"Strelitski isn't married, is he?" asked Sidney.

"No," said Mr. Goldsmith, "not yet. The congregation expects him to, though. I don't care to give him the hint myself; he is a little queer sometimes."

"He owes it to his position," said Miss Cissy Levine.

"That is what we think," said Mrs. Henry Goldsmith, with the majestic manner that suited her opulent beauty.

"I wish we had him in our synagogue," said Raphael. "Michaels is a well-meaning worthy man, but he is dreadfully dull."

"Poor Raphael!" said Sidney. "Why did you abolish the old style of minister who had to slaughter the sheep? Now the minister reserves all his powers of destruction for his own flock."

"I have given him endless hints to preach only once a month," said Mr. Montagu Samuels dolefully. "But every Saturday our hearts sink as we see him walk to the pulpit."

"You see, Addie, how a sense of duty makes a man criminal," said Sidney. "Isn't Michaels the minister who defends orthodoxy in a way that makes the orthodox rage over his unconscious heresies, while the heterodox enjoy themselves by looking out for his historical and grammatical blunders!"

"Poor man, he works hard," said Raphael, gently. "Let him be."

Over the dessert the conversation turned by way of the Rev. Strelitski's marriage, to the growing willingness of the younger generation to marry out of Judaism. The table discerned in inter-marriage the beginning of the end.

"But why postpone the inevitable?" asked Sidney calmly. "What is this mania for keeping up an effete *ism*? Are we to cripple our lives for the sake of a word? It's all romantic fudge, the idea of perpetual isolation. You get into little cliques and mistaken narrow-mindedness for fidelity to an ideal. I can live for months and forget there are such beings as Jews in the world. I have floated down the Nile in a *dahabiya* while you were beating your breasts in the Synagogue, and the palm-trees and pelicans knew nothing of your sacrosanct chronological crisis, your annual epidemic of remorse."

The table thrilled with horror, without, however, quite believing in the speaker's wickedness. Addie looked troubled.

"A man and wife of different religions can never know true happiness," said the hostess.

"Granted," retorted Sidney. "But why shouldn't Jews without Judaism marry Christians without Christianity? Must a Jew needs have a Jewess to help him break the Law?"

"Inter-marriage must not be tolerated," said Raphael. "It would hurt us less if we had a country. Lacking that, we must preserve our human boundaries."

"You have good phrases sometimes," admitted Sidney. "But why must we preserve any boundaries? Why must we exist at all as a separate people?"

"To fulfil the mission of Israel," said Mr. Montagu Samuels solemnly.

"Ah, what is that? That is one of the things nobody ever seems able to tell me."

"We are God's witnesses," said Mrs. Henry Goldsmith, snipping off for herself a little bunch of hot-house grapes.

"False witnesses, mostly then," said Sidney. "A Christian friend of mine, an artist, fell in love with a girl and courted her regularly at her house for four years. Then he proposed; she told him to ask her father, and he then learned for the first time that the family were Jewish, and his suit could not therefore be entertained. Could a satirist have invented anything funnier? Whatever it was Jews have to bear witness to, these people had been bearing witness to so effectually that a daily visitor never heard a word of the evidence during four years. And this family is not an exception; it is a type. Abroad the English Jew keeps his Judaism in the background, at home in the back kitchen. When he travels, his Judaism is not packed up among his *impedimenta*. He never obtrudes his creed, and even his Jewish newspaper is sent to him in a wrapper labelled something else. How's that for witnesses? Mind you, I'm not blaming the men, being one of 'em. They may be the best fellows going, honorable, high-minded, generous—why expect them to be martyrs more than other Englishmen? Isn't life hard enough without inventing a new hardship? I declare there's no narrower creature in the world than your idealist; he sets up a moral standard which suits his own line of business, and rails at men of the world for not conforming to it. God's witnesses, indeed! I say nothing of those who are rather the Devil's witnesses, but think of the host of Jews like myself who, whether they marry Christians or not, simply drop out, and whose absence of all religion escapes notice in the medley of creeds. We no more give evidence than those old Spanish Jews—Marannos, they were called, weren't they?—who wore the Christian mask for generations. Practically, many of us are Marannos still; I don't mean the Jews who are on the stage and the press and all that, but the Jews who have gone on believing. One Day of Atonement I amused myself by noting the pretexts on the shutters of shops that were closed in the Strand. 'Our annual holiday,' 'Stock-taking day,' 'Our annual bean-feast.' 'Closed for repairs.'"

"Well, it's something if they keep the Fast at all," said Mr. Henry Goldsmith. "It shows spirituality is not dead in them."

"Spirituality!" sneered Sidney. "Sheer superstition, rather. A dread of thunderbolts. Besides, fasting is a sensuous *attraction*. But for the fasting, the Day of Atonement would have long since died out for these men. 'Our annual bean-feast'! There's witnesses for you."

"We cannot help if we have false witnesses among us," said Raphael Leon quietly. "Our mission is to spread the truth of the Torah till the earth is filled with the knowledge of the Lord as the waters cover the sea."

"But we don't spread it."

"We do. Christianity and Mohammedanism are offshoots of Judaism; through them we have won the world from Paganism and taught it that God is one with the moral law."

"Then we are somewhat in the position of an ancient school-master lagging superfluous in the school-room where his whilom pupils are teaching."

"By no means. Rather of one who stays on to protest against the false additions of his whilom pupils."

"But we don't protest."

"Our mere existence since the Dispersion is a protest," urged Raphael. "When the stress of persecution lightens, we may protest more consciously. We cannot have been preserved in vain through so many centuries of horrors, through the invasions of the Goths and Huns, through the Crusades, through the Holy Roman Empire, through the times of Torquemada. It is not for nothing that a handful of Jews loom so large in the history of the world that their past is bound up with every noble human effort, every high ideal, every development of science, literature and art. The ancient faith that has united us so long must not be lost just as it is on the very eve of surviving the faiths that sprang from it, even as it has survived Egypt, Assyria, Rome, Greece and the Moors. If any of us fancy we have lost it, let us keep together still. Who knows but that it will be born again in us if we are only patient? Race affinity is a potent force; why be in a hurry to dissipate it? The Marannos you speak of were but maimed heroes, yet one day the olden flame burst through the layers of three generations of Christian profession and inter-marriage, and a brilliant company of illustrious Spaniards threw up their positions and sailed away in voluntary exile to serve the God of Israel. We shall yet see a spiritual revival even among our brilliant English Jews who have hid their face from their own flesh."

The dark little girl looked up into his face with ill-suppressed wonder.

"Have you done preaching at me, Raphael?" inquired Sidney. "If so, pass me a banana."

Raphael smiled sadly and obeyed.

"I'm afraid if I see much of Raphael I shall be converted to Judaism," said Sidney, peeling the banana. "I had better take a hansom to the Riviera at once. I intended to spend Christmas there; I never dreamed I should be talking theology in London."

"Oh, I think Christmas in London is best," said the hostess unguardedly.

"Oh, I don't know. Give me Brighton," said the host.

"Well, yes, I suppose Brighton *is* pleasanter," said Mr. Montagu Samuels.

"Oh, but so many Jews go there," said Percy Saville.

"Yes, that *is* the drawback," said Mrs. Henry Goldsmith. "Do you know, some years ago I discovered a delightful village in Devonshire, and took the household there in the summer. The very next year when I went down I found no less than two Jewish families temporarily located there. Of course, I have never gone there since."

"Yes, it's wonderful how Jews scent out all the nicest places," agreed Mrs. Montagu Samuels. "Five years ago you could escape them by not going to Ramsgate; now even the Highlands are getting impossible."

Thereupon the hostess rose and the ladies retired to the drawing-room, leaving the gentlemen to discuss coffee, cigars and the paradoxes of Sidney, who, tired of religion, looked to dumb show plays for the salvation of dramatic literature.

There was a little milk-jug on the coffee-tray, it represented a victory over Mary O'Reilly. The late Aaron Goldsmith never took milk till six hours after meat, and it was with some trepidation that the present Mr. Goldsmith ordered it to be sent up one evening after dinner. He took an early opportunity of explaining apologetically to Mary that some of his guests were not so pious as himself, and hospitality demanded the concession.

Mr. Henry Goldsmith did not like his coffee black. His dinner-table was hardly ever without a guest.

II

RAPHAEL LEON

When the gentlemen joined the ladies, Raphael instinctively returned to his companion of the dinner-table. She had been singularly silent during the meal, but her manner had attracted him. Over his black coffee and cigarette it struck him that she might have been unwell, and that he had been insufficiently attentive to the little duties of the table, and he hastened to ask if she had a headache.

"No, no," she said, with a grateful smile. "At least not more than usual." Her smile was full of pensive sweetness, which made her face beautiful. It was a face that would have been almost plain but for the soul behind. It was dark, with great earnest eyes. The profile was disappointing, the curves were not perfect, and there was a reminder of Polish origin in the lower jaw and the cheek-bone. Seen from the front, the face fascinated again, in the Eastern glow of its coloring, in the flash of the white teeth, in the depths of the brooding eyes, in the strength of the features that yet softened to womanliest tenderness and charm when flooded by the sunshine of a smile. The figure was *petite* and graceful, set off by a simple tight-fitting, high-necked dress of ivory silk draped with lace, with a spray of Neapolitan violets at the throat. They sat in a niche of the spacious and artistically furnished drawing-room, in the soft light of the candles, talking quietly while Addie played Chopin.

Mrs. Henry Goldsmith's aesthetic instincts had had full play in the elaborate carelessness of the *ensemble*, and the result was a triumph, a medley of Persian luxury and Parisian grace, a dream of somniferous couches and arm-chairs, rich tapestry, vases, fans, engravings, books, bronzes, tiles, plaques and flowers. Mr. Henry Goldsmith was himself a connoisseur in the arts, his own and his father's fortunes having been built up in the curio and antique business, though to old Aaron Goldsmith appreciation had meant strictly pricing, despite his genius for detecting false Correggios and sham Louis Quatorze cabinets.

"Do you suffer from headaches?" inquired Raphael solicitously.

"A little. The doctor says I studied too much and worked too hard when a little girl. Such is the punishment of perseverance. Life isn't like the copy-books."

"Oh, but I wonder your parents let you over-exert yourself."

A melancholy smile played about the mobile lips. "I brought myself up," she said. "You look puzzled—Oh, I know! Confess you think I'm Miss Goldsmith!"

"Why—are—you—not?" he stammered.

"No, my name is Ansell, Esther Ansell."

"Pardon me. I am so bad at remembering names in introductions. But I've just come back from Oxford and it's the first time I've been to this house, and seeing you here without a cavalier when we arrived, I thought you lived here."

"You thought rightly, I do live here." She laughed gently at his changing expression.

"I wonder Sidney never mentioned you to me," he said.

"Do you mean Mr. Graham?" she said with a slight blush.

"Yes, I know he visits here."

"Oh, he is an artist. He has eyes only for the beautiful." She spoke quickly, a little embarrassed.

"You wrong him; his interests are wider than that."

"Do you know I am so glad you didn't pay me the obvious compliment?" she said, recovering herself. "It looked as if I were fishing for it. I'm so stupid."

He looked at her blankly.

"*I'm* stupid," he said, "for I don't know what compliment I missed paying."

"If you regret it I shall not think so well of you," she said. "You know I've heard all about your brilliant success at Oxford."

"They put all those petty little things in the Jewish papers, don't they?"

"I read it in the *Times*," retorted Esther. "You took a double first and the prize for poetry and a heap of other things, but I noticed the prize for poetry, because it is so rare to find a Jew writing poetry."

"Prize poetry is not poetry," he reminded her. "But, considering the Jewish Bible contains the finest poetry in the world, I do not see why you should be surprised to find a Jew trying to write some."

"Oh, you know what I mean," answered Esther. "What is the use of talking about the old Jews? We seem to be a different race now. Who cares for poetry?"

"Our poet's scroll reaches on uninterruptedly through the Middle Ages. The passing phenomenon of today must not blind us to the real traits of our race," said Raphael.

"Nor must we be blind to the passing phenomenon of today," retorted Esther. "We have no ideals now."

"I see Sidney has been infecting you," he said gently.

"No, no; I beg you will not think that," she said, flushing almost resentfully. "I have thought these things, as the Scripture tells us to meditate on the Law, day and night, sleeping and waking, standing up and sitting down."

"You cannot have thought of them without prejudice, then," he answered, "if you say we have no ideals."

"I mean, we're not responsive to great poetry—to the message of a Browning for instance."

"I deny it. Only a small percentage of his own race is responsive. I would wager our percentage is proportionally higher. But Browning's philosophy of religion is already ours, for hundreds of years every Saturday night every Jew has been proclaiming the view of life and Providence in 'Pisgah Sights.'"

> *All's lend and borrow,*
> *Good, see, wants evil,*
> *Joy demands sorrow,*
> *Angel weds devil.*

"What is this but the philosophy of our formula for ushering out the Sabbath and welcoming in the days of toil, accepting the holy and the profane, the light and the darkness?"

"Is that in the prayer-book?" said Esther astonished.

"Yes; you see you are ignorant of our own ritual while admiring everything non-Jewish. Excuse me if I am frank, Miss Ansell, but there are many people among us who rave over Italian antiquities but can see nothing poetical in Judaism. They listen eagerly to Dante but despise David."

"I shall certainly look up the liturgy," said Esther. "But that will not alter my opinion. The Jew may say these fine things, but they are only a tune to him. Yes, I begin to recall the passage in Hebrew—I see my father making *Havdolah*—the melody goes in my head like a sing-song. But I never in my life thought of the meaning. As a little girl I always got my conscious religious inspiration out of the New Testament. It sounds very shocking, I know."

"Undoubtedly you put your finger on an evil. But there is religious

ISRAEL ZANGWILL

edification in common prayers and ceremonies even when divorced from meaning. Remember the Latin prayers of the Catholic poor. Jews may be below Judaism, but are not all men below their creed? If the race which gave the world the Bible knows it least—" He stopped suddenly, for Addie was playing pianissimo, and although she was his sister, he did not like to put her out.

"It comes to this," said Esther when Chopin spoke louder, "our prayer-book needs depolarization, as Wendell Holmes says of the Bible."

"Exactly," assented Raphael. "And what our people need is to make acquaintance with the treasure of our own literature. Why go to Browning for theism, when the words of his 'Rabbi Ben Ezra' are but a synopsis of a famous Jewish argument:

> *'I see the whole design.*
> *I, who saw Power, see now Love, perfect too.*
> *Perfect I call Thy plan,*
> *Thanks that I was a man!*
> *Maker, remaker, complete, I trust what thou shalt do.'"*

"It sounds like a bit of Bachja. That there is a Power outside us nobody denies; that this Power works for our good and wisely, is not so hard to grant when the facts of the soul are weighed with the facts of Nature. Power, Love, Wisdom—there you have a real trinity which makes up the Jewish God. And in this God we trust, incomprehensible as are His ways, unintelligible as is His essence. 'Thy ways are not My ways nor Thy thoughts My thoughts.' That comes into collision with no modern philosophies; we appeal to experience and make no demands upon the faculty for believing things 'because they are impossible.' And we are proud and happy in that the dread Unknown God of the infinite Universe has chosen our race as the medium by which to reveal His will to the world. We are sanctified to His service. History testifies that this has verily been our mission, that we have taught the world religion as truly as Greece has taught beauty and science. Our miraculous survival through the cataclysms of ancient and modern dynasties is a proof that our mission is not yet over."

The sonata came to an end; Percy Saville started a comic song, playing his own accompaniment. Fortunately, it was loud and rollicking.

"And do you really believe that we are sanctified to God's service?" said Esther, casting a melancholy glance at Percy's grimaces.

"Can there be any doubt of it? God made choice of one race to be messengers and apostles, martyrs at need to His truth. Happily, the sacred duty is ours," he said earnestly, utterly unconscious of the incongruity that struck Esther so keenly. And yet, of the two, he had by far the greater gift of humor. It did not destroy his idealism, but kept it in touch with things mundane. Esther's vision, though more penetrating, lacked this corrective of humor, which makes always for breadth of view. Perhaps it was because she was a woman, that the trivial, sordid details of life's comedy hurt her so acutely that she could scarcely sit out the play patiently. Where Raphael would have admired the lute, Esther was troubled by the little rifts in it.

"But isn't that a narrow conception of God's revelation?" she asked.

"No. Why should God not teach through a great race as through a great man?"

"And you really think that Judaism is not dead, intellectually speaking?"

"How can it die? Its truths are eternal, deep in human nature and the constitution of things. Ah, I wish I could get you to see with the eyes of the great Rabbis and sages in Israel; to look on this human life of ours, not with the pessimism of Christianity, but as a holy and precious gift, to be enjoyed heartily yet spent in God's service—birth, marriage, death, all holy; good, evil, alike holy. Nothing on God's earth common or purposeless. Everything chanting the great song of God's praise; the morning stars singing together, as we say in the Dawn Service."

As he spoke Esther's eyes filled with strange tears. Enthusiasm always infected her, and for a brief instant her sordid universe seemed to be transfigured to a sacred joyous reality, full of infinite potentialities of worthy work and noble pleasure. A thunder of applausive hands marked the end of Percy Saville's comic song. Mr. Montagu Samuels was beaming at his brother's grotesque drollery. There was an interval of general conversation, followed by a round game in which Raphael and Esther had to take part. It was very dull, and they were glad to find themselves together again.

"Ah, yes," said Esther, sadly, resuming the conversation as if there had been no break, "but this is a Judaism of your own creation. The real Judaism is a religion of pots and pans. It does not call to the soul's depths like Christianity."

"Again, it is a question of the point of view taken. From a practical, our ceremonialism is a training in self-conquest, while it links the generations 'bound each to each by natural piety,' and unifies our atoms dispersed to the four corners of the earth as nothing else could. From a theoretical, it is but an extension of the principle I tried to show you. Eating, drinking, every act of life is holy, is sanctified by some relation to heaven. We will not arbitrarily divorce some portions of life from religion, and say these are of the world, the flesh, or the devil, anymore than we will save up our religion for Sundays. There is no devil, no original sin, no need of salvation from it, no need of a mediator. Every Jew is in as direct relation with God as the Chief Rabbi. Christianity is an historical failure—its counsels of perfection, its command to turn the other cheek—a farce. When a modern spiritual genius, a Tolstoi, repeats it, all Christendom laughs, as at a new freak of insanity. All practical, honorable men are Jews at heart. Judaism has never tampered with human dignity, nor perverted the moral consciousness. Our housekeeper, a Christian, once said to my sifter Addie, 'I'm so glad to see you do so much charity, Miss; I need not, because I'm saved already.' Judaism is the true 'religion of humanity.' It does not seek to make men and women angels before their time. Our marriage service blesses the King of the Universe, who has created 'joy and gladness, bridegroom and bride, mirth and exultation, pleasure and delight, love, brotherhood, peace and fellowship.'"

"It is all very beautiful in theory," said Esther. "But so is Christianity, which is also not to be charged with its historical caricatures, nor with its superiority to average human nature. As for the doctrine of original sin, it is the one thing that the science of heredity has demonstrated, with a difference. But do not be alarmed, I do not call myself a Christian because I see some relation between the dogmas of Christianity and the truths of experience, nor even because"—here she smiled, wistfully—"I should like to believe in Jesus. But you are less logical. When you said there was no devil, I felt sure I was right; that you belong to the modern schools, who get rid of all the old beliefs but cannot give up the old names. You know, as well as I do, that, take away the belief in hell, a real old-fashioned hell of fire and brimstone, even such Judaism as survives would freeze to death without that genial warmth."

"I know nothing of the kind," he said, "and I am in no sense a modern. I am (to adopt a phrase which is, to me, tautologous) an orthodox Jew."

Esther smiled. "Forgive my smiling," she said. "I am thinking of the orthodox Jews I used to know, who used to bind their phylacteries on their arms and foreheads every morning."

"I bind my phylacteries on my arm and forehead every morning," he said, simply.

"What!" gasped Esther. "You an Oxford man!"

"Yes," he said, gravely. "Is it so astonishing to you?"

"Yes, it is. You are the first educated Jew I have ever met who believed in that sort of thing."

"Nonsense?" he said, inquiringly. "There are hundreds like me."

She shook her head.

"There's the Rev. Joseph Strelitski. I suppose *he* does, but then he's paid for it."

"Oh, why will you sneer at Strelitski?" he said, pained. "He has a noble soul. It is to the privilege of his conversation that I owe my best understanding of Judaism."

"Ah, I was wondering why the old arguments sounded so different, so much more convincing, from your lips," murmured Esther. "Now I know; because he wears a white tie. That sets up all my bristles of contradiction when he opens his mouth."

"But I wear a white tie, too," said Raphael, his smile broadening in sympathy with the slow response on the girl's serious face.

"That's not a trade-mark," she protested. "But forgive me; I didn't know Strelitski was a friend of yours. I won't say a word against him anymore. His sermons really are above the average, and he strives more than the others to make Judaism more spiritual."

"More spiritual!" he repeated, the pained expression returning. "Why, the very theory of Judaism has always been the spiritualization of the material."

"And the practice of Judaism has always been the materialization of the spiritual," she answered.

He pondered the saying thoughtfully, his face growing sadder.

"You have lived among your books," Esther went on. "I have lived among the brutal facts. I was born in the Ghetto, and when you talk of the mission of Israel, silent sardonic laughter goes through me as I think of the squalor and the misery."

"God works through human suffering; his ways are large," said Raphael, almost in a whisper.

"And wasteful," said Esther. "Spare me clerical platitudes à la Strelitski. I have seen so much."

"And suffered much?" he asked gently.

She nodded scarce perceptibly. "Oh, if you only knew my life!"

"Tell it me," he said. His voice was soft and caressing. His frank soul seemed to pierce through all conventionalities, and to go straight to hers.

"I cannot, not now," she murmured. "There is so much to tell."

"Tell me a little," he urged.

She began to speak of her history, scarce knowing why, forgetting he was a stranger. Was it racial affinity, or was it merely the spiritual affinity of souls that feel their identity through all differences of brain?

"What is the use?" she said. "You, with your childhood, could never realize mine. My mother died when I was seven; my father was a Russian pauper alien who rarely got work. I had an elder brother of brilliant promise. He died before he was thirteen. I had a lot of brothers and sisters and a grandmother, and we all lived, half starved, in a garret."

Her eyes grew humid at the recollection; she saw the spacious drawing-room and the dainty bric-à-brac through a mist.

"Poor child!" murmured Raphael.

"Strelitski, by the way, lived in our street then. He sold cigars on commission and earned an honest living. Sometimes I used to think that is why he never cares to meet my eye; he remembers me and knows I remember him; at other times I thought he knew that I saw through his professions of orthodoxy. But as you champion him, I suppose I must look for a more creditable reason for his inability to look me straight in the face. Well, I grew up, I got on well at school, and about ten years ago I won a prize given by Mrs. Henry Goldsmith, whose kindly interest I excited thenceforward. At thirteen I became a teacher. This had always been my aspiration: when it was granted I was more unhappy than ever. I began to realize acutely that we were terribly poor. I found it difficult to dress so as to insure the respect of my pupils and colleagues; the work was unspeakably hard and unpleasant; tiresome and hungry little girls had to be ground to suit the inspectors, and fell victims to the then prevalent competition among teachers for a high percentage of passes. I had to teach Scripture history and I didn't believe in it. None of us believed in it; the talking serpent, the Egyptian miracles, Samson, Jonah and the whale, and all that. Everything about me was sordid and unlovely. I yearned for a fuller, wider life, for larger knowledge. I hungered for the sun. In short, I was intensely miserable. At home things went from bad to worse; often I was the sole bread-winner, and my few shillings a week were our only income. My brother Solomon grew up, but could not get into a decent situation because he must not work on the Sabbath. Oh, if you knew how young lives are cramped and shipwrecked at the start by this one curse of the Sabbath, you would not wish us to persevere in our isolation. It sent a mad thrill of indignation through me to find my father daily entreating the deaf heavens."

He would not argue now. His eyes were misty.

"Go on!" he murmured.

"The rest is nothing. Mrs. Henry Goldsmith stepped in as the *dea ex machina*. She had no children, and she took it into her head to adopt me. Naturally I was dazzled, though anxious about my brothers and sisters. But my father looked upon it as a godsend. Without consulting me, Mrs. Goldsmith arranged that he and the other children should be shipped to America: she got him some work at a relative's in Chicago. I suppose she was afraid of having the family permanently hanging about the Terrace. At first I was grieved; but when the pain of parting was over I found myself relieved to be rid of them, especially of my father. It sounds shocking, I know, but I can confess all my vanities now, for I have learned all is vanity. I thought Paradise was opening before me; I was educated by the best masters, and graduated at the London University. I travelled and saw the Continent; had my fill of sunshine and beauty. I have had many happy moments, realized many childish ambitions, but happiness is as far away as ever. My old school-colleagues envy me, yet I do not know whether I would not go back without regret."

"Is there anything lacking in your life, then?" he asked gently.

"No, I happen to be a nasty, discontented little thing, that is all," she said, with a faint smile. "Look on me as a psychological paradox, or a text for the preacher."

"And do the Goldsmiths know of your discontent?"

"Heaven forbid! They have been so very kind to me. We get along very well together. I never discuss religion with them, only the services and the minister."

"And your relatives?"

"Ah, they are all well and happy. Solomon has a store in Detroit. He is only nineteen and dreadfully enterprising. Father is a pillar of a Chicago *Chevra*. He still talks Yiddish. He has escaped learning American just as he escaped learning English. I buy him a queer old Hebrew book sometimes with my pocket-money and he is happy. One little sister is a typewriter, and the other is just out of school and does the housework. I suppose I shall go out and see them all some day."

"What became of the grandmother you mentioned?"

"She had a Charity Funeral a year before the miracle happened. She was very weak and ill, and the Charity Doctor warned her that she must not fast on the Day of Atonement. But she wouldn't even moisten her parched lips with a drop of cold water. And so she died; exhorting my father with her last breath to beware of Mrs. Simons (a good-hearted widow who was very kind to us), and to marry a pious Polish woman."

"And did he?"

"No, I am still stepmotherless. Your white tie's gone wrong. It's all on one side."

"It generally is," said Raphael, fumbling perfunctorily at the little bow.

"Let me put it straight. There! And now you know all about me. I hope you are going to repay my confidences in kind."

"I am afraid I cannot oblige with anything so romantic," he said smiling. "I was born of rich but honest parents, of a family settled in England for three generations, and went to Harrow and Oxford in due course. That is all. I saw a little of the Ghetto, though, when I was a boy. I had some correspondence on Hebrew Literature with a great Jewish scholar, Gabriel Hamburg (he lives in Stockholm now), and one day when I was up from Harrow I went to see him. By good fortune I assisted at the foundation of the Holy Land League, now presided over by Gideon, the member for Whitechapel. I was moved to tears by the enthusiasm; it was there I made the acquaintance of Strelitski. He spoke as if inspired. I also met a poverty-stricken poet, Melchitsedek Pinchas, who afterwards sent me his work, *Metatoron's Flames*, to Harrow. A real neglected genius. Now there's the man to bear in mind when one speaks of Jews and poetry. After that night I kept up a regular intercourse with the Ghetto, and have been there several times lately."

"But surely you don't also long to return to Palestine?"

"I do. Why should we not have our own country?"

"It would be too chaotic! Fancy all the Ghettos of the world amalgamating. Everybody would want to be ambassador at Paris, as the old joke says."

"It would be a problem for the statesmen among us. Dissenters, Churchmen, Atheists, Slum Savages, Clodhoppers, Philosophers,

Aristocrats—make up Protestant England. It is the popular ignorance of the fact that Jews are as diverse as Protestants that makes such novels as we were discussing at dinner harmful."

"But is the author to blame for that? He does not claim to present the whole truth but a facet. English society lionized Thackeray for his pictures of it. Good heavens! Do Jews suppose they alone are free from the snobbery, hypocrisy and vulgarity that have shadowed every society that has ever existed?"

"In no work of art can the spectator be left out of account," he urged. "In a world full of smouldering prejudices a scrap of paper may start the bonfire. English society can afford to laugh where Jewish society must weep. That is why our papers are always so effusively grateful for Christian compliments. You see it is quite true that the author paints not the Jews but bad Jews, but, in the absence of paintings of good Jews, bad Jews are taken as identical with Jews."

"Oh, then you agree with the others about the book?" she said in a disappointed tone.

"I haven't read it; I am speaking generally. Have you?"

"Yes."

"And what did you think of it? I don't remember your expressing an opinion at table."

She pondered an instant.

"I thought highly of it and agreed with every word of it." She paused. He looked expectantly into the dark intense face. He saw it was charged with further speech.

"Till I met you," she concluded abruptly.

A wave of emotion passed over his face.

"You don't mean that?" he murmured.

"Yes, I do. You have shown me new lights."

"I thought I was speaking platitudes," he said simply. "It would be nearer the truth to say you have given *me* new lights."

The little face flushed with pleasure; the dark skin shining, the eyes sparkling. Esther looked quite pretty.

"How is that possible?" she said. "You have read and thought twice as much as I"

"Then you must be indeed poorly off," he said, smiling. "But I am really glad we met. I have been asked to edit a new Jewish paper, and our talk has made me see more clearly the lines on which it must be run, if it is to do any good. I am awfully indebted to you."

"A new Jewish paper?" she said, deeply interested. "We have so many already. What is its *raison d'être*?"

"To convert you," he said smiling, but with a ring of seriousness in the words.

"Isn't that like a steam-hammer cracking a nut or Hoti burning down his house to roast a pig? And suppose I refuse to take in the new Jewish paper? Will it suspend publication?" He laughed.

"What's this about a new Jewish paper?" said Mrs. Goldsmith, suddenly appearing in front of them with her large genial smile. "Is that what you two have been plotting? I noticed you've laid your heads together all the evening. Ah well, birds of a feather flock together. Do you know my little Esther took the scholarship for logic at London? I wanted her to proceed to the M.A. at once, but the doctor said she must have a rest." She laid her hand affectionately on the girl's hair.

Esther looked embarrassed.

"And so she is still a Bachelor," said Raphael, smiling but evidently impressed.

"Yes, but not for long I hope," returned Mrs. Goldsmith. "Come, darling, everybody's dying to hear one of your little songs."

"The dying is premature," said Esther. "You know I only sing for my own amusement."

"Sing for mine, then," pleaded Raphael.

"To make you laugh?" queried Esther. "I know you'll laugh at the way I play the accompaniment. One's fingers have to be used to it from childhood—"

Her eyes finished the sentence, "and you know what mine was."

The look seemed to seal their secret sympathy.

She went to the piano and sang in a thin but trained soprano. The song was a ballad with a quaint air full of sadness and heartbreak. To Raphael, who had never heard the psalmic wails of "The Sons of the Covenant" or the Polish ditties of Fanny Belcovitch, it seemed also full of originality. He wished to lose himself in the sweet melancholy, but Mrs. Goldsmith, who had taken Esther's seat at his side, would not let him.

"Her own composition—words and music," she whispered. "I wanted her to publish it, but she is so shy and retiring. Who would think she was the child of a pauper emigrant, a rough jewel one has picked up and polished? If you really are going to start a new Jewish paper, she might be of use to you. And then there is Miss Cissy Levine—you have read her novels, of course? Sweetly pretty! Do you know, I think we are badly in want of a new paper, and you are the only man in the community who could give it us. We want educating, we poor people, we know so little of our faith and our literature."

"I am so glad you feel the want of it," whispered Raphael, forgetting Esther in his pleasure at finding a soul yearning for the light.

"Intensely. I suppose it will be advanced?"

Raphael looked at her a moment a little bewildered.

"No, it will be orthodox. It is the orthodox party that supplies the funds."

A flash of light leaped into Mrs. Goldsmith's eyes.

"I am so glad it is not as I feared." she said. "The rival party has hitherto monopolized the press, and I was afraid that like most of our young men of talent you would give it that tendency. Now at last we poor orthodox will have a voice. It will be written in English?"

"As far as I can," he said, smiling.

"No, you know what I mean. I thought the majority of the orthodox couldn't read English and that they have their jargon papers. Will you be able to get a circulation?"

"There are thousands of families in the East End now among whom English is read if not written. The evening papers sell as well there as anywhere else in London."

"Bravo!" murmured Mrs. Goldsmith, clapping her hands.

Esther had finished her song. Raphael awoke to the remembrance of her. But she did not come to him again, sitting down instead on a lounge near the piano, where Sidney bantered Addie with his most paradoxical persiflage.

Raphael looked at her. Her expression was abstracted, her eyes had an inward look. He hoped her headache had not got worse. She did not look at all pretty now. She seemed a frail little creature with a sad thoughtful face and an air of being alone in the midst of a merry company. Poor little thing! He felt as if he had known her for years. She seemed curiously out of harmony with all these people. He doubted even his own capacity to commune with her inmost soul. He wished he could be of service to her, could do anything for her that might lighten her gloom and turn her morbid thoughts in healthier directions.

The butler brought in some claret negus. It was the break-up signal. Raphael drank his negus with a pleasant sense of arming himself against the cold air. He wanted to walk home smoking his pipe, which he always carried in his overcoat. He clasped Esther's hand with a cordial smile of farewell.

"We shall meet again soon, I trust," he said.

"I hope so," said Esther; "put me down as a subscriber to that paper."

"Thank you," he said; "I won't forget."

"What's that?" said Sidney, pricking up his ears; "doubled your circulation already?"

Sidney put his cousin Addie into a hansom, as she did not care to walk, and got in beside her.

"My feet are tired," she said; "I danced a lot last night, and was out a lot this afternoon. It's all very well for Raphael, who doesn't know whether he's walking on his head or his heels. Here, put your collar up, Raphael, not like that, it's all crumpled. Haven't you got a handkerchief to put round your throat? Where's that one I gave you? Lend him yours, Sidney."

"You don't mind if *I* catch my death of cold; I've got to go on a Christmas dance when I deposit you on your doorstep," grumbled Sidney. "Catch! There, you duffer! It's gone into the mud. Sure you won't jump in? Plenty of room. Addie can sit on my knee. Well, ta, ta! Merry Christmas."

Raphael lit his pipe and strode off with long ungainly strides. It was a clear frosty night, and the moonlight glistened on the silent spaces of street and square.

"Go to bed, my dear," said Mrs. Goldsmith, returning to the lounge where Esther still sat brooding. "You look quite worn out."

Left alone, Mrs. Goldsmith smiled pleasantly at Mr. Goldsmith, who, uncertain of how he had behaved himself, always waited anxiously for the verdict. He was pleased to find it was "not guilty" this time.

"I think that went off very well," she said. She was looking very lovely tonight, the low bodice emphasizing the voluptuous outlines of the bust.

"Splendidly," he returned. He stood with his coat-tails to the fire, his coarse-grained face beaming like an extra lamp. "The people and those croquettes were A1. The way Mary's picked up French cookery is wonderful."

"Yes, especially considering she denies herself butter. But I'm not thinking of that nor of our guests." He looked at her wonderingly. "Henry," she continued impressively, "how would you like to get into Parliament?"

"Eh, Parliament? Me?" he stammered.

"Yes, why not? I've always had it in my eye."

His face grew gloomy. "It is not practicable," he said, shaking the head with the prominent teeth and ears.

"Not practicable?" she echoed sharply. "Just think of what you've achieved already, and don't tell me you're going to stop now. Not practicable, indeed! Why, that's the very word you used years ago in the provinces when I said you ought to be President. You said old Winkelstein had been in the position too long to be ousted. And yet I felt certain your superior English would tell in the long run in such a miserable congregation of foreigners, and when Winkelstein had made that delicious blunder about the 'university' of the Exodus instead of the 'anniversary,' and I went about laughing over it in all the best circles, the poor man's day was over. And when we came to London, and seemed to fall again to the bottom of the ladder because our greatness was swallowed up in the vastness, didn't you despair then? Didn't you tell me that we should never rise to the surface?"

"It didn't seem probable, did it?" he murmured in self-defence.

"Of course not. That's just my point. Your getting into the House of Commons doesn't seem probable now. But in those days your getting merely to know M.P.'s was equally improbable. The synagogal dignities were all filled up by old hands, there was no way of getting on the Council and meeting our magnates."

"Yes, but your solution of that difficulty won't do here. I had not much difficulty in persuading the United Synagogue that a new synagogue was a crying want in Kensington, but I could hardly persuade the government that a new constituency is a crying want in London." He spoke pettishly; his ambition always required rousing and was easily daunted.

"No, but somebody's going to start a new something else, Henry," said Mrs. Goldsmith with enigmatic cheerfulness. "Trust in me; think of what we have done in less than a dozen years at comparatively trifling costs, thanks to that happy idea of a new synagogue—you the representative of the Kensington synagogue, with a 'Sir' for a colleague and a congregation that from exceptionally small beginnings has sprung up to be the most fashionable in London; likewise a member of the Council of the Anglo-Jewish Association and an honorary officer of the *Shechitah* Board; I, connected with several first-class charities, on the Committee of our leading school, and the acknowledged discoverer of a girl who gives promise of doing something notable in literature or music. We have a reputation for wealth, culture and hospitality, and it is quite two years since we shook off the last of the Maida Vale lot, who are so graphically painted in that novel of Mr. Armitage's. Who are our guests now? Take tonight's! A celebrated artist, a brilliant young Oxford man, both scions of the same wealthy and well-considered family, an authoress of repute who dedicates her books (by permission) to the very first families of the community; and lastly the Montagu Samuels with the brother, Percy Saville, who both go only to the best houses. Is there any other house, where the company is so exclusively Jewish, that could boast of a better gathering?"

"I don't say anything against the company," said her husband awkwardly, "it's better than we got in the Provinces. But your company isn't your constituency. What constituency would have me?"

"Certainly, no ordinary constituency would have you," admitted his wife frankly. "I am thinking of Whitechapel."

"But Gideon represents Whitechapel."

"Certainly; as Sidney Graham says, he represents it very well. But he has made himself unpopular, his name has appeared in print as a guest at City banquets, where the food can't be *kosher*. He has alienated a goodly proportion of the Jewish vote."

"Well?" said Mr. Goldsmith, still wonderingly.

"Now is the time to bid for his shoes. Raphael Leon is about to establish a new Jewish paper. I was mistaken about that young man. You remember my telling you I had heard he was eccentric and despite his brilliant career a little touched on religious matters. I naturally supposed his case was like that of one or two other Jewish young men we know and that he yearned for spirituality, and his remarks at table rather confirmed the impression. But he is worse than that—and I nearly put my foot in it—his craziness is on the score of orthodoxy! Fancy that! A man who has been to Harrow and Oxford longing for a gaberdine and side curls! Well, well, live and learn. What a sad trial for his parents!" She paused, musing.

"But, Rosetta, what has Raphael Leon to do with my getting into Parliament?"

"Don't be stupid, Henry. Haven't I explained to you that Leon is going to start an orthodox paper which will be circulated among your future constituents. It's extremely fortunate that we have always kept our religion. We have a widespread reputation for orthodoxy. We are friends with Leon, and we can get Esther to write for the paper (I could see he was rather struck by her). Through this paper we can keep you and your orthodoxy constantly before the constituency. The poor people are quite fascinated by the idea of rich Jews like us keeping a strictly *kosher* table; but the image of a Member of Parliament with phylacteries on his forehead will simply intoxicate them." She smiled, herself, at the image; the smile that always intoxicated Percy Saville.

"You're a wonderful woman, Rosetta," said Henry, smiling in response with admiring affection and making his incisors more prominent. He drew her head down to him and kissed her lips. She returned his kiss lingeringly and they had a flash of that happiness which is born of mutual fidelity and trust.

"Can I do anything for you, mum, afore I go to bed?" said stout old Mary O'Reilly, appearing at the door. Mary was a privileged person, unappalled even by the butler. Having no relatives, she never took a holiday and never went out except to Chapel.

"No, Mary, thank you. The dinner was excellent. Goodnight and merry Christmas."

"Same to you, mum," and as the unconscious instrument of Henry Goldsmith's candidature turned away, the Christmas bells broke merrily upon the night. The peals fell upon the ears of Raphael Leon, still striding along, casting a gaunt shadow on the hoar-frosted pavement, but he marked them not; upon Addie sitting by her bedroom mirror thinking of Sidney speeding to the Christmas dance; upon Esther turning restlessly on the luxurious eider-down, oppressed by panoramic pictures of the martyrdom of her race. Lying between sleep and waking, especially when her brain had been excited, she had the faculty of seeing wonderful vivid visions, indistinguishable from realities. The martyrs who mounted the scaffold and the stake all had the face of Raphael.

"The mission of Israel" buzzed through her brain. Oh, the irony of history! Here was another life going to be wasted on an illusory dream. The figures of Raphael and her father suddenly came into grotesque juxtaposition. A bitter smile passed across her face.

The Christmas bells rang on, proclaiming Peace in the name of Him who came to bring a sword into the world.

"Surely," she thought, "the people of Christ has been the Christ of peoples."

And then she sobbed meaninglessly in the darkness.

III

"The Flag of Judah"

The call to edit the new Jewish paper seemed to Raphael the voice of Providence. It came just when he was hesitating about his future, divided between the attractions of the ministry, pure Hebrew scholarship and philanthropy. The idea of a paper destroyed these conflicting claims by comprehending them all. A paper would be at once a pulpit, a medium for organizing effective human service, and an incentive to serious study in the preparation of scholarly articles.

The paper was to be the property of the Co-operative Kosher Society, an association originally founded to supply unimpeachable Passover cakes. It was suspected by the pious that there was a taint of heresy in the flour used by the ordinary bakers, and it was remarked that the Rabbinate itself imported its *Matzoth* from abroad. Successful in its first object, the Co-operative Kosher Society extended its operations to more perennial commodities, and sought to save Judaism from dubious cheese and butter, as well as to provide public baths for women in accordance with the precepts of Leviticus. But these ideals were not so easy to achieve, and so gradually the idea of a paper to preach them to a godless age formed itself. The members of the Society met in Aaron Schlesinger's back office to consider them. Schlesinger was a cigar merchant, and the discussions of the Society were invariably obscured by gratuitous smoke Schlesinger's junior partner, Lewis De Haan, who also had a separate business as a surveyor, was the soul of the Society, and talked a great deal. He was a stalwart old man, with a fine imagination and figure, boundless optimism, a big biceps, a long venerable white beard, a keen sense of humor, and a versatility which enabled him to turn from the price of real estate to the elucidation of a Talmudical difficulty, and from the consignment of cigars to the organization of apostolic movements. Among the leading spirits were our old friends, Karlkammer the red-haired zealot, Sugarman the *Shadchan*, and Guedalyah the greengrocer, together with Gradkoski the scholar, fancy goods merchant and man of the world. A furniture-dealer, who was always failing, was also an important personage, while Ebenezer Sugarman, a young man who had once translated a romance from the

Dutch, acted as secretary. Melchitsedek Pinchas invariably turned up at the meetings and smoked Schlesinger's cigars. He was not a member; he had not qualified himself by taking ten pound shares (far from fully paid up), but nobody liked to eject him, and no hint less strong than a physical would have moved the poet.

All the members of the Council of the Co-operative Kosher Society spoke English volubly and more or less grammatically, but none had sufficient confidence in the others to propose one of them for editor, though it is possible that none would have shrunk from having a shot. Diffidence is not a mark of the Jew. The claims of Ebenezer Sugarman and of Melchitsedek Pinchas were put forth most vehemently by Ebenezer and Melchitsedek respectively, and their mutual accusations of incompetence enlivened Mr. Schlesinger's back office.

"He ain't able to spell the commonest English words," said Ebenezer, with a contemptuous guffaw that sounded like the croak of a raven.

The young littérateur, the sumptuousness of whose *Barmitzvah*-party was still a memory with his father, had lank black hair, with a long nose that supported blue spectacles.

"What does he know of the Holy Tongue?" croaked Melchitsedek witheringly, adding in a confidential whisper to the cigar merchant: "I and you, Schlesinger, are the only two men in England who can write the Holy Tongue grammatically."

The little poet was as insinutive and volcanic (by turns) as ever. His beard was, however, better trimmed and his complexion healthier, and he looked younger than ten years ago. His clothes were quite spruce. For several years he had travelled about the Continent, mainly at Raphael's expense. He said his ideas came better in touring and at a distance from the unappreciative English Jewry. It was a pity, for with his linguistic genius his English would have been immaculate by this time. As it was, there was a considerable improvement in his writing, if not so much in his accent.

"What do I know of the Holy Tongue!" repeated Ebenezer scornfully. "Hold yours!"

The Committee laughed, but Schlesinger, who was a serious man, said, "Business, gentlemen, business."

"Come, then! I'll challenge you to translate a page of *Metatoron's Flames*," said Pinchas, skipping about the office like a sprightly flea. "You know no more than the Reverend Joseph Strelitski with his vite tie and his princely income."

De Haan seized the poet by the collar, swung him off his feet and tucked him up in the coal-scuttle.

"Yah!" croaked Ebenezer. "Here's a fine editor. Ho! Ho! Ho!"

"We cannot have either of them. It's the only way to keep them quiet," said the furniture-dealer who was always failing.

Ebenezer's face fell and his voice rose.

"I don't see why I should be sacrificed to '*im*. There ain't a man in England who can write English better than me. Why, everybody says so. Look at the success of my book, *The Old Burgomaster*, the best Dutch novel ever written. The *St. Pancras Press* said it reminded them of Lord Lytton, it did indeed. I can show you the paper. I can give you one each if you like. And then it ain't as if I didn't know 'Ebrew, too. Even if I was in doubt about anything, I could always go to my father. You give me this paper to manage and I'll make your fortunes for you in a twelvemonth; I will as sure as I stand here."

Pinchas had made spluttering interruptions as frequently as he could in resistance of De Haan's brawny, hairy hand which was pressed against his nose and mouth to keep him down in the coal-scuttle, but now he exploded with a force that shook off the hand like a bottle of soda water expelling its cork.

"You Man-of-the-Earth," he cried, sitting up in the coal-scuttle. "You are not even orthodox. Here, my dear gentlemen, is the very position created by Heaven for me—in this disgraceful country where genius starves. Here at last you have the opportunity of covering yourselves vid eternal glory. Have I not given you the idea of starting this paper? And vas I not born to be a Rédacteur, a Editor, as you call it? Into the paper I vill pour all the fires of my song—"

"Yes, burn it up," croaked Ebenezer.

"I vill lead the Freethinkers and the Reformers back into the fold. I vill be Elijah and my vings shall be quill pens. I vill save Judaism." He started up, swelling, but De Haan caught him by his waistcoat and readjusted him in the coal-scuttle.

"Here, take another cigar, Pinchas," he said, passing Schlesinger's private box, as if with a twinge of remorse for his treatment of one he admired as a poet though he could not take him seriously as a man.

The discussion proceeded; the furniture-dealer's counsel was followed; it was definitely decided to let the two candidates neutralize each other.

"Vat vill you give me, if I find you a Rédacteur?" suddenly asked Pinchas. "I give up my editorial seat—"

"Editorial coal-scuttle," growled Ebenezer.

"Pooh! I find you a first-class Rédacteur who vill not want a big salary; perhaps he vill do it for nothing. How much commission vill you give me?"

"Ten shillings on every pound if he does not want a big salary," said De Haan instantly, "and twelve and sixpence on every pound if he does it for nothing."

And Pinchas, who was easily bamboozled when finance became complex, went out to find Raphael.

Thus at the next meeting the poet produced Raphael in triumph, and Gradkoski, who loved a reputation for sagacity, turned a little green with disgust at his own forgetfulness. Gradkoski was among those founders of the Holy Land League with whom Raphael had kept up relations, and he could not deny that the young enthusiast was the ideal man for the post. De Haan, who was busy directing the clerks to write out ten thousand wrappers for the first number, and who had never heard of Raphael before, held a whispered confabulation with Gradkoski and Schlesinger and in a few moments Raphael was rescued from obscurity and appointed to the editorship of the *Flag of Judah* at a salary of nothing a year. De Haan immediately conceived a vast contemptuous admiration of the man.

"You von't forget me," whispered Pinchas, buttonholing the editor at the first opportunity, and placing his forefinger insinuatingly alongside his nose. "You vill remember that I expect a commission on your salary."

Raphael smiled good-naturedly and, turning to De Haan, said: "But do you think there is any hope of a circulation?"

"A circulation, sir, a circulation!" repeated De Haan. "Why, we shall not be able to print fast enough. There are seventy-thousand orthodox Jews in London alone."

"And besides," added Gradkoski, in a corroboration strongly like a contradiction, "we shall not have to rely on the circulation. Newspapers depend on their advertisements."

"Do they?" said Raphael, helplessly.

"Of course," said Gradkoski with his air of worldly wisdom, "And don't you see, being a religious paper we are bound to get all the communal advertisements. Why, we get the Co-operative Kosher Society to start with."

"Yes, but we ain't: going to pay for that,'" said Sugarman the *Shadchan*.

"That doesn't matter," said De Haan. "It'll look well—we can fill up a whole page with it. You know what Jews are—they won't ask 'is this paper wanted?' they'll balance it in their hand, as if weighing up the value of the advertisements, and ask 'does it pay?' But it *will* pay, it must pay; with you at the head of it, Mr. Leon, a man whose fame and piety are known and respected wherever a *Mezuzah* adorns a door-post, a man who is in sympathy with the East End, and has the ear of the West, a man who will preach the purest Judaism in the best English, with such a man at the head of it, we shall be able to ask bigger prices for advertisements than the existing Jewish papers."

Raphael left the office in a transport of enthusiasm, full of Messianic emotions. At the next meeting he announced that he was afraid he could not undertake the charge of the paper. Amid universal consternation, tempered by the exultation of Ebenezer, he explained that he had been thinking it over and did not see how it could be done. He said he had been carefully studying the existing communal organs, and saw that they dealt with many matters of which he knew nothing; whilst he might be competent to form the taste of the community in religious and literary matters, it appeared that the community was chiefly excited about elections and charities. "Moreover," said he, "I noticed that it is expected of these papers to publish obituaries of communal celebrities, for whose biographies no adequate materials are anywhere extant. It would scarcely be decent to obtrude upon the sacred grief of the bereaved relatives with a request for particulars."

"Oh, that's all right," laughed De Haan. "I'm sure *my* wife would be glad to give you any information."

"Of course, of course," said Gradkoski, soothingly. "You will get the obituaries sent in of themselves by the relatives."

Raphael's brow expressed surprise and incredulity.

"And besides, we are not going to crack up the same people as the other papers," said De Haan; "otherwise we should not supply a want. We must dole out our praise and blame quite differently, and we must be very scrupulous to give only a little praise so that it shall be valued the more." He stroked his white, beard tranquilly.

"But how about meetings?" urged Raphael. "I find that sometimes two take place at once. I can go to one, but I can't be at both."

"Oh, that will be all right," said De Haan airily. "We will leave out one and people will think it is unimportant. We are bringing out a paper for our own ends, not to report the speeches of busybodies."

Raphael was already exhibiting a conscientiousness which must be nipped in the bud. Seeing him silenced, Ebenezer burst forth anxiously:

"But Mr. Leon is right. There must be a sub-editor."

"Certainly there must be a sub-editor," cried Pinchas eagerly.

"Very well, then," said De Haan, struck with a sudden thought. "It is true Mr. Leon cannot do all the work. I know a young fellow who'll be just the very thing. He'll come for a pound a week."

"But I'll come for a pound a week," said Ebenezer.

"Yes, but you won't get it," said Schlesinger impatiently.

"*Sha*, Ebenezer," said old Sugarman imperiously.

De Haan thereupon hunted up a young gentleman, who dwelt in his mind as "Little Sampson," and straightway secured him at the price named. He was a lively young Bohemian born in Australia, who had served an apprenticeship on the Anglo-Jewish press, worked his way up into the larger journalistic world without, and was now engaged in organizing a comic-opera touring company, and in drifting back again into Jewish journalism. This young gentleman, who always wore long curling locks, an eye-glass and a romantic cloak which covered a multitude of shabbinesses, fully allayed Raphael's fears as to the difficulties of editorship.

"Obituaries!" he said scornfully. "You rely on me for that! The people who are worth chronicling are sure to have lived in the back numbers of our contemporaries, and I can always hunt them up in the Museum. As for the people who are not, their families will send them in, and your only trouble will be to conciliate the families of those you ignore."

"But about all those meetings?" said Raphael.

"I'll go to some," said the sub-editor good-naturedly, "whenever they don't interfere with the rehearsals of my opera. You know of course I am bringing out a comic-opera, composed by myself, some lovely tunes in it; one goes like this: Ta ra ra ta, ta dee dum dee—that'll knock 'em. Well, as I was saying, I'll help you as much as I can find time for. You rely on me for that."

"Yes," said poor Raphael with a sickly smile, "but suppose neither of us goes to some important meeting."

"No harm done. God bless you, I know the styles of all our chief speakers—ahem—ha!—pauperization of the East End, ha!—I would emphatically say that this scheme—ahem!—his lordship's untiring zeal for hum!—the welfare of—and so on. Ta dee dum da, ta, ra, rum dee. They always send on the agenda beforehand. That's all I want, and I'll lay you twenty to one I'll turn out as good a report as any of our rivals. You rely on me for *that*! I know exactly how debates go. At the worst I can always swop with another reporter—a prize distribution for an obituary, or a funeral for a concert."

"And do you really think we two between us can fill up the paper every week?" said Raphael doubtfully.

Little Sampson broke into a shriek of laughter, dropped his eyeglass and collapsed helplessly into the coal-scuttle. The Committeemen looked up from their confabulations in astonishment.

"Fill up the paper! Ho! Ho! Ho!" roared little Sampson, still doubled up. "Evidently *you've* never had anything to do with papers. Why, the reports of London and provincial sermons alone would fill three papers a week."

"Yes, but how are we to get these reports, especially from the provinces?"

"How? Ho! Ho! Ho!" And for sometime little Sampson was physically incapable of speech. "Don't you know," he gasped, "that the ministers always send up their own sermons, pages upon pages of foolscap?"

"Indeed?" murmured Raphael.

"What, haven't you noticed all Jewish sermons are eloquent?".

"They write that themselves?"

"Of course; sometimes they put 'able,' and sometimes 'learned,' but, as a rule, they prefer to be 'eloquent.' The run on that epithet is tremendous. Ta dee dum da. In holiday seasons they are also very fond of 'enthralling the audience,' and of 'melting them to tears,' but this is chiefly during the Ten Days of Repentance, or when a boy is *Barmitzvah*. Then, think of the people who send in accounts of the oranges they gave away to distressed widows, or of the prizes won by their children at fourth-rate schools, or of the silver pointers they present to the synagogue. Whenever a reader sends a letter to an evening paper, he will want you to quote it; and, if he writes a paragraph in the obscurest leaflet, he will want you to note it as 'Literary Intelligence.' Why, my dear fellow, your chief task will be to cut down. Ta, ra, ra, ta! Any Jewish paper could be entirely supported by voluntary contributions—as, for the matter of that, could any newspaper in the world." He got up and shook the coal-dust languidly from his cloak.

"Besides, we shall all be helping you with articles," said De Haan, encouragingly.

"Yes, we shall all be helping you," said Ebenezer.

"I vill give you from the Pierian spring—bucketsful," said Pinchas in a flush of generosity.

"Thank you, I shall be much obliged," said Raphael, heartily, "for I don't quite see the use of a paper filled up as Mr. Sampson suggests." He flung his arms out and drew them in again. It was a way he had when in earnest. "Then, I should like to have some foreign news. Where's that to come from?"

"You rely on me for *that*," said little Sampson, cheerfully. "I will write at once to all the chief Jewish papers in the world, French, German, Dutch, Italian, Hebrew, and American, asking them to exchange with us. There is never any dearth of foreign news. I translate a thing from the Italian *Vessillo Israelitico*, and the *Israelitische Nieuwsbode* copies it from us; *Der Israelit* then translates it into German, whence it gets into Hebrew, in *Hamagid*, thence into *L'Univers Israélite*, of Paris, and thence into the *American Hebrew*. When I see it in American, not having to translate it, it strikes me as fresh, and so I transfer it bodily to our columns, whence it gets translated into Italian, and so the merry-go-round goes eternally on. Ta dee rum day. You rely on me for your foreign news. Why, I can get you foreign telegrams if you'll only allow me to stick 'Trieste, December 21,' or things of that sort at the top. Ti, tum, tee ti." He went on humming a sprightly air, then, suddenly interrupting himself, he said, "but have you got an advertisement canvasser, Mr. De Haan?"

"No, not yet," said De Haan, turning around. The committee had resolved itself into animated groups, dotted about the office, each group marked by a smoke-drift. The clerks were still writing the ten thousand wrappers, swearing inaudibly.

"Well, when are you going to get him?"

"Oh, we shall have advertisements rolling in of themselves," said De Haan, with a magnificent sweep of the arm. "And we shall all assist in that department! Help yourself to another cigar, Sampson." And he passed Schlesinger's box. Raphael and Karlkammer were the only two men in the room not smoking cigars—Raphael, because he preferred his pipe, and Karlkammer for some more mystic reason.

"We must not ignore Cabalah," the zealot's voice was heard to observe.

"You can't get advertisements by Cabalah," drily interrupted Guedalyah, the greengrocer, a practical man, as everybody knew.

"No, indeed," protested Sampson. "The advertisement canvasser is a more important man than the editor."

Ebenezer pricked up his ears.

"I thought *you* undertook to do some canvassing for your money," said De Haan.

"So I will, so I will; rely on me for that. I shouldn't be surprised if I get the capitalists who are backing up my opera to give you the advertisements of the tour, and I'll do all I can in my spare time. But I feel sure you'll want another man—only, you must pay him well and give him a good commission. It'll pay best in the long run to have a good man, there are so many seedy duffers about," said little Sampson, drawing his faded cloak loftily around him. "You want an eloquent, persuasive man, with a gift of the gab—"

"Didn't I tell you so?" interrupted Pinchas, putting his finger to his nose. "I vill go to the advertisers and speak burning words to them. I vill—"

"Garn! They'd kick you out!" croaked Ebenezer. "They'll only listen to an Englishman." His coarse-featured face glistened with spite.

"My Ebenezer has a good appearance," said old Sugarman, "and his English is fine, and dat is half de battle."

Schlesinger, appealed to, intimated that Ebenezer might try, but that they could not well spare him any percentage at the start. After much haggling, Ebenezer consented to waive his commission, if the committee would consent to allow an original tale of his to appear in the paper.

The stipulation having been agreed to, he capered joyously about the office and winked periodically at Pinchas from behind the battery of his blue spectacles. The poet was, however, rapt in a discussion as to the best printer. The Committee were for having Gluck, who had done odd jobs for most of them, but Pinchas launched into a narrative of how, when he edited a great organ in Buda-Pesth, he had effected vast economies by starting a little printing-office of his own in connection with the paper.

"You vill set up a little establishment," he said. "I vill manage it for a few pounds a veek. Then I vill not only print your paper, I vill get you large profits from extra printing. Vith a man of great business talent at the head of it—"

De Haan made a threatening movement, and Pinchas edged away from the proximity of the coal-scuttle.

"Gluck's our printer!" said De Haan peremptorily. "He has Hebrew type. We shall want a lot of that. We must have a lot of Hebrew quotations—not spell Hebrew words in English like the other papers. And the Hebrew date must come before the English. The public must see at once that our principles are superior. Besides, Gluck's a Jew, which will save us from the danger of having any of the printing done on Saturdays."

"But shan't we want a publisher?" asked Sampson.

"That's vat I say," cried Pinchas. "If I set up this office, I can be your publisher too. Ve must do things business-like."

"Nonsense, nonsense! We are our own publishers," said De Haan. "Our clerks will send out the invoices and the subscription copies, and an extra office-boy can sell the papers across the counter."

Sampson smiled in his sleeve.

"All right. That will do—for the first number," he said cordially. "Ta ra ra ta."

"Now then, Mr. Leon, everything is settled," said De Haan, stroking his beard briskly. "I think I'll ask you to help us to draw up the posters. We shall cover all London, sir, all London."

"But wouldn't that be wasting money?" said Raphael.

"Oh, we're going to do the thing properly. I don't believe in meanness."

"It'll be enough if we cover the East End," said Schlesinger, drily.

"Quite so. The East End *is* London as far as we're concerned," said De Haan readily.

Raphael took the pen and the paper which De Haan tendered him and wrote *The Flag of Judah*, the title having been fixed at their first interview.

"The only orthodox paper!" dictated De Haan. "Largest circulation of any Jewish paper in the world!"

"No, how can we say that?" said Raphael, pausing.

"No, of course not," said De Haan. "I was thinking of the subsequent posters. Look out for the first number—on Friday, January 1st. The best Jewish writers! The truest Jewish teachings! Latest Jewish news and finest Jewish stories. Every Friday. Twopence."

"Twopence?" echoed Raphael, looking up. "I thought you wanted to appeal to the masses. I should say it must be a penny."

"It *will* be a penny," said De Haan oracularly.

"We have thought it all over," interposed Gradkoski. "The first number will be bought up out of curiosity, whether at a penny or at twopence. The second will go almost as well, for people will be anxious to see how it compares with the first. In that number we shall announce that owing to the enormous success we have been able to reduce it to a penny; meantime we make all the extra pennies."

"I see," said Raphael dubiously.

"We must have *Chochma*" said De Haan. "Our sages recommend that."

Raphael still had his doubts, but he had also a painful sense of his lack of the "practical wisdom" recommended by the sages cited. He thought these men were probably in the right. Even religion could not be pushed on the masses without business methods, and so long as they were in earnest about the doctrines to be preached, he could even feel a dim admiration for their superior shrewdness in executing a task in which he himself would have hopelessly broken down. Raphael's mind was large; and larger by being conscious of its cloistral limitations. And the men were in earnest; not even their most intimate friends could call this into question.

"We are going to save London," De Haan put it in one of his dithyrambic moments. "Orthodoxy has too long been voiceless, and yet it is five-sixths of Judaea. A small minority has had all the say. We must redress the balance. We must plead the cause of the People against the Few."

Raphael's breast throbbed with similar hopes. His Messianic emotions resurged. Sugarman's solicitous request that he should buy a Hamburg Lottery Ticket scarcely penetrated his consciousness. Carrying the copy of the poster, he accompanied De Haan to Gluck's. It was a small shop in a back street with jargon-papers and hand-bills in the window and a pervasive heavy oleaginous odor. A hand-press occupied the centre of the interior, the back of which was partitioned of and marked "Private." Gluck came forward, grinning welcome. He wore an unkempt beard and a dusky apron.

"Can you undertake to print an eight-page paper?" inquired De Haan.

"If I can print at all, I can print anything," responded Gluck reproachfully. "How many shall you want?"

"It's the orthodox paper we've been planning so long," said De Haan evasively.

Gluck nodded his head.

"There are seventy thousand orthodox Jews in London alone," said De Haan, with rotund enunciation. "So you see what you may have to print. It'll be worth your while to do it extra cheap."

Gluck agreed readily, naming a low figure. After half an hour's discussion it was reduced by ten percent.

"Goodbye, then," said De Haan. "So let it stand. We shall start with a thousand copies of the first number, but where we shall end, the Holy One, blessed be He, alone knows. I will now leave you and the editor to talk over the rest. Today's Monday. We must have the first number out by Friday week. Can you do that, Mr. Leon?"

"Oh, that will be ample," said Raphael, shooting out his arms.

He did not remain of that opinion. Never had he gone through such an awful, anxious time, not even in his preparations for the stiffest exams. He worked sixteen hours a day at the paper. The only evening he allowed himself off was when he dined with Mrs. Henry Goldsmith and met Esther. First numbers invariably take twice as long to produce as second numbers, even in the best regulated establishments. All sorts of mysterious sticks and leads, and fonts and forms, are found wanting at the eleventh hour. As a substitute for gray hair-dye there is nothing in the market to compete with the production of first numbers. But in Gluck's establishment, these difficulties were multiplied by a hundred. Gluck spent a great deal of time in going round the corner to get something from a brother printer. It took an enormous time to get a proof of any article out of Gluck.

"My men are so careful," Gluck explained. "They don't like to pass anything till it's free from typos."

The men must have been highly disappointed, for the proofs were invariably returned bristling with corrections and having a highly hieroglyphic appearance. Then Gluck would go in and slang his men. He kept them behind the partition painted "Private."

The fatal Friday drew nearer and nearer. By Thursday not a single page had been made up. Still Gluck pointed out that there were only eight, and the day was long. Raphael had not the least idea in the world how to make up a paper, but about eleven little Sampson kindly strolled into Gluck's, and explained to his editor his own method of pasting the proofs on sheets of paper of the size of the pages. He even made up one page himself to a blithe vocal accompaniment. When the busy composer and acting-manager hurried off to conduct a rehearsal, Raphael expressed his gratitude warmly. The hours flew; the paper evolved as by geologic stages. As the fateful day wore on, Gluck was scarcely visible for a moment. Raphael was left alone eating his heart out in the shop, and solacing himself with huge whiffs of smoke. At immense intervals

ISRAEL ZANGWILL

Gluck appeared from behind the partition bearing a page or a galley slip. He said his men could not be trusted to do their work unless he was present. Raphael replied that he had not seen the compositors come through the shop to get their dinners, and he hoped Gluck would not find it necessary to cut off their meal-times. Gluck reassured him on this point; he said his men were so loyal that they preferred to bring their food with them rather than have the paper delayed. Later on he casually mentioned that there was a back entrance. He would not allow Raphael to talk to his workmen personally, arguing that it spoiled their discipline. By eleven o'clock at night seven pages had been pulled and corrected: but the eighth page was not forthcoming. The *Flag* had to be machined, dried, folded, and a number of copies put into wrappers and posted by three in the morning. The situation looked desperate. At a quarter to twelve, Gluck explained that a column of matter already set up had been "pied" by a careless compositor. It happened to be the column containing the latest news and Raphael had not even seen a proof of it. Still, Gluck conjured him not to trouble further: he would give his reader strict injunctions not to miss the slightest error. Raphael had already seen and passed the first column of this page, let him leave it to Gluck to attend to this second column; all would be well without his remaining later, and he would receive a copy of the *Flag* by the first post. The poor editor, whose head was splitting, weakly yielded; he just caught the midnight train to the West End and he went to bed feeling happy and hopeful.

At seven o'clock the next morning the whole Leon household was roused by a thunderous double rat-tat at the door. Addie was even heard to scream. A housemaid knocked at Raphael's door and pushed a telegram under it. Raphael jumped out of bed and read: "Third of column more matter wanted. Come at once. Gluck."

"How can that be?" he asked himself in consternation. "If the latest news made a column when it was first set up before the accident, how can it make less now?"

He dashed up to Gluck's office in a hansom and put the conundrum to him.

"You see we had no time to distribute the 'pie,' and we had no more type of that kind, so we had to reset it smaller," answered Gluck glibly. His eyes were blood-shot, his face was haggard. The door of the private compartment stood open.

"Your men are not come yet, I suppose," said Raphael.

"No," said Gluck. "They didn't go away till two, poor fellows. Is that the copy?" he asked, as Raphael handed him a couple of slips he had distractedly scribbled in the cab under the heading of "Talmudic Tales." "Thank you, it's just about the size. I shall have to set it myself."

"But won't we be terribly late?" said poor Raphael.

"We shall be out today," responded Gluck cheerfully. "We shall be in time for the Sabbath, and that's the important thing. Don't you see they're half-printed already?" He indicated a huge pile of sheets. Raphael examined them with beating heart. "We've only got to print 'em on the other side and the thing's done," said Gluck.

"Where are your machines?"

"There," said Gluck, pointing.

"That hand-press!" cried Raphael, astonished. "Do you mean to say you print them all with your own hand?"

"Why not?" said the dauntless Gluck. "I shall wrap them up for the post, too." And he shut himself up with the last of the "copy."

Raphael having exhausted his interest in the half-paper, fell to striding about the little shop, when who should come in but Pinchas, smoking a cigar of the Schlesinger brand.

"Ah, my Prince of Rédacteurs," said Pinchas, darting at Raphael's hand and kissing it. "Did I not say you vould produce the finest paper in the kingdom? But vy have I not my copy by post? You must not listen to Ebenezer ven he says I must not be on the free list, the blackguard."

Raphael explained to the incredulous poet that Ebenezer had not said anything of the kind. Suddenly Pinchas's eye caught sight of the sheets. He swooped down upon them like a hawk. Then he uttered a shriek of grief.

"Vere's my poem, my great poesie?"

Raphael looked embarrassed.

"This is only half the paper," he said evasively.

"Ha, then it vill appear in the other half, *hein*?" he said with hope tempered by a terrible suspicion.

"N—n—o," stammered Raphael timidly.

"No?" shrieked Pinchas.

"You see—the—fact is, it wouldn't scan. Your Hebrew poetry is perfect, but English poetry is made rather differently and I've been too busy to correct it."

"But it is exactly like Lord Byron's!" shrieked Pinchas. "Mein Gott! All night I lie avake—vaiting for the post. At eight o'clock the post comes—but *The Flag of Judah* she vaves not! I rush round here—and now my beautiful poem vill not appear." He seized the sheet again, then cried fiercely: "You have a tale, 'The Waters of Babylon,' by Ebenezer the fool-boy, but my poesie have you not. *Gott in Himmel!*" He tore the sheet frantically across and rushed from the shop. In five minutes he reappeared. Raphael was absorbed in reading the last proof. Pinchas plucked timidly at his coat-tails.

"You vill put it in next veek?" he said winningly.

"I dare say," said Raphael gently.

"Ah, promise me. I vill love you like a brother, I vill be grateful to you forever and ever. I vill never ask another favor of you in all my life. Ve are already like brothers—*hein*? I and you, the only two men—"

"Yes, yes," interrupted Raphael, "it shall appear next week."

"God bless you!" said Pinchas, kissing Raphael's coat-tails passionately and rushing without.

Looking up accidentally some minutes afterwards, Raphael was astonished to see the poet's carneying head thrust through the half-open door with a finger laid insinuatingly on the side of the nose. The head was fixed there as if petrified, waiting to catch the editor's eye.

The first number of *The Flag of Judah* appeared early in the afternoon.

IV

The Troubles of an Editor

The new organ did not create a profound impression. By the rival party it was mildly derided, though many fair-minded persons were impressed by the rather unusual combination of rigid orthodoxy with a high spiritual tone and Raphael's conception of Judaism as outlined in his first leader, his view of it as a happy human compromise between an empty unpractical spiritualism and a choked-up over-practical formalism, avoiding the opposite extremes of its offshoots, Christianity and Mohammedanism, was novel to many of his readers, unaccustomed to think about their faith. Dissatisfied as Raphael was with the number, he felt he had fluttered some of the dove-cotes at least. Several people of taste congratulated him during Saturday and Sunday, and it was with a continuance of Messianic emotions and with agreeable anticipations that he repaired on Monday morning to the little den which had been inexpensively fitted up for him above the offices of Messrs. Schlesinger and De Haan. To his surprise he found it crammed with the committee; all gathered round little Sampson, who, with flushed face and cloak tragically folded, was expostulating at the top of his voice. Pinchas stood at the back in silent amusement. As Raphael entered jauntily, from a dozen lips, the lowering faces turned quickly towards him. Involuntarily Raphael started back in alarm, then stood rooted to the threshold. There was a dread ominous silence. Then the storm burst.

"*Du Shegetz! Du Pasha Yisroile!*" came from all quarters of the compass.

To be called a graceless Gentile and a sinner in Israel is not pleasant to a pious Jew: but all Raphael's minor sensations were swallowed up in a great wonderment.

"We are ruined!" moaned the furniture-dealer, who was always failing.

"You have ruined us!" came the chorus from the thick, sensuous lips, and swarthy fists were shaken threateningly. Sugarman's hairy paw was almost against his face. Raphael turned cold, then a rush of red-hot blood flooded his veins. He put out his good right hand and smote the nearest fist aside. Sugarman blenched and skipped back and the line of fists wavered.

"Don't be fools, gentlemen," said De Haan, his keen sense of humor asserting itself. "Let Mr. Leon sit down."

Raphael, still dazed, took his seat on the editorial chair. "Now, what can I do for you?" he said courteously. The fists dropped at his calm.

"Do for us," said Schlesinger drily. "You've done for the paper. It's not worth twopence."

"Well, bring it out at a penny at once then," laughed little Sampson, reinforced by the arrival of his editor.

Guedalyah the greengrocer glowered at him.

"I am very sorry, gentlemen, I have not been able to satisfy you," said Raphael. "But in a first number one can't do much."

"Can't they?" said De Haan. "You've done so much damage to orthodoxy that we don't know whether to go on with the paper."

"You're joking," murmured Raphael.

"I wish I was," laughed De Haan bitterly.

"But you astonish me." persisted Raphael. "Would you be so good as to point out where I have gone wrong?"

"With pleasure. Or rather with pain," said De Haan. Each of the committee drew a tattered copy from his pocket, and followed De Haan's demonstration with a murmured accompaniment of lamentation.

"The paper was founded to inculcate the inspection of cheese, the better supervision of the sale of meat, the construction of ladies' baths, and all the principles of true Judaism," said De Haan gloomily, "and there's not one word about these things, but a great deal about spirituality and the significance of the ritual. But I will begin at the beginning. Page 1—"

"But that's advertisements," muttered Raphael.

"The part surest to be read! The very first line of the paper is simply shocking. It reads:

"Death: On the 59th ult., at 22 Buckley St., the Rev. Abraham Barnett, in his fifty-fourth—"

"But death is always shocking; what's wrong about that?" interposed little Sampson.

"Wrong!" repeated De Haan, witheringly. "Where did you get that from? That was never sent in."

"No, of course not," said the sub-editor. "But we had to have at least one advertisement of that kind; just to show we should be pleased to advertise our readers' deaths. I looked in the daily papers to see if there were any births or marriages with Jewish names, but I couldn't find any, and that was the only Jewish-sounding death I could see."

"But the Rev. Abraham Barnett was a *Meshumad*," shrieked Sugarman the *Shadchan*. Raphael turned pale. To have inserted an advertisement about an apostate missionary was indeed terrible. But little Sampson's audacity did not desert him.

"I thought the orthodox party would be pleased to hear of the death of a *Meshumad*," he said suavely, screwing his eyeglass more tightly into its orbit, "on the same principle that anti-Semites take in the Jewish papers to hear of the death of Jews."

For a moment De Haan was staggered. "That would be all very well," he said; "let him be an atonement for us all, but then you've gone and put 'May his soul be bound up in the bundle of life.'"

It was true. The stock Hebrew equivalent for R.I.P. glared from the page.

"Fortunately, that taking advertisement of *kosher* trousers comes just underneath," said De Haan, "and that may draw off the attention. On page 2 you actually say in a note that Rabbenu Bachja's great poem on repentance should be incorporated in the ritual and might advantageously replace the obscure *Piyut* by Kalir. But this is rank Reform—it's worse than the papers we come to supersede."

"But surely you know it is only the Printing Press that has stereotyped our liturgy, that for Maimonides and Ibn Ezra, for David Kimchi and Joseph Albo, the contents were fluid, that—"

"We don't deny that," interrupted Schlesinger drily. "But we can't have anymore alterations now-a-days. Who is there worthy to alter them? You?"

"Certainly not. I merely suggest."

"You are playing into the hands of our enemies," said De Haan, shaking his head. "We must not let our readers even imagine that the prayer-book can be tampered with. It's the thin end of the wedge. To trim our liturgy is like trimming living flesh; wherever you cut, the blood oozes. The four cubits of the *Halacha*—that is what is wanted, not changes in the liturgy. Once touch anything, and where are you to stop? Our religion becomes a flux. Our old Judaism is like an old family mansion, where each generation has left a memorial and where every room is hallowed with traditions of merrymaking and mourning. We do not want our fathers' home decorated in the latest style; the next step will be removal to a new dwelling altogether. On page 3 you refer to the second Isaiah."

"But I deny that there were two Isaiahs."

"So you do; but it is better for our readers not to hear of such impious

ISRAEL ZANGWILL

theories. The space would be much better occupied in explaining the Portion for the week. The next leaderette has a flippant tone, which has excited unfavorable comment among some of the most important members of the Dalston Synagogue. They object to humor in a religious paper. On page 4 you have deliberately missed an opportunity of puffing the Kosher Co-operative Society. Indeed, there is not a word throughout about our Society. But I like Mr. Henry Goldsmith's letter on this page, though; he is a good orthodox man and he writes from a good address. It will show we are not only read in the East End. Pity he's such a Man-of-the-Earth, though. Yes, and that's good—the communication from the Rev. Joseph Strelitski. I think he's a bit of an *Epikouros* but it looks as if the whole of the Kensington Synagogue was with us. I understand he is a friend of yours: it will be as well for you to continue friendly. Several of us here knew him well in *Olov Hasholom* times, but he is become so grand and rarely shows himself at the Holy Land League Meetings. He can help us a lot if he will."

"Oh, I'm sure he will," said Raphael.

"That's good," said De Haan, caressing his white beard. Then growing gloomy again, he went on, "On page 5 you have a little article by Gabriel Hamburg, a well-known *Epikouros*."

"Oh, but he's one of the greatest scholars in Europe!" broke in Raphael. "I thought you'd be extra pleased to have it. He sent it to me from Stockholm as a special favor." He did not mention he had secretly paid for it. "I know some of his views are heterodox, and I don't agree with half he says, but this article is perfectly harmless."

"Well, let it pass—very few of our readers have ever heard of him. But on the same page you have a Latin quotation. I don't say there's anything wrong in that, but it smacks of Reform. Our readers don't understand it and it looks as if our Hebrew were poor. The Mishna contains texts suited for all purposes. We are in no need of Roman writers. On page 6 you speak of the Reform *Shool*, as if it were to be reasoned with. Sir, if we mention these freethinkers at all, it must be in the strongest language. By worshipping bare-headed and by seating the sexes together they have denied Judaism."

"Stop a minute!" interrupted Raphael warmly. "Who told you the Reformers do this?"

"Who told me, indeed? Why, it's common knowledge. That's how they've been going on for the last fifty years." "Everybody knows it," said the Committee in chorus.

"Has one of you ever been there?" said Raphael, rising in excitement.

"God forbid!" said the chorus.

"Well, I have, and it's a lie," said Raphael. His arms whirled round to the discomfort of the Committee.

"You ought not to have gone there," said Schlesinger severely. "Besides, will you deny they have the organ in their Sabbath services?"

"No, I won't!"

"Well, then!" said De Haan, triumphantly. "If they are capable of that, they are capable of any wickedness. Orthodox people can have nothing to do with them."

"But orthodox immigrants take their money," said Raphael.

"Their money is *kosher*, they are *tripha*," said De Haan sententiously. "Page 7, now we get to the most dreadful thing of all!" A solemn silence fell on the room, Pinchas sniggered unobtrusively.

"You have a little article headed, 'Talmudic Tales.' Why in heaven's name you couldn't have finished the column with bits of news I don't know. Satan himself must have put the thought into your head. Just at the end of the paper, too! For I can't reckon page 8, which is simply our own advertisement."

"I thought it would be amusing," said Raphael.

"Amusing! If you had simply told the tales, it might have been. But look how you introduce them! 'These amusing tales occur in the fifth chapter of Baba Bathra, and are related by Rabbi Bar Bar Channah. Our readers will see that they are parables or allegories rather than actual facts.'"

"But do you mean to say you look upon them as facts?" cried Raphael, sawing the air wildly and pacing about on the toes of the Committee.

"Surely!" said De Haan, while a low growl at his blasphemous doubts ran along the lips of the Committee.

"Was it treacherously to undermine Judaism that you so eagerly offered to edit for nothing?" said the furniture-dealer who was always failing.

"But listen here!" cried Raphael, exasperated. "Harmez, the son of Lilith, a demon, saddled two mules and made them stand on opposite sides of the River Doneg. He then jumped from the back of one to that of the other. He had, at the time, a cup of wine in each hand, and as he jumped, he threw the wine from each cup into the other without spilling a drop, although a hurricane was blowing at the time. When the King of demons heard that Harmez had been thus showing off to mortals, he slew him. Does any of you believe that?"

ISRAEL ZANGWILL

"Vould our Sages (their memories for a blessing) put anything into the Talmud that vasn't true?" queried Sugarman. "Ve know there are demons because it stands that Solomon knew their language."

"But then, what about this?" pursued Raphael. "'I saw a frog which was as big as the district of Akra Hagronia. A sea-monster came and swallowed the frog, and a raven came and ate the sea-monster. The raven then went and perched on a tree' Consider how strong that tree must have been. R. Papa ben Samuel remarks, 'Had I not been present, I should not have believed it.' Doesn't this appendix about ben Samuel show that it was never meant to be taken seriously?"

"It has some high meaning we do not understand in these degenerate times," said Guedalyah the greengrocer. "It is not for our paper to weaken faith in the Talmud."

"Hear, hear!" said De Haan, while "*Epikouros*" rumbled through the air, like distant thunder.

"Didn't I say an Englishman could never master the Talmud?" Sugarman asked in triumph.

This reminder of Raphael's congenital incompetence softened their minds towards him, so that when he straightway resigned his editorship, their self-constituted spokesman besought him to remain. Perhaps they remembered, too, that he was cheap.

"But we must all edit the paper," said De Haan enthusiastically, when peace was re-established. "We must have meetings everyday and every article must he read aloud before it is printed."

Little Sampson winked cynically, passing his hand pensively through his thick tangled locks, but Raphael saw no objection to the arrangement. As before, he felt his own impracticability borne in upon him, and he decided to sacrifice himself for the Cause as far as conscience permitted. Excessive as it was the zeal of these men, it was after all in the true groove. His annoyance returned for a while, however, when Sugarman the *Shadchan* seized the auspicious moment of restored amity to inquire insinuatingly if his sister was engaged. Pinchas and little Sampson went down the stairs, quivering with noiseless laughter, which became boisterous when they reached the street. Pinchas was in high feather.

"The fool-men!" he said, as he led the sub-editor into a public-house and regaled him on stout and sandwiches. "They believe any *Narrischkeit*. I and you are the only two sensible Jews in England. You vill see that my poesie goes in next week—promise me that! To your life!" here they touched glasses. "Ah, it is beautiful poesie. Such high tragic ideas!

You vill kiss me when you read them!" He laughed in childish light-heartedness. "Perhaps I write you a comic opera for your company—*hein*? Already I love you like a brother. Another glass stout? Bring us two more, thou Hebe of the hops-nectar. You have seen my comedy 'The Hornet of Judah'—No?—Ah, she vas a great comedy, Sampson. All London talked of her. She has been translated into every tongue. Perhaps I play in your company. I am a great actor—*hein*? You know not my forte is voman's parts—I make myself so lovely complexion vith red paint, I fall in love with me." He sniggered over his stout. "The Rédacteur vill not redact long, *hein*?" he said presently. "He is a fool-man. If he work for nothing they think that is what he is worth. They are orthodox, he, he!"

"But he is orthodox too," said little Sampson.

"Yes," replied Pinchas musingly. "It is strange. It is very strange. I cannot understand him. Never in all my experience have I met another such man. There vas an Italian exile I talked with once in the island of Chios, his eyes were like Leon's, soft with a shining splendor like the stars vich are the eyes of the angels of love. Ah, he is a good man, and he writes sharp; he has ideas, not like an English Jew at all. I could throw my arms round him sometimes. I love him like a brother." His voice softened. "Another glass stout; ve vill drink to him."

Raphael did not find the editing by Committee feasible. The friction was incessant, the waste of time monstrous. The second number cost him even more headaches than the first, and this, although the gallant Gluck abandoning his single-handed emprise fortified himself with a real live compositor and had arranged for the paper to be printed by machinery. The position was intolerable. It put a touch of acid into his dulciferous mildness! Just before going to press he was positively rude to Pinchas. It would seem that little Sampson sheltering himself behind his capitalists had refused to give the poet a commission for a comic opera, and Pinchas raved at Gideon, M.P., who he was sure was Sampson's financial backer, and threatened to shoot him and danced maniacally about the office.

"I have written an attack on the Member for Vitechapel," he said, growing calmer, "to hand him down to the execration of posterity, and I have brought it to the *Flag*. It must go in this veek."

"We have already your poem," said Raphael.

"I know, but I do not grudge my work, I am not like your money-making English Jews."

"There is no room. The paper is full."

"Leave out Ebenezer's tale—with the blue spectacles."

"There is none. It was completed in one number."

"Well, must you put in your leader?"

"Absolutely; please go away. I have this page to read."

"But you can leave out some advertisements?"

"I must not. We have too few as it is."

The poet put his finger alongside his nose, but Raphael was adamant.

"Do me this one favor," he pleaded. "I love you like a brother; just this one little thing. I vill never ask another favor of you all my life."

"I would not put it in, even if there was room. Go away," said Raphael, almost roughly.

The unaccustomed accents gave Pinchas a salutary shock. He borrowed two shillings and left, and Raphael was afraid to look up lest he should see his head wedged in the doorway. Soon after Gluck and his one compositor carried out the forms to be machined. Little Sampson, arriving with a gay air on his lips, met them at the door.

On the Friday, Raphael sat in the editorial chair, utterly dispirited, a battered wreck. The Committee had just left him. A heresy had crept into a bit of late news not inspected by them, and they declared that the paper was not worth twopence and had better be stopped. The demand for this second number was, moreover, rather poor, and each man felt his ten pound share melting away, and resolved not to pay up the half yet unpaid. It was Raphael's first real experience of men—after the enchanted towers of Oxford, where he had foregathered with dreamers.

His pipe hung listless in his mouth; an extinct volcano. His first fit of distrust in human nature, nay, even in the purifying powers of orthodoxy, was racking him. Strangely enough this wave of scepticism tossed up the thought of Esther Ansell, and stranger still on the top of this thought, in walked Mr. Henry Goldsmith. Raphael jumped up and welcomed his late host, whose leathery countenance shone with the polish of a sweet smile. It appeared that the communal pillar had been passing casually, and thought he'd look Raphael up.

"So you don't pull well together," he said, when he had elicited an outline of the situation from the editor.

"No, not altogether," admitted Raphael.

"Do you think the paper'll live?"

"I can't say," said Raphael, dropping limply into his chair. "Even if it does. I don't know whether it will do much good if run on their lines, for although it is of great importance that we get *kosher* food and baths. I hardly think they go about it in the right spirit. I may be wrong. They are older men than I and have seen more of actual life, and know the class we appeal to better."

"No, no, you are not wrong," said Mr. Goldsmith vehemently. "I am myself dissatisfied with some of the Committee's contributions to this second number. It is a great opportunity to save English Judaism, but it is being frittered away."

"I am afraid it is," said Raphael, removing his empty pipe from his mouth, and staring at it blankly.

Mr. Goldsmith brought his fist down sharp on the soft litter that covered the editorial table.

"It shall not be frittered away!" he cried. "No, not if I have to buy the paper!"

Raphael looked up eagerly.

"What do you say?" said Goldsmith. "Shall I buy it up and let you work it on your lines?"

"I shall be very glad," said Raphael, the Messianic look returning to his face.

"How much will they want for it?"

"Oh, I think they'll be glad to let you take it over. They say it's not worth twopence, and I'm sure they haven't got the funds to carry it on," replied Raphael, rising. "I'll go down about it at once. The Committee have just been here, and I dare say they are still in Schlesinger's office."

"No, no," said Goldsmith, pushing him down into his seat. "It will never do if people know I'm the proprietor."

"Why not?"

"Oh, lots of reasons. I'm not a man to brag; if I want to do a good thing for Judaism, there's no reason for all the world to know it. Then again, from my position on all sorts of committees I shall be able to influence the communal advertisements in a way I couldn't if people knew I had any connection with the paper. So, too, I shall be able to recommend it to my wealthy friends (as no doubt it will deserve to be recommended) without my praise being discounted."

"Well, but then what am I to say to the Committee?"

"Can't you say you want to buy it for yourself? They know you can afford it."

Raphael hesitated. "But why shouldn't I buy it for myself?"

"Pooh! Haven't you got better use for your money?"

It was true. Raphael had designs more tangibly philanthropic for the five thousand pounds left him by his aunt. And he was business-like enough to see that Mr. Goldsmith's money might as well be utilized for the good of Judaism. He was not quite easy about the little fiction that would he necessary for the transaction, but the combined assurances of Mr. Goldsmith and his own common sense that there was no real deception or harm involved in it, ultimately prevailed. Mr. Goldsmith left, promising to call again in an hour, and Raphael, full of new hopes, burst upon the Committee.

But his first experience of bargaining was no happier than the rest of his worldly experience. When he professed his willingness to relieve them of the burden of carrying on the paper they first stared, then laughed, then shook their fists. As if they would leave him to corrupt the Faith! When they understood he was willing to pay something, the value of *The Flag of Judah* went up from less than twopence to more than two hundred pounds. Everybody was talking about it, its reputation was made, they were going to print double next week.

"But it has not cost you forty pounds yet?" said the astonished Raphael.

"What are you saying? Look at the posters alone!" said Sugarman.

"But you don't look at it fairly," argued De Haan, whose Talmudical studies had sharpened wits already super-subtle. "Whatever it has cost us, it would have cost as much more if we had had to pay our editor, and it is very unfair of you to leave that out of account."

Raphael was overwhelmed. "It's taking away with the left hand what you gave us with the right," added De Haan, with infinite sadness. "I had thought better of you, Mr. Leon."

"But you got a good many twopences back," murmured Raphael.

"It's the future profits that we're losing," explained Schlesinger.

In the end Raphael agreed to give a hundred pounds, which made the members inwardly determine to pay up the residue on their shares at once. De Haan also extorted a condition that the *Flag* should continue to be the organ of the Kosher Co-operative Society, for at least six months, doubtless perceiving that should the paper live and thrive over that period, it would not then pay the proprietor to alter its principles. By which bargain the Society secured for itself a sum of money together with an organ, gratis, for six months and, to all seeming, in perpetuity, for at bottom they knew well that Raphael's heart was sound. They were all on the free list, too, and they knew he would not trouble to remove them.

Mr. Henry Goldsmith, returning, was rather annoyed at the price, but did not care to repudiate his agent.

"Be economical," he said. "I will get you a better office and find a proper publisher and canvasser. But cut it as close as you can."

Raphael's face beamed with joy. "Oh, depend upon me," he said.

"What is your own salary?" asked Goldsmith.

"Nothing," said Raphael.

A flash passed across Goldsmith's face, then he considered a moment.

"I wish you would let it be a guinea," he said. "Quite nominal, you know. Only I like to have things in proper form. And if you ever want to go, you know, you'll give me a month's notice and," here he laughed genially, "I'll do ditto when I want to get rid of you. Ha! Ha! Ha! Is that a bargain?"

Raphael smiled in reply and the two men's hands met in a hearty clasp.

"Miss Ansell will help you, I know," said Goldsmith cheerily. "That girl's got it in her, I can tell you. She'll take the shine out of some of our West Enders. Do you know I picked her out of the gutter, so to speak?"

"Yes, I know," said Raphael. "It was very good and discriminating of you. How is she?"

"She's all right. Come up and see her about doing something for you. She goes to the Museum sometimes in the afternoons, but you'll always find her in on Sundays, or most Sundays. Come up and dine with us again soon, will you? Mrs. Goldsmith will be so pleased."

"I will," said Raphael fervently. And when the door closed upon the communal pillar, he fell to striding feverishly about his little den. His trust in human nature was restored and the receding wave of scepticism bore off again the image of Esther Ansell. Now to work for Judaism!

The sub-editor made his first appearance that day, carolling joyously.

"Sampson," said Raphael abruptly, "your salary is raised by a guinea a week."

The joyous song died away on little Sampson's lips. His eyeglass dropped. He let himself fall backwards, impinging noiselessly upon a heap of "returns" of number one.

V

A Woman's Growth

The sloppy Sunday afternoon, which was the first opportunity Raphael had of profiting by Mr. Henry Goldsmith's general invitation to call and see Esther, happened to be that selected by the worthy couple for a round of formal visits. Esther was left at home with a headache, little expecting pleasanter company. She hesitated about receiving Raphael, but on hearing that he had come to see her rather than her patrons, she smoothed her hair, put on a prettier frock, and went down into the drawing-room, where she found him striding restlessly in bespattered boots and moist overcoat. When he became aware of her presence, he went towards her eagerly, and shook her hand with jerky awkwardness.

"How are you?" he said heartily.

"Very well, thank you," she replied automatically. Then a twinge, as of reproach at the falsehood, darted across her brow, and she added, "A trifle of the usual headache. I hope you are well."

"Quite, thank you," he rejoined.

His face rather contradicted him. It looked thin, pale, and weary. Journalism writes lines on the healthiest countenance. Esther looked at him disapprovingly; she had the woman's artistic instinct if not the artist's, and Raphael, with his damp overcoat, everlastingly crumpled at the collar, was not an aesthetic object. Whether in her pretty moods or her plain, Esther was always neat and dainty. There was a bit of ruffled lace at her throat, and the heliotrope of her gown contrasted agreeably with the dark skin of the vivid face.

"Do take off your overcoat and dry yourself at the fire," she said.

While he was disposing of it, she poked the fire into a big cheerful blaze, seating herself opposite him in a capacious arm-chair, where the flame picked her out in bright tints upon the dusky background of the great dim room.

"And how is *The Flag of Judah*?" she said.

"Still waving," he replied. "It is about that that I have come."

"About that?" she said wonderingly. "Oh, I see; you want to know if the one person it is written at has read it. Well, make your mind easy. I have. I have read it religiously—No, I don't mean that; yes, I do; it's the appropriate word."

"Really?" He tried to penetrate behind the bantering tone.

"Yes, really. You put your side of the case eloquently and well. I look forward to Friday with interest. I hope the paper is selling?"

"So, so," he said. "It is uphill work. The Jewish public looks on journalism as a branch of philanthropy, I fear, and Sidney suggests publishing our free-list as a 'Jewish Directory.'"

She smiled. "Mr. Graham is very amusing. Only, he is too well aware of it. He has been here once since that dinner, and we discussed you. He says he can't understand how you came to be a cousin of his, even a second cousin. He says he is *L'Homme qui rit*, and you are *L'Homme qui prie*."

"He has let that off on me already, supplemented by the explanation that every extensive Jewish family embraces a genius and a lunatic. He admits that he is the genius. The unfortunate part for me," ended Raphael, laughing, "is, that he *is* a genius."

"I saw two of his little things the other day at the Impressionist Exhibition in Piccadilly. They are very clever and dashing."

"I am told he draws ballet-girls," said Raphael, moodily.

"Yes, he is a disciple of Degas."

"You don't like that style of art?" he said, a shade of concern in his voice.

"I do not," said Esther, emphatically. "I am a curious mixture. In art, I have discovered in myself two conflicting tastes, and neither is for the modern realism, which I yet admire in literature. I like poetic pictures, impregnated with vague romantic melancholy; and I like the white lucidity of classic statuary. I suppose the one taste is the offspring of temperament, the other of thought; for intellectually, I admire the Greek ideas, and was glad to hear you correct Sidney's perversion of the adjective. I wonder," she added, reflectively, "if one can worship the gods of the Greeks without believing in them."

"But you wouldn't make a cult of beauty?"

"Not if you take beauty in the narrow sense in which I should fancy your cousin uses the word; but, in a higher and broader sense, is it not the one fine thing in life which is a certainty, the one ideal which is not illusion?"

"Nothing is illusion," said Raphael, earnestly. "At least, not in your sense. Why should the Creator deceive us?"

"Oh well, don't let us get into metaphysics. We argue from different platforms," she said. "Tell me what you really came about in connection with the *Flag*."

"Mr. Goldsmith was kind enough to suggest that you might write for it."

"What!" exclaimed Esther, sitting upright in her arm-chair. "I? I write for an orthodox paper?"

"Yes, why not?"

"Do you mean I'm to take part in my own conversion?"

"The paper is not entirely religious," he reminded her.

"No, there are the advertisements." she said slily.

"Pardon me," he said. "We don't insert any advertisements contrary to the principles of orthodoxy. Not that we are much tempted."

"You advertise soap," she murmured.

"Oh, please! Don't you go in for those cheap sarcasms."

"Forgive me," she said. "Remember my conceptions of orthodoxy are drawn mainly from the Ghetto, where cleanliness, so far from being next to godliness, is nowhere in the vicinity. But what can I do for you?"

"I don't know. At present the staff, the *Flag*-staff as Sidney calls it, consists of myself and a sub-editor, who take it in turn to translate the only regular outside contributor's articles into English."

"Who's that?"

"Melchitsedek Pinchas, the poet I told you of."

"I suppose he writes in Hebrew."

"No, if he did the translation would be plain sailing enough. The trouble is that he will write in English. I must admit, though, he improves daily. Our correspondents, too, have the same weakness for the vernacular, and I grieve to add that when they do introduce a Hebrew word, they do not invariably spell it correctly."

She smiled; her smile was never so fascinating as by firelight.

Raphael rose and paced the room nervously, flinging out his arms in uncouth fashion to emphasize his speech.

"I was thinking you might introduce a secular department of some sort which would brighten up the paper. My articles are so plaguy dull."

"Not so dull, for religious articles," she assured him.

"Could you treat Jewish matters from a social standpoint—gossipy sort of thing."

She shook her head. "I'm afraid to trust myself to write on Jewish subjects. I should be sure to tread on somebody's corns."

"Oh, I have it!" he cried, bringing his arms in contact with a small Venetian vase which Esther, with great presence of mind, just managed to catch ere it reached the ground.

"No, I have it," she said, laughing. "Do sit down, else nobody can answer for the consequences."

She half pushed him into his chair, where he fell to warming his hands contemplatively.

"Well?" she said after a pause. "I thought you had an idea."

"Yes, yes," he said, rousing himself. "The subject we were just discussing—Art."

"But there is nothing Jewish about art."

"All noble work has its religious aspects. Then there are Jewish artists."

"Oh yes! your contemporaries do notice their exhibits, and there seem to be more of them than the world ever hears of. But if I went to a gathering for you how should I know which were Jews?"

"By their names, of course."

"By no means of course. Some artistic Jews have forgotten their own names."

"That's a dig at Sidney."

"Really, I wasn't thinking of him for the moment," she said a little sharply. "However, in any case there's nothing worth doing till May, and that's some months ahead. I'll do the Academy for you if you like."

"Thank you. Won't Sidney stare if you pulverize him in *The Flag of Judah*? Some of the pictures have also Jewish subjects, you know."

"Yes, but if I mistake not, they're invariably done by Christian artists."

"Nearly always," he admitted pensively. "I wish we had a Jewish allegorical painter to express the high conceptions of our sages."

"As he would probably not know what they are,"—she murmured. Then, seeing him rise as if to go, she said: "Won't you have a cup of tea?"

"No, don't trouble," he answered.

"Oh yes, do!" she pleaded. "Or else I shall think you're angry with me for not asking you before." And she rang the bell. She discovered, to her amusement, that Raphael took two pieces of sugar per cup, but that if they were not inserted, he did not notice their absence. Over tea, too, Raphael had a new idea, this time fraught with peril to the Sèvres tea-pot.

"Why couldn't you write us a Jewish serial story?" he said suddenly. "That would be a novelty in communal journalism."

Esther looked startled by the proposition.

"How do you know I could?" she said after a silence.

"I don't know," he replied. "Only I fancy you could. Why not?" he said encouragingly. "You don't know what you can do till you try. Besides you write poetry."

"The Jewish public doesn't like the looking-glass," she answered him, shaking her head.

"Oh, you can't say that. They've only objected as yet to the distorting mirror. You're thinking of the row over that man Armitage's book. Now, why not write an antidote to that book? There now, there's an idea for you."

"It *is* an idea!" said Esther with overt sarcasm. "You think art can be degraded into an antidote."

"Art is not a fetish," he urged. "What degradation is there in art teaching a noble lesson?"

"Ah, that is what you religious people will never understand," she said scathingly. "You want everything to preach."

"Everything does preach something," he retorted. "Why not have the sermon good?"

"I consider the original sermon *was* good," she said defiantly. "It doesn't need an antidote."

"How can you say that? Surely, merely as one who was born a Jewess, you wouldn't care for the sombre picture drawn by this Armitage to stand as a portrait of your people."

She shrugged her shoulders—the ungraceful shrug of the Ghetto. "Why not? It is one-sided, but it is true."

"I don't deny that; probably the man was sincerely indignant at certain aspects. I am ready to allow he did not even see he was one-sided. But if *you* see it, why not show the world the other side of the shield?"

She put her hand wearily to her brow.

"Do not ask me," she said. "To have my work appreciated merely because the moral tickled the reader's vanity would be a mockery. The suffrages of the Jewish public—I might have valued them once; now I despise them." She sank further back on the chair, pale and silent.

"Why, what harm have they done you?" he asked.

"They are so stupid," she said, with a gesture of distaste.

"That is a new charge against the Jews."

"Look at the way they have denounced this Armitage, saying his book is vulgar and wretched and written for gain, and all because it does not flatter them."

"Can you wonder at it? To say 'you're another' may not be criticism, but it is human nature."

Esther smiled sadly. "I cannot make you out at all," she said.

"Why? What is there strange about me?"

"You say such shrewd, humorous things sometimes; I wonder how you can remain orthodox."

"Now I can't understand *you*," he said, puzzled.

"Oh well. Perhaps if you could, you wouldn't be orthodox. Let us remain mutual enigmas. And will you do me a favor?"

"With pleasure," he said, his face lighting up.

"Don't mention Mr. Armitage's book to me again. I am sick of hearing about it."

"So am I," he said, rather disappointed. "After that dinner I thought it only fair to read it, and although I detect considerable crude power in it, still I am very sorry it was ever published. The presentation of Judaism is most ignorant. All the mystical yearnings of the heroine might have found as much satisfaction in the faith of her own race as they find expression in its poetry."

He rose to go. "Well, I am to take it for granted you will not write that antidote?"

"I'm afraid it would be impossible for me to undertake it," she said more mildly than before, and pressed her hand again to her brow.

"Pardon me," he said in much concern. "I am too selfish. I forgot you are not well. How is your head feeling now?"

"About the same, thank you," she said, forcing a grateful smile. "You may rely on me for art; yes, and music, too, if you like."

"Thank you," he said. "You read a great deal, don't you?"

She nodded her head. "Well, every week books are published of more or less direct Jewish interest. I should be glad of notes about such to brighten up the paper."

"For anything strictly unorthodox you may count on me. If that antidote turns up, I shall not fail to cackle over it in your columns. By the by, are you going to review the poison? Excuse so many mixed metaphors," she added, with a rather forced laugh.

"No, I shan't say anything about it. Why give it an extra advertisement by slating it?"

"Slating," she repeated with a faint smile. "I see you have mastered all the slang of your profession."

"Ah, that's the influence of my sub-editor," he said, smiling in return. "Well, goodbye."

"You're forgetting your overcoat," she said, and having smoothed out that crumpled collar, she accompanied him down the wide soft-carpeted staircase into the hall with its rich bronzes and glistening statues.

"How are your people in America?" he bethought himself to ask on the way down.

"They are very well, thank you," she said. "I send my brother Solomon *The Flag of Judah*. He is also, I am afraid, one of the unregenerate. You see I am doing my best to enlarge your congregation."

He could not tell whether it was sarcasm or earnest.

"Well, goodbye," he said, holding out his hand. "Thank you for your promise."

"Oh, that's not worth thanking me for," she said, touching his long white fingers for an instant. "Look at the glory of seeing myself in print. I hope you're not annoyed with me for refusing to contribute fiction," she ended, growing suddenly remorseful at the moment of parting.

"Of course not. How could I be?"

"Couldn't your sister Adelaide do you a story?"

"Addle?" he repeated laughing, "Fancy Addie writing stories! Addie has no literary ability."

"That's always the way with brothers. Solomon says—" She paused suddenly.

"I don't remember for the moment that Solomon has any proverb on the subject," he said, still amused at the idea of Addie as an authoress.

"I was thinking of something else. Goodbye. Remember me to your sister, please."

"Certainly," he said. Then he exclaimed, "Oh, what a block-head I am! I forgot to remember her to you. She says she would be so pleased if you would come and have tea and a chat with her some day. I should like you and Addie to know each other."

"Thanks, I will. I will write to her some day. Goodbye, once more."

He shook hands with her and fumbled at the door.

"Allow me!" she said, and opened it upon the gray dulness of the dripping street. "When may I hope for the honor of another visit from a real live editor?"

"I don't know," he said, smiling. "I'm awfully busy, I have to read a paper on Ibn Ezra at Jews' College today fortnight."

"Outsiders admitted?" she asked.

"The lectures *are* for outsiders," he said. "To spread the knowledge of our literature. Only they won't come. Have you never been to one?"

She shook her head.

"There!" he said. "You complain of our want of culture, and you don't even know what's going on."

She tried to take the reproof with a smile, but the corners of her mouth quivered. He raised his hat and went down the steps.

She followed him a little way along the Terrace, with eyes growing dim with tears she could not account for. She went back to the drawing-room and threw herself into the arm-chair where he had sat, and made her headache worse by thinking of all her unhappiness. The great room was filling with dusk, and in the twilight pictures gathered and dissolved. What girlish dreams and revolts had gone to make that unfortunate book, which after endless boomerang-like returns from the publishers, had appeared, only to be denounced by Jewry, ignored by its journals and scantily noticed by outside criticisms. *Mordecai Josephs* had fallen almost still-born from the press; the sweet secret she had hoped to tell her patroness had turned bitter like that other secret of her dead love for Sidney, in the reaction from which she had written most of her book. How fortunate at least that her love had flickered out, had proved but the ephemeral sentiment of a romantic girl for the first brilliant man she had met. Sidney had fascinated her by his verbal audacities in a world of narrow conventions; he had for the moment laughed away spiritual aspirations and yearnings with a raillery that was almost like ozone to a young woman avid of martyrdom for the happiness of the world. How, indeed, could she have expected the handsome young artist to feel the magic that hovered about her talks with him, to know the thrill that lay in the formal hand-clasp, to be aware that he interpreted for her poems and pictures, and incarnated the undefined ideal of girlish day-dreams? How could he ever have had other than an intellectual thought of her; how could any man, even the religious Raphael? Sickly, ugly little thing that she was! She got up and looked in the glass now to see herself thus, but the shadows had gathered too thickly. She snatched up a newspaper that lay on a couch, lit it, and held it before the glass; it flared up threateningly and she beat it out, laughing hysterically and asking herself if she was mad. But she had seen the ugly little face; its expression frightened her. Yes, love was not for her; she could only love a man of brilliancy and culture, and she was nothing but a Petticoat Lane girl, after all. Its coarseness, its vulgarity underlay all her veneer. They had got into her book; everybody said so. Raphael said so. How dared she write disdainfully of Raphael's people? She an upstart, an outsider? She went to the library, lit the gas, got down a volume of

Graetz's history of the Jews, which she had latterly taken to reading, and turned over its wonderful pages. Then she wandered restlessly back to the great dim drawing-room and played amateurish fantasias on the melancholy Polish melodies of her childhood till Mr. and Mrs. Henry Goldsmith returned. They had captured the Rev. Joseph Strelitski and brought him back to dinner, Esther would have excused herself from the meal, but Mrs. Goldsmith insisted the minister would think her absence intentionally discourteous. In point of fact, Mrs. Goldsmith, like all Jewesses a born match-maker, was not disinclined to think of the popular preacher as a sort of adopted son-in-law. She did not tell herself so, but she instinctively resented the idea of Esther marrying into the station of her patroness. Strelitski, though his position was one of distinction for a Jewish clergyman, was, like Esther, of humble origin; it would be a match which she could bless from her pedestal in genuine goodwill towards both parties.

The fashionable minister was looking careworn and troubled. He had aged twice ten years since his outburst at the Holy Land League. The black curl hung disconsolately on his forehead. He sat at Esther's side, but rarely looking at her, or addressing her, so that her taciturnity and scarcely-veiled dislike did not noticeably increase his gloom. He rallied now and again out of politeness to his hostess, flashing out a pregnant phrase or two. But prosperity did not seem to have brought happiness to the whilom, poor Russian student, even though he had fought his way to it unaided.

VI

COMEDY OR TRAGEDY?

The weeks went on and Passover drew nigh. The recurrence of the feast brought no thrill to Esther now. It was no longer a charmed time, with strange things to eat and drink, and a comparative plenty of them—stranger still. Lack of appetite was the chief dietary want now. Nobody had any best clothes to put on in a world where everything was for the best in the way of clothes. Except for the speckled Passover cakes, there was hardly any external symptom of the sacred Festival. While the Ghetto was turning itself inside out, the Kensington Terrace was calm in the dignity of continuous cleanliness. Nor did Henry Goldsmith himself go prowling about the house in quest of vagrant crumbs. Mary O'Reilly attended to all that, and the Goldsmiths had implicit confidence in her fidelity to the traditions of their faith. Wherefore, the evening of the day before Passover, instead of being devoted to frying fish and provisioning, was free for more secular occupations; Esther, for example, had arranged to go to see the *début* of a new Hamlet with Addie. Addie had asked her to go, mentioned that Raphael, who was taking her, had suggested that she should bring her friend. For they had become great friends, had Addie and Esther, ever since Esther had gone to take that cup of tea, with the chat that is more essential than milk or sugar.

The girls met or wrote every week. Raphael, Esther never met nor heard from directly. She found Addie a sweet, lovable girl, full of frank simplicity and unquestioning piety. Though dazzlingly beautiful, she had none of the coquetry which Esther, with a touch of jealousy, had been accustomed to associate with beauty, and she had little of the petty malice of girlish gossip. Esther summed her up as Raphael's heart without his head. It was unfair, for Addie's own head was by no means despicable. But Esther was not alone in taking eccentric opinions as the touchstone of intellectual vigor. Anyhow, she was distinctly happier since Addie had come into her life, and she admired her as a mountain torrent might admire a crystal pool—half envying her happier temperament.

The Goldsmiths were just finishing dinner, when the expected ring

ISRAEL ZANGWILL

came. To their surprise, the ringer was Sidney. He was shown into the dining-room.

"Good evening, all," he said. "I've come as a substitute for Raphael."

Esther grew white. "Why, what has happened to him?" she asked.

"Nothing, I had a telegram to say he was unexpectedly detained in the city, and asking me to take Addie and to call for you."

Esther turned from white to red. How rude of Raphael! How disappointing not to meet him, after all! And did he think she could thus unceremoniously be handed over to somebody else? She was about to beg to be excused, when it struck her a refusal would look too pointed. Besides, she did not fear Sidney now. It would be a test of her indifference. So she murmured instead, "What can detain him?"

"Charity, doubtless. Do you know, that after he is fagged out with upholding the *Flag* from early morning till late eve, he devotes the later eve to gratuitous tuition, lecturing and the like."

"No," said Esther, softened. "I knew he came home late, but I thought he had to report communal meetings."

"That, too. But Addie tells me he never came home at all one night last week. He was sitting up with some wretched dying pauper."

"He'll kill himself," said Esther, anxiously.

"People are right about him. He is quite hopeless," said Percy Saville, the solitary guest, tapping his forehead significantly.

"Perhaps it is we who are hopeless," said Esther, sharply.

"I wish we were all as sensible," said Mrs. Henry Goldsmith, turning on the unhappy stockbroker with her most superior air. "Mr. Leon always reminds me of Judas Maccabaeus."

He shrank before the blaze of her mature beauty, the fulness of her charms revealed by her rich evening dress, her hair radiating strange, subtle perfume. His eye sought Mr. Goldsmith's for refuge and consolation.

"That is so," said Mr. Goldsmith, rubbing his red chin. "He is an excellent young man."

"May I trouble you to put on your things at once, Miss Ansell?" said Sidney. "I have left Addie in the carriage, and we are rather late. I believe it is usual for ladies to put on 'things,' even when in evening dress. I may mention that there is a bouquet for you in the carriage, and, however unworthy a substitute I may be for Raphael, I may at least claim he would have forgotten to bring you that."

Esther smiled despite herself as she left the room to get her cloak. She was chagrined and disappointed, but she resolved not to inflict her ill-humor on her companions.

She had long since got used to carriages, and when they arrived at the theatre, she took her seat in the box without heart-fluttering. It was an old discovery now that boxes had no connection with oranges nor stalls with costers' barrows.

The house was brilliant. The orchestra was playing the overture.

"I wish Mr. Shakspeare would write a new play," grumbled Sidney. "All these revivals make him lazy. Heavens! what his fees must tot up to! If I were not sustained by the presence of you two girls, I should no more survive the fifth act than most of the characters. Why don't they brighten the piece up with ballet-girls?"

"Yes, I suppose you blessed Mr. Leon when you got his telegram," said Esther. "What a bore it must be to you to be saddled with his duties!"

"Awful!" admitted Sidney gravely. "Besides, it interferes with my work."

"Work?" said Addie. "You know you only work by sunlight."

"Yes, that's the best of my profession—in England. It gives you such opportunities of working—at other professions."

"Why, what do you work at?" inquired Esther, laughing.

"Well, there's amusement, the most difficult of all things to achieve! Then there's poetry. You don't know what a dab I am at rondeaux and barcarolles. And I write music, too, lovely little serenades to my lady-loves and reveries that are like dainty pastels."

"All the talents!" said Addie, looking at him with a fond smile. "But if you have anytime to spare from the curling of your lovely silken moustache, which is entirely like a delicate pastel, will you kindly tell me what celebrities are present?"

"Yes, do," added Esther, "I have only been to two first nights, and then I had nobody to point out the lions."

"Well, first of all I see a very celebrated painter in a box—a man who has improved considerably on the weak draughtsmanship displayed by Nature in her human figures, and the amateurishness of her glaring sunsets."

"Who's that?" inquired Addie and Esther eagerly.

"I think he calls himself Sidney Graham—but that of course is only a *nom de pinceau*."

"Oh!" said, the girls, with a reproachful smile.

"Do be serious!" said Esther. "Who is that stout gentleman with the bald head?" She peered down curiously at the stalls through her opera-glass.

"What, the lion without the mane? That's Tom Day, the dramatic critic of a dozen papers. A terrible Philistine. Lucky for Shakspeare he didn't flourish in Elizabethan times."

He rattled on till the curtain rose and the hushed audience settled down to the enjoyment of the tragedy.

"This looks as if it is going to be the true Hamlet," said Esther, after the first act.

"What do you mean by the true Hamlet?" queried Sidney cynically.

"The Hamlet for whom life is at once too big and too little," said Esther.

"And who was at once mad and sane," laughed Sidney. "The plain truth is that Shakspeare followed the old tale, and what you take for subtlety is but the blur of uncertain handling. Aha! You look shocked. Have I found your religion at last?"

"No; my reverence for our national bard is based on reason," rejoined Esther seriously. "To conceive Hamlet, the typical nineteenth-century intellect, in that bustling picturesque Elizabethan time was a creative feat bordering on the miraculous. And then, look at the solemn inexorable march of destiny in his tragedies, awful as its advance in the Greek dramas. Just as the marvels of the old fairy-tales were an instinctive prevision of the miracles of modern science, so this idea of destiny seems to me an instinctive anticipation of the formulas of modern science. What we want today is a dramatist who shall show us the great natural silent forces, working the weal and woe of human life through the illusions of consciousness and free will."

"What you want tonight, Miss Ansell, is black coffee," said Sidney, "and I'll tell the attendant to get you a cup, for I dragged you away from dinner before the crown and climax of the meal; I have always noticed myself that when I am interrupted in my meals, all sorts of bugbears, scientific or otherwise, take possession of my mind."

He called the attendant.

"Esther has the most nonsensical opinions," said Addie gravely. "As if people weren't responsible for their actions! Do good and all shall be well with thee, is sound Bible teaching and sound common sense."

"Yes, but isn't it the Bible that says, 'The fathers have eaten a sour grape and the teeth of the children are set on edge'?" Esther retorted.

Addie looked perplexed. "It sounds contradictory," she said honestly.

"Not at all, Addie," said Esther. "The Bible is a literature, not a book. If you choose to bind Tennyson and Milton in one volume that doesn't make them a book. And you can't complain if you find contradictions in the text. Don't you think the sour grape text the truer, Mr. Graham?"

"Don't ask me, please. I'm prejudiced against anything that appears in the Bible."

In his flippant way Sidney spoke the truth. He had an almost physical repugnance for his fathers' ways of looking at things.

"I think you're the two most wicked people in the world," exclaimed Addie gravely.

"We are," said Sidney lightly. "I wonder you consent to sit in the same box with us. How you can find my company endurable I can never make out."

Addie's lovely face flushed and her lip quivered a little.

"It's your friend who's the wickeder of the two," pursued Sidney. "For she's in earnest and I'm not. Life's too short for us to take the world's troubles on our shoulders, not to speak of the unborn millions. A little light and joy, the flush of sunset or of a lovely woman's face, a fleeting strain of melody, the scent of a rose, the flavor of old wine, the flash of a jest, and ah, yes, a cup of coffee—here's yours, Miss Ansell— that's the most we can hope for in life. Let us start a religion with one commandment: 'Enjoy thyself.'"

"That religion has too many disciples already," said Esther, stirring her coffee.

"Then why not start it if you wish to reform the world," asked Sidney. "All religions survive merely by being broken. With only one commandment to break, everybody would jump at the chance. But so long as you tell people they mustn't enjoy themselves, they will, it's human nature, and you can't alter that by Act of Parliament or Confession of Faith. Christ ran amuck at human nature, and human nature celebrates his birthday with pantomimes."

"Christ understood human nature better than the modern young man," said Esther scathingly, "and the proof lies in the almost limitless impress he has left on history."

"Oh, that was a fluke," said Sidney lightly. "His real influence is only superficial. Scratch the Christian and you find the Pagan—spoiled."

"He divined by genius what science is slowly finding out," said Esther, "when he said, 'Forgive them for they know not what they do'!—"

Sidney laughed heartily. "That seems to be your King Charles's head—seeing divinations of modern science in all the old ideas. Personally I honor him for discovering that the Sabbath was made for man, not man for the Sabbath. Strange he should have stopped half-way to the truth!"

"What is the truth?" asked Addie curiously.

"Why, that morality was made for man, not man for morality," said Sidney. "That chimera of meaningless virtue which the Hebrew has brought into the world is the last monster left to slay. The Hebrew view of life is too one-sided. The Bible is a literature without a laugh in it. Even Raphael thinks the great Radical of Galilee carried spirituality too far."

"Yes, he thinks he would have been reconciled to the Jewish doctors and would have understood them better," said Addie, "only he died so young."

"That's a good way of putting it!" said Sidney admiringly. "One can see Raphael is my cousin despite his religious aberrations. It opens up new historical vistas. Only it is just like Raphael to find excuses for everybody, and Judaism in everything. I am sure he considers the devil a good Jew at heart; if he admits any moral obliquity in him, he puts it down to the climate."

This made Esther laugh outright, even while there were tears for Raphael in the laugh. Sidney's intellectual fascination reasserted itself over her; there seemed something inspiring in standing with him on the free heights that left all the clogging vapors and fogs of moral problems somewhere below; where the sun shone and the clear wind blew and talk was a game of bowls with Puritan ideals for ninepins. He went on amusing her till the curtain rose, with a pretended theory of Mohammedology which he was working at. Just as for the Christian Apologist the Old Testament was full of hints of the New, so he contended was the New Testament full of foreshadowings of the Koran, and he cited as a most convincing text, "In Heaven, there shall be no marrying, nor giving in marriage." He professed to think that Mohammedanism was the dark horse that would come to the front in the race of religions and win in the west as it had won in the east.

"There's a man staring dreadfully at you, Esther," said Addie, when the curtain fell on the second act.

"Nonsense!" said Esther, reluctantly returning from the realities of the play to the insipidities of actual life. "Whoever it is, it must be at you."

She looked affectionately at the great glorious creature at her side, tall and stately, with that winning gentleness of expression which spiritualizes the most voluptuous beauty. Addie wore pale sea-green, and there were lilies of the valley at her bosom, and a diamond star in her hair. No man could admire her more than Esther, who felt quite vain of her friend's beauty and happy to bask in its reflected sunshine. Sidney followed her glance and his cousin's charms struck him with almost novel freshness. He was so much with Addie that he always took her for granted. The semi-unconscious liking he had for her society was based on other than physical traits. He let his eyes rest upon her for a moment in half-surprised appreciation, figuring her as half-bud, half-blossom. Really, if Addie had not been his cousin and a Jewess! She was not much of a cousin, when he came to cipher it out, but then she was a good deal of a Jewess!

"I'm sure it's you he's staring at," persisted Addie.

"Don't be ridiculous," persisted Esther. "Which man do you mean?"

"There! The fifth row of stalls, the one, two, four, seven, the seventh man from the end! He's been looking at you all through, but now he's gone in for a good long stare. There! next to that pretty girl in pink."

"Do you mean the young man with the dyed carnation in his buttonhole and the crimson handkerchief in his bosom?"

"Yes, that's the one. Do you know him?"

"No," said Esther, lowering her eyes and looking away. But when Addie informed her that the young man had renewed his attentions to the girl in pink, she levelled her opera-glass at him. Then she shook her head.

"There seems something familiar about his face, but I cannot for the life of me recall who it is."

"The something familiar about his face is his nose," said Addie laughing, "for it is emphatically Jewish."

"At that rate," said Sidney, "nearly half the theatre would be familiar, including a goodly proportion of the critics, and Hamlet and Ophelia themselves. But I know the fellow."

"You do? Who is he?" asked the girls eagerly.

"I don't know. He's one of the mashers of the *Frivolity*. I'm another, and so we often meet. But we never speak as we pass by. To tell the truth, I resent him."

"It's wonderful how fond Jews are of the theatre," said Esther, "and how they resent other Jews going."

ISRAEL ZANGWILL

"Thank you," said Sidney. "But as I'm not a Jew the arrow glances off."

"Not a Jew?" repeated Esther in amaze.

"No. Not in the current sense. I always deny I'm a Jew."

"How do you justify that?" said Addie incredulously.

"Because it would be a lie to say I was. It would be to produce a false impression. The conception of a Jew in the mind of the average Christian is a mixture of Fagin, Shylock, Rothschild and the caricatures of the American comic papers. I am certainly not like that, and I'm not going to tell a lie and say I am. In conversation always think of your audience. It takes two to make a truth. If an honest man told an old lady he was an atheist, that would be a lie, for to her it would mean he was a dissolute reprobate. To call myself 'Abrahams' would be to live a daily lie. I am not a bit like the picture called up by Abrahams. Graham is a far truer expression of myself."

"Extremely ingenious," said Esther smiling. "But ought you not rather to utilize yourself for the correction of the portrait of Abrahams?"

Sidney shrugged his shoulders. "Why should I subject myself to petty martyrdom for the sake of an outworn creed and a decaying sect?"

"We are not decaying," said Addie indignantly.

"Personally you are blossoming," said Sidney, with a mock bow. "But nobody can deny that our recent religious history has been a series of dissolving views. Look at that young masher there, who is still ogling your fascinating friend; rather, I suspect, to the annoyance of the young lady in pink, and compare him with the old hard-shell Jew. When I was a lad named Abrahams, painfully training in the way I wasn't going to go, I got an insight into the lives of my ancestors. Think of the people who built up the Jewish prayer-book, who added line to line and precept to precept, and whose whole thought was intertwined with religion, and then look at that young fellow with the dyed carnation and the crimson silk handkerchief, who probably drives a drag to the Derby, and for aught I know runs a music hall. It seems almost incredible he should come of that Puritan old stock."

"Not at all," said Esther. "If you knew more of our history, you would see it is quite normal. We were always hankering after the gods of the heathen, and we always loved magnificence; remember our Temples. In every land we have produced great merchants and rulers, prime-ministers, viziers, nobles. We built castles in Spain (solid ones) and palaces in Venice. We have had saints and sinners, free livers and ascetics, martyrs and money-lenders. Polarity, Graetz calls the self-contradiction which runs through our history. I figure the Jew as the eldest-born of Time, touching the Creation and reaching forward into the future, the true *blasé* of the Universe; the Wandering Jew who has been everywhere, seen everything, done everything, led everything, thought everything and suffered everything."

"Bravo, quite a bit of Beaconsfieldian fustian," said Sidney laughing, yet astonished. "One would think you were anxious to assert yourself against the ancient peerage of this mushroom realm."

"It is the bare historical truth," said Esther, quietly. "We are so ignorant of our own history—can we wonder at the world's ignorance of it? Think of the part the Jew has played—Moses giving the world its morality, Jesus its religion, Isaiah its millennial visions, Spinoza its cosmic philosophy, Ricardo its political economy, Karl Marx and Lassalle its socialism, Heine its loveliest poetry, Mendelssohn its most restful music, Rachael its supreme acting—and then think of the stock Jew of the American comic papers! There lies the real comedy, too deep for laughter."

"Yes, but most of the Jews you mention were outcasts or apostates," retorted Sidney. "There lies the real tragedy, too deep for tears. Ah, Heine summed it up best: 'Judaism is not a religion; it is a misfortune.' But do you wonder at the intolerance of every nation towards its Jews? It is a form of homage. Tolerate them and they spell 'Success,' and patriotism is an ineradicable prejudice. Since when have you developed this extraordinary enthusiasm for Jewish history? I always thought you were an anti-Semite."

Esther blushed and meditatively sniffed at her bouquet, but fortunately the rise of the curtain relieved her of the necessity far a reply. It was only a temporary relief, however, for the quizzical young artist returned to the subject immediately the act was over.

"I know you're in charge of the aesthetic department of the *Flag*," he said. "I had no idea you wrote the leaders."

"Don't be absurd!" murmured Esther.

"I always told Addie Raphael could never write so eloquently; didn't I, Addie? Ah, I see you're blushing to find it fame, Miss Ansell."

Esther laughed, though a bit annoyed. "How can you suspect me of writing orthodox leaders?" she asked.

"Well, who else *is* there?" urged Sidney, with mock *naïveté*. "I went down there once and saw the shanty. The editorial sanctum was crowded. Poor Raphael was surrounded by the queerest looking set of creatures I ever clapped eyes on. There was a quaint lunatic in a check suit, describing his apocalyptic visions; a dragoman with sore eyes and a grievance against the Board of Guardians; a venerable son of Jerusalem with a most artistic white beard, who had covered the editorial table with carved nick-nacks in olive and sandal-wood; an inventor who had squared the circle and the problem of perpetual motion, but could not support himself; a Roumanian exile with a scheme for fertilizing Palestine; and a wild-eyed hatchet-faced Hebrew poet who told me I was a famous patron of learning, and sent me his book soon after with a Hebrew inscription which I couldn't read, and a request for a cheque which I didn't write. I thought I just capped the company of oddities, when in came a sallow red-haired chap, with the extraordinary name of Karlkammer, and kicked up a deuce of a shine with Raphael for altering his letter. Raphael mildly hinted that the letter was written in such unintelligible English that he had to grapple with it for an hour before he could reduce it to the coherence demanded of print. But it was no use; it seems Raphael had made him say something heterodox he didn't mean, and he insisted on being allowed to reply to his own letter! He had brought the counter-blast with him; six sheets of foolscap with all the t's uncrossed, and insisted on signing it with his own name. I said, 'Why not? Set a Karlkammer to answer to a Karlkammer.' But Raphael said it would make the paper a laughing-stock, and between the dread of that and the consciousness of having done the man a wrong, he was quite unhappy. He treats all his visitors with angelic consideration, when in another newspaper office the very office-boy would snub them. Of course, nobody has a bit of consideration for him or his time or his purse."

"Poor Raphael!" murmured Esther, smiling sadly at the grotesque images conjured up by Sidney's description.

"I go down there now whenever I want models," concluded Sidney gravely.

"Well, it is only right to hear what those poor people have to say," Addie observed. "What is a paper for except to right wrongs?"

"Primitive person!" said Sidney. "A paper exists to make a profit."

"Raphael's doesn't," retorted Addie.

"Of course not," laughed Sidney. "It never will, so long as there's a conscientious editor at the helm. Raphael flatters nobody and reserves his praises for people with no control of the communal advertisements. Why, it quite preys upon his mind to think that he is linked to an advertisement canvasser with a gorgeous imagination, who goes about representing to the unwary Christian that the *Flag* has a circulation of fifteen hundred."

"Dear me!" said Addie, a smile of humor lighting up her beautiful features.

"Yes," said Sidney, "I think he salves his conscience by an extra hour's slumming in the evening. Most religious folks do their moral book-keeping by double entry. Probably that's why he's not here tonight."

"It's too bad!" said Addie, her face growing grave again. "He comes home so late and so tired that he always falls asleep over his books."

"I don't wonder," laughed Sidney. "Look what he reads! Once I found him nodding peacefully over Thomas à Kempis."

"Oh, he often reads that," said Addie. "When we wake him up and tell him to go to bed, he says he wasn't sleeping, but thinking, turns over a page and falls asleep again."

They all laughed.

"Oh, he's a famous sleeper," Addie continued. "It's as difficult to get him out of bed as into it. He says himself he's an awful lounger and used to idle away whole days before he invented time-tables. Now, he has every hour cut and dried—he says his salvation lies in regular hours."

"Addie, Addie, don't tell tales out of school," said Sidney.

"Why, what tales?" asked Addie, astonished. "Isn't it rather to his credit that he has conquered his bad habits?"

"Undoubtedly; but it dissipates the poetry in which I am sure Miss Ansell was enshrouding him. It shears a man of his heroic proportions, to hear he has to be dragged out of bed. These things should be kept in the family."

Esther stared hard at the house. Her cheeks glowed as if the limelight man had turned his red rays on them. Sidney chuckled mentally over his insight. Addie smiled.

"Oh, nonsense. I'm sure Esther doesn't think less of him because he keeps a time-table."

"You forget your friend has what you haven't—artistic instinct. It's ugly. A man should be a man, not a railway system. If I were you, Addie, I'd capture that time-table, erase lecturing and substitute 'cricketing.' Raphael would never know, and every afternoon, say at 2 P.M., he'd consult his time-table, and seeing he had to cricket, he'd take up his stumps and walk to Regent's Park."

"Yes, but he can't play cricket," said Esther, laughing and glad of the opportunity.

"Oh, can't he?" Sidney whistled. "Don't insult him by telling him that. Why, he was in the Harrow eleven and scored his century in the match with Eton; those long arms of his send the ball flying as if it were a drawing-room ornament."

"Oh yes," affirmed Addie. "Even now, cricket is his one temptation."

Esther was silent. Her Raphael seemed toppling to pieces. The silence seemed to communicate itself to her companions. Addie broke it by sending Sidney to smoke a cigarette in the lobby. "Or else I shall feel quite too selfish," she said. "I know you're just dying to talk to some sensible people. Oh, I beg your pardon, Esther."

The squire of dames smiled but hesitated.

"Yes, do go," said Esther. "There's six or seven minutes more interval. This is the longest wait."

"Ladies' will is my law," said Sidney, gallantly, and, taking a cigarette case from his cloak, which was hung on a peg at the back of a box, he strolled out. "Perhaps," he said, "I shall skip some Shakspeare if I meet a congenial intellectual soul to gossip with."

He had scarce been gone two minutes when there came a gentle tapping at the door and, the visitor being invited to come in, the girls were astonished to behold the young gentleman with the dyed carnation and the crimson silk handkerchief. He looked at Esther with an affable smile.

"Don't you remember me?" he said. The ring of his voice woke some far-off echo in her brain. But no recollection came to her.

"I remembered you almost at once," he went on, in a half-reproachful tone, "though I didn't care about coming up while you had another fellow in the box. Look at me carefully, Esther."

The sound of her name on the stranger's lips set all the chords of memory vibrating—she looked again at the dark oval face with the aquiline nose, the glittering eyes, the neat black moustache, the close-shaved cheeks and chin, and in a flash the past resurged and she murmured almost incredulously, "Levi!"

The young man got rather red. "Ye-e-s!" he stammered. "Allow me to present you my card." He took it out of a little ivory case and handed it to her. It read, "Mr. Leonard James."

An amused smile flitted over Esther's face, passing into one of welcome. She was not at all displeased to see him.

"Addie," she said. "This is Mr. Leonard James, a friend I used to know in my girlhood."

"Yes, we were boys together, as the song says," said Leonard James, smiling facetiously.

Addie inclined her head in the stately fashion which accorded so well with her beauty and resumed her investigation of the stalls. Presently she became absorbed in a tender reverie induced by the passionate waltz music and she forgot all about Esther's strange visitor, whose words fell as insensibly on her ears as the ticking of a familiar clock. But to Esther, Leonard James's conversation was full of interest. The two ugly ducklings of the back-pond had become to all appearance swans of the ornamental water, and it was natural that they should gabble of auld lang syne and the devious routes by which they had come together again.

"You see, I'm like you, Esther," explained the young man. "I'm not fitted for the narrow life that suits my father and mother and my sister. They've got no ideas beyond the house, and religion, and all that sort of thing. What do you think my father wanted me to be? A minister! Think of it! Ha! ha! ha! Me a minister! I actually did go for a couple of terms to Jews' College. Oh, yes, you remember! Why, I was there when you were a school-teacher and got taken up by the swells. But our stroke of fortune came soon after yours. Did you never hear of it? My, you must have dropped all your old acquaintances if no one ever told you that! Why, father came in for a couple of thousand pounds! I thought I'd make you stare. Guess who from?"

"I give it up," said Esther.

"Thank you. It was never yours to give," said Leonard, laughing jovially at his wit. "Old Steinwein—you remember his death. It was in all the papers; the eccentric old buffer, who was touched in the upper story, and used to give so much time and money to Jewish affairs, setting up lazy old rabbis in Jerusalem to shake themselves over their Talmuds. You remember his gifts to the poor—six shillings sevenpence each because he was seventy-nine years old and all that. Well, he used to send the pater a basket of fruit every *Yomtov*. But he used to do that to every Rabbi, all around, and my old man had not the least idea he was the object of special regard till the old chap pegged out. Ah, there's nothing like Torah, after all."

"You don't know what you may have lost through not becoming a minister," suggested Esther slily.

"Ah, but I know what I've gained. Do you think I could stand having my hands and feet tied with phylacteries?" asked Leonard, becoming vividly metaphoric in the intensity of his repugnance to the galling bonds of orthodoxy. "Now, I do as I like, go where I please, eat what I please. Just fancy not being able to join fellows at supper, because you mustn't eat oysters or steak? Might as well go into a monastery at once. All very well in ancient Jerusalem, where everybody was rowing in the same boat. Have you ever tasted pork, Esther?"

"No," said Esther, with a faint smile.

"I have," said Leonard. "I don't say it to boast, but I have had it times without number. I didn't like it the first time—thought it would choke me, you know, but that soon wears off. Now I breakfast off ham and eggs regularly. I go the whole hog, you see. Ha! ha! ha!"

"If I didn't see from your card you're not living at home, that would have apprised me of it," said Esther.

"Of course, I couldn't live at home. Why the guvnor couldn't bear to let me shave. Ha! ha! ha! Fancy a religion that makes you keep your hair on unless you use a depilatory. I was articled to a swell solicitor. The old man resisted a long time, but he gave in at last, and let me live near the office."

"Ah, then I presume you came in for some of the two thousand, despite your non-connection with Torah?"

"There isn't much left of it now," said Leonard, laughing. "What's two thousand in seven years in London? There were over four hundred guineas swallowed up by the premium, and the fees, and all that."

"Well, let us hope it'll all come back in costs."

"Well, between you and me," said Leonard, seriously, "I should be surprised if it does. You see, I haven't yet scraped through the Final; they're making the beastly exam. stiffer every year. No, it isn't to that quarter I look to recoup myself for the outlay on my education."

"No?" said Esther.

"No. Fact is—between you and me—I'm going to be an actor."

"Oh!" said Esther.

"Yes. I've played several times in private theatricals; you know we Jews have a knack for the stage; you'd be surprised to know how many pros are Jews. There's heaps of money to be made now-a-days on the boards. I'm in with lots of 'em, and ought to know. It's the only profession where you don't want any training, and these law books are as dry as the Mishna the old man used to make me study. Why, they say tonight's 'Hamlet' was in a counting-house four years ago."

"I wish you success," said Esther, somewhat dubiously. "And how is your sister Hannah? Is she married yet?"

"Married! Not she! She's got no money, and you know what our Jewish young men are. Mother wanted her to have the two thousand pounds for a dowry, but fortunately Hannah had the sense to see that it's the man that's got to make his way in the world. Hannah is always certain of her bread and butter, which is a good deal in these hard times. Besides, she's naturally grumpy, and she doesn't go out of her way to make herself agreeable to young men. It's my belief she'll die an old maid. Well, there's no accounting for tastes."

"And your father and mother?"

"They're all right, I believe. I shall see them tomorrow night—Passover, you know. I haven't missed a single *Seder* at home," he said, with conscious virtue. "It's an awful bore, you know. I often laugh to think of the chappies' faces if they could see me leaning on a pillow and gravely asking the old man why we eat Passover cakes." He laughed now to think of it. "But I never miss; they'd cut up rough, I expect, if I did."

"Well, that's something in your favor," murmured Esther gravely.

He looked at her sharply; suddenly suspecting that his auditor was not perfectly sympathetic. She smiled a little at the images passing through her mind, and Leonard, taking her remark for badinage, allowed his own features to relax to their original amiability.

"You're not married, either, I suppose," he remarked.

"No," said Esther. "I'm like your sister Hannah."

He shook his head sceptically.

"Ah, I expect you'll be looking very high," he said.

"Nonsense," murmured Esther, playing with her bouquet.

A flash passed across his face, but he went on in the same tone. "Ah, don't tell me. Why shouldn't you? Why, you're looking perfectly charming tonight."

"Please, don't," said Esther, "Every girl looks perfectly charming when she's nicely dressed. Who and what am I? Nothing. Let us drop the subject."

"All right; but you *must* have grand ideas, else you'd have sometimes gone to see my people as in the old days."

"When did I visit your people? You used to come and see me sometimes." A shadow of a smile hovered about the tremulous lips. "Believe me, I didn't consciously drop any of my old acquaintances. My life changed; my family went to America; later on I travelled. It is the currents of life, not their wills, that bear old acquaintances asunder."

He seemed pleased with her sentiments and was about to say something, but she added: "The curtain's going up. Hadn't you better go down to your friend? She's been looking up at us impatiently."

"Oh, no, don't bother about her." said Leonard, reddening a little. "She—she won't mind. She's only—only an actress, you know, I have to keep in with the profession in case any opening should turn up. You never know. An actress may become a lessee at any moment. Hark! The orchestra is striking up again; the scene isn't set yet. Of course I'll go if you want me to!"

"No, stay by all means if you want to," murmured Esther. "We have a chair unoccupied."

"Do you expect that fellow Sidney Graham back?"

"Yes, sooner or later. But how do you know his name?" queried Esther in surprise.

"Everybody about town knows Sidney Graham, the artist. Why, we belong to the same club—the Flamingo—though he only turns up for the great glove-fights. Beastly cad, with all due respect to your friends, Esther. I was introduced to him once, but he stared at me next time so haughtily that I cut him dead. Do you know, ever since then I've suspected he's one of us; perhaps you can tell me, Esther? I dare say he's no more Sidney Graham than I am."

"Hush!" said Esther, glancing warningly towards Addie, who, however, betrayed no sign of attention.

"Sister?" asked Leonard, lowering his voice to a whisper.

Esther shook her head. "Cousin; but Mr. Graham is a friend of mine as well and you mustn't talk of him like that."

"Ripping fine girl!" murmured Leonard irrelevantly. "Wonder at his taste." He took a long stare at the abstracted Addie.

"What do you mean?" said Esther, her annoyance increasing. Her old friend's tone jarred upon her.

"Well, I don't know what he could see in the girl he's engaged to."

Esther's face became white. She looked anxiously towards the unconscious Addie.

"You are talking nonsense," she said, in a low cautious tone. "Mr. Graham is too fond of his liberty to engage himself to any girl."

"Oho!" said Leonard, with a subdued whistle. "I hope you're not sweet on him yourself."

Esther gave an impatient gesture of denial. She resented Leonard's rapid resumption of his olden familiarity.

"Then take care not to be," he said. "He's engaged privately to Miss Hannibal, a daughter of the M.P. Tom Sledge, the sub-editor of the *Cormorant*, told me. You know they collect items about everybody and publish them at what they call the psychological moment. Graham goes to the Hannibals' every Saturday afternoon. They're very strict people; the father, you know, is a prominent Wesleyan and she's not the sort of girl to be played with."

"For Heaven's sake speak more softly," said Esther, though the orchestra was playing *fortissimo* now and they had spoken so quietly all along that Addie could scarcely have heard without a special effort. "It can't be true; you are repeating mere idle gossip."

"Why, they know everything at the *Cormorant*," said Leonard, indignantly. "Do you suppose a man can take such a step as that without its getting known? Why, I shall be chaffed—enviously—about you two tomorrow! Many a thing the world little dreams of is an open secret in Club smoking-rooms. Generally more discreditable than Graham's, which must be made public of itself sooner or later."

To Esther's relief, the curtain rose. Addie woke up and looked round, but seeing that Sidney had not returned, and that Esther was still in colloquy with the invader, she gave her attention to the stage. Esther could no longer bend her eye on the mimic tragedy; her eyes rested pityingly upon Addie's face, and Leonard's eyes rested admiringly upon Esther's. Thus Sidney found the group, when he returned in the middle of the act, to his surprise and displeasure. He stood silently at the back of the box till the act was over. Leonard James was the first to perceive him; knowing he had been telling tales about him, he felt uneasy under his supercilious gaze. He bade Esther goodbye, asking and receiving permission to call upon her. When he was gone, constraint fell upon the party. Sidney was moody; Addie pensive, Esther full of stifled wrath and anxiety. At the close of the performance Sidney took down the girls' wrappings from the pegs. He helped Esther courteously, then hovered over his cousin with a solicitude that brought a look of calm happiness into Addie's face, and an expression of pain into Esther's. As they moved slowly along the crowded corridors, he allowed Addie to get a few paces in advance. It was his last opportunity of saying a word to Esther alone.

"If I were you, Miss Ansell, I would not allow that cad to presume on any acquaintance he may have."

ISRAEL ZANGWILL

All the latent irritation in Esther's breast burst into flame at the idea of Sidney's constituting himself a judge.

"If I had not cultivated his acquaintance I should not have had the pleasure of congratulating you on your engagement," she replied, almost in a whisper. To Sidney it sounded like a shout. His color heightened; he was visibly taken aback.

"What are you talking about?" he murmured automatically.

"About your engagement to Miss Hannibal."

"That blackguard told you!" he whispered angrily, half to himself. "Well, what of it? I am not bound to advertise it, am I? It's my private business, isn't it? You don't expect me to hang a placard round my breast like those on concert-room chairs—'Engaged'!"

"Certainly not," said Esther. "But you might have told your friends, so as to enable them to rejoice sympathetically."

"You turn your sarcasm prettily," he said mildly, "but the sympathetic rejoicing was just what I wanted to avoid. You know what a Jewish engagement is, how the news spreads like wildfire from Piccadilly to Petticoat Lane, and the whole house of Israel gathers together to discuss the income and the prospects of the happy pair. I object to sympathetic rejoicing from the slums, especially as in this case it would probably be exchanged for curses. Miss Hannibal is a Christian, and for a Jew to embrace a Christian is, I believe, the next worse thing to his embracing Christianity, even when the Jew is a pagan." His wonted flippancy rang hollow. He paused suddenly and stole a look at his companion's face, in search of a smile, but it was pale and sorrowful. The flush on his own face deepened; his features expressed internal conflict. He addressed a light word to Addie in front. They were nearing the portico; it was raining outside and a cold wind blew in to meet them; he bent his head down to the delicate little face at his side, and his tones were changed.

"Miss Ansell," he said tremulously, "if I have in anyway misled you by my reticence, I beg you to believe it was unintentionally. The memory of the pleasant quarters of an hour we have spent together will always—"

"Good God!" said Esther hoarsely, her cheeks flaming, her ears tingling. "To whom are you apologising?" He looked at her perplexed. "Why have you not told Addie?" she forced herself to say.

In the press of the crowd, on the edge of the threshold, he stood still. Dazzled as by a flash of lightning, he gazed at his cousin, her beautifully poised head, covered with its fleecy white shawl, dominating the throng. The shawl became an aureole to his misty vision.

"Have you told her?" he whispered with answering hoarseness.

"No," said Esther.

"Then don't tell her," he whispered eagerly.

"I must. She must hear it soon. Such things must ooze out sooner or later."

"Then let it be later. Promise me this."

"No good can come of concealment."

"Promise me, for a little while, till I give you leave."

His pleading, handsome face was close to hers. She wondered how she could ever have cared for a creature so weak and pitiful.

"So be it," she breathed.

"Miss Leon's carriage," bawled the commissionaire. There was a confusion of rain-beaten umbrellas, gleaming carriage-lamps, zigzag rejections on the black pavements, and clattering omnibuses full inside. But the air was fresh.

"Don't go into the rain, Addie," said Sidney, pressing forwards anxiously. "You're doing all my work tonight. Hallo! where did *you* spring from?"

It was Raphael who had elicited the exclamation. He suddenly loomed upon the party, bearing a decrepit dripping umbrella. "I thought I should be in time to catch you—and to apologize," he said, turning to Esther.

"Don't mention it," murmured Esther, his unexpected appearance completing her mental agitation.

"Hold the umbrella over the girls, you beggar," said Sidney.

"Oh, I beg your pardon," said Raphael, poking the rim against a policeman's helmet in his anxiety to obey.

"Don't mention it," said Addie smiling.

"All right, sir," growled the policeman good-humoredly.

Sidney laughed heartily.

"Quite a general amnesty," he said. "Ah! here's the carriage. Why didn't you get inside it out of the rain or stand in the entrance—you're wringing wet."

"I didn't think of it," said Raphael. "Besides, I've only been here a few minutes. The 'busses are so full when it rains I had to walk all the way from Whitechapel."

"You're incorrigible," grumbled Sidney. "As if you couldn't have taken a hansom."

"Why waste money?" said Raphael. They got into the carriage.

"Well, did you enjoy yourselves?" he asked cheerfully.

"Oh yes, thoroughly," said Sidney. "Addie wasted two pocket-handkerchiefs over Ophelia; almost enough to pay for that hansom. Miss Ansell doated on the finger of destiny and I chopped logic and swopped cigarettes with O'Donovan. I hope you enjoyed yourself equally."

Raphael responded with a melancholy smile. He was seated opposite Esther, and ever and anon some flash of light from the street revealed clearly his sodden, almost shabby, garments and the weariness of his expression. He seemed quite out of harmony with the dainty pleasure-party, but just on that account the more in harmony with Esther's old image, the heroic side of him growing only more lovable for the human alloy. She bent towards him at last and said: "I am sorry you were deprived of your evening's amusement. I hope the reason didn't add to the unpleasantness."

"It was nothing," he murmured awkwardly. "A little unexpected work. One can always go to the theatre."

"Ah, I am afraid you overwork yourself too much. You mustn't. Think of your own health."

His look softened. He was in a harassed, sensitive state. The sympathy of her gentle accents, the concern upon the eager little face, seemed to flood his own soul with a self-compassion new to him.

"My health doesn't matter," he faltered. There were sweet tears in his eyes, a colossal sense of gratitude at his heart. He had always meant to pity her and help her; it was sweeter to be pitied, though of course she could not help him. He had no need of help, and on second thoughts he wondered what room there was for pity.

"No, no, don't talk like that," said Esther. "Think of your parents—and Addle."

VII

WHAT THE YEARS BROUGHT

The next morning Esther sat in Mrs. Henry Goldsmith's boudoir, filling up some invitation forms for her patroness, who often took advantage of her literary talent in this fashion. Mrs. Goldsmith herself lay back languidly upon a great easy-chair before an asbestos fire and turned over the leaves of the new number of the *Acadaeum*. Suddenly she uttered a little exclamation.

"What is it?" said Esther.

"They've got a review here of that Jewish novel."

"Have they?" said Esther, glancing up eagerly. "I'd given up looking for it."

"You seem very interested in it," said Mrs. Goldsmith, with a little surprise.

"Yes, I—I wanted to know what they said about it," explained Esther quickly; "one hears so many worthless opinions."

"Well, I'm glad to see we were all right about it," said Mrs. Goldsmith, whose eye had been running down the column. "Listen here. 'It is a disagreeable book at best; what might have been a powerful tragedy being disfigured by clumsy workmanship and sordid superfluous detail. The exaggerated unhealthy pessimism, which the very young mistake for insight, pervades the work and there are some spiteful touches of observation which seem to point to a woman's hand. Some of the minor personages have the air of being sketched from life. The novel can scarcely be acceptable to the writer's circle. Readers, however, in search of the unusual will find new ground broken in this immature study of Jewish life.'"

"There, Esther, isn't that just what I've been saying in other words?"

"It's hardly worth bothering about the book now," said Esther in low tones, "it's such a long time ago now since it came out. I don't know what's the good of reviewing it now. These literary papers always seem so cold and cruel to unknown writers."

"Cruel, it isn't half what he deserves," said Mrs. Goldsmith, "or ought I to say she? Do you think there's anything, Esther, in that idea of its being a woman?"

"Really, dear, I'm sick to death of that book," said Esther. "These reviewers always try to be very clever and to see through brick walls. What does it matter if it's a he, or a she?"

"It doesn't matter, but it makes it more disgraceful, if it's a woman. A woman has no business to know the seamy side of human nature."

At this instant, a domestic knocked and announced that Mr. Leonard James had called to see Miss Ansell. Annoyance, surprise and relief struggled to express themselves on Esther's face.

"Is the gentleman waiting to see me?" she said.

"Yes, miss, he's in the hall."

Esther turned to Mrs. Goldsmith. "It's a young man I came across unexpectedly last night at the theatre. He's the son of Reb Shemuel, of whom you may have heard. I haven't met him since we were boy and girl together. He asked permission to call, but I didn't expect him so soon."

"Oh, see him by all means, dear. He is probably anxious to talk over old times."

"May I ask him up here?"

"No—unless you particularly want to introduce him to me. I dare say he would rather have you to himself." There was a touch of superciliousness about her tone, which Esther rather resented, although not particularly anxious for Levi's social recognition.

"Show him into the library," she said to the servant. "I will be down in a minute." She lingered a few indifferent remarks with her companion and then went down, wondering at Levi's precipitancy in renewing the acquaintance. She could not help thinking of the strangeness of life. That time yesterday she had not dreamed of Levi, and now she was about to see him for the second time and seemed to know him as intimately as if they had never been parted.

Leonard James was pacing the carpet. His face was perturbed, though his stylishly cut clothes were composed and immaculate. A cloak was thrown loosely across his shoulders. In his right hand he held a bouquet of Spring flowers, which he transferred to his left in order to shake hands with her.

"Good afternoon, Esther," he said heartily. "By Jove, you have got among tip-top people. I had no idea. Fancy you ordering Jeames de la Pluche about. And how happy you must be among all these books! I've brought you a bouquet. There! Isn't it a beauty? I got it at Covent Garden this morning."

"It's very kind of you," murmured Esther, not so pleased as she might have been, considering her love of beautiful things. "But you really ought not to waste your money like that."

"What nonsense, Esther! Don't forget I'm not in the position my father was. I'm going to be a rich man. No, don't put it into a vase; put it in your own room where it will remind you of me. Just smell those violets, they are awfully sweet and fresh. I flatter myself, it's quite as swell and tasteful as the bouquet you had last night. Who gave you that. Esther?" The "Esther" mitigated the off-handedness of the question, but made the sentence jar doubly upon her ear. She might have brought herself to call him "Levi" in exchange, but then she was not certain he would like it. "Leonard" was impossible. So she forbore to call him by any name.

"I think Mr. Graham brought it. Won't you sit down?" she said indifferently.

"Thank you. I thought so. Luck that fellow's engaged. Do you know, Esther. I didn't sleep all night."

"No?" said Esther. "You seemed quite well when I saw you."

"So I was, but seeing you again, so unexpectedly, excited me. You have been whirling in my brain ever since. I hadn't thought of you for years—"

"I hadn't thought of you," Esther echoed frankly.

"No, I suppose not," he said, a little ruefully. "But, anyhow, fate has brought us together again. I recognized you the moment I set eyes on you, for all your grand clothes and your swell bouquets. I tell you I was just struck all of a heap; of course, I knew about your luck, but I hadn't realized it. There wasn't anyone in the whole theatre who looked the lady more—'pon honor; you'd have no cause to blush in the company of duchesses. In fact I know a duchess or two who don't look near so refined. I was quite surprised. Do you know, if anyone had told me you used to live up in a garret—"

"Oh, please don't recall unpleasant things," interrupted Esther, petulantly, a little shudder going through her, partly at the picture he called up, partly at his grating vulgarity. Her repulsion to him was growing. Why had he developed so disagreeably? She had not disliked him as a boy, and he certainly had not inherited his traits of coarseness from his father, whom she still conceived as a courtly old gentleman.

"Oh well, if you don't like it, I won't. I see you're like me; I never think of the Ghetto if I can help it. Well, as I was saying, I haven't had a wink of sleep since I saw you. I lay tossing about, thinking all sorts of things, till I could stand it no longer, and I got up and dressed and walked about the streets and strayed into Covent Garden Market, where the inspiration came upon me to get you this bouquet. For, of course, it was about you that I had been thinking."

"About me?" said Esther, turning pale.

"Yes, of course. Don't make *Schnecks*—you know what I mean. I can't help using the old expression when I look at you; the past seems all come back again. They were happy days, weren't they, Esther, when I used to come up to see you in Royal Street; I think you were a little sweet on me in those days, Esther, and I know I was regular mashed on you."

He looked at her with a fond smile.

"I dare say you were a silly boy," said Esther, coloring uneasily under his gaze. "However, you needn't reproach yourself now."

"Reproach myself, indeed! Never fear that. What I have been reproaching myself with all night is never having looked you up. Somehow, do you know, I kept asking myself whether I hadn't made a fool of myself lately, and I kept thinking things might have been different if—"

"Nonsense, nonsense," interrupted Esther with an embarrassed laugh. "You've been doing very well, learning to know the world and studying law and mixing with pleasant people."

"Ah, Esther," he said, shaking his head, "it's very good of you to say that. I don't say I've done anything particularly foolish or out of the way. But when a man is alone, he sometimes gets a little reckless and wastes his time, and you know what it is. I've been thinking if I had someone to keep me steady, someone I could respect, it would be the best thing that could happen to me."

"Oh, but surely you ought to have sense enough to take care of yourself. And there is always your father. Why don't you see more of him?"

"Don't chaff a man when you see he's in earnest. You know what I mean. It's you I am thinking of."

"Me? Oh well, if you think my friendship can be of any use to you I shall be delighted. Come and see me sometimes and tell me of your struggles."

"You know I don't mean that," he said desperately. "Couldn't we be more than friends? Couldn't we commence again—where we left off"

"How do you mean?" she murmured.

"Why are you so cold to me?" he burst out. "Why do you make it so hard for me to speak? You know I love you, that I fell in love with you all over again last night. I never really forgot you; you were always deep down in my breast. All that I said about steadying me wasn't a lie. I felt that, too. But the real thing I feel is the need of you. I want you to care for me as I care for you. You used to, Esther; you know you did."

"I know nothing of the kind," said Esther, "and I can't understand why a young fellow like you wants to bother his head with such ideas. You've got to make your way in the world—"

"I know, I know; that's why I want you. I didn't tell you the exact truth last night, Esther, but I must really earn some money soon. All that two thousand is used up, and I only get along by squeezing some money out of the old man every now and again. Don't frown; he got a rise of screw three years ago and can well afford it. Now that's what I said to myself last night; if I were engaged, it would be an incentive to earning something."

"For a Jewish young man, you are fearfully unpractical," said Esther, with a forced smile. "Fancy proposing to a girl without even prospects of prospects."

"Oh, but I *have* got prospects. I tell you I shall make no end of money on the stage."

"Or no beginning," she said, finding the facetious vein easiest.

"No fear. I know I've got as much talent as Bob Andrews (he admits it himself), and *he* draws his thirty quid a week."

"Wasn't that the man who appeared at the police-court the other day for being drunk and disorderly?"

"Y-e-es," admitted Leonard, a little disconcerted. "He is a very good fellow, but he loses his head when he's in liquor."

"I wonder you can care for society of that sort," said Esther.

"Perhaps you're right. They're not a very refined lot. I tell you what—I'd like to go on the stage, but I'm not mad on it, and if you only say the word I'll give it up. There! And I'll go on with my law studies; honor bright, I will."

"I should, if I were you," she said.

"Yes, but I can't do it without encouragement. Won't you say 'yes'? Let's strike the bargain. I'll stick to law and you'll stick to me."

She shook her head. "I am afraid I could not promise anything you mean. As I said before, I shall be always glad to see you. If you do well, no one will rejoice more than I"

"Rejoice! What's the good of that to me? I want you to care for me; I want you to took forward to your being my wife."

"Really, I cannot take advantage of a moment of folly like this. You don't know what you're saying. You saw me last night, after many years, and in your gladness at seeing an old friend you flare up and fancy you're in love with me. Why, who ever heard of such foolish haste? Go back to your studies, and in a day or two you will find the flame sinking as rapidly as it leaped up."

"No, no! Nothing of the kind!" His voice was thicker and there was real passion in it. She grew dearer to him as the hope of her love receded. "I couldn't forget you. I care for you awfully. I realized last night that my feeling for you is quite unlike what I have ever felt towards any other girl. Don't say no! Don't send me away despairing. I can hardly realize that you have grown so strange and altered. Surely you oughtn't to put on any side with me. Remember the times we have had together."

"I remember," she said gently. "But I do not want to marry anyone: indeed, I don't."

"Then if there is no one else in your thoughts, why shouldn't it be me? There! I won't press you for an answer now. Only don't say it's out of the question."

"I'm afraid I must."

"No, you mustn't, Esther, you mustn't," he exclaimed excitedly. "Think of what it means for me. You are the only Jewish girl I shall ever care for; and father would be pleased if I were to marry you. You know if I wanted to marry a *Shiksah* there'd be awful rows. Don't treat me as if I were some outsider with no claim upon you. I believe we should get on splendidly together, you and me. We've been through the same sort of thing in childhood, we should understand each other, and be in sympathy with each other in a way I could never be with another girl and I doubt if you could with another fellow."

The words burst from him like a torrent, with excited foreign-looking gestures. Esther's headache was coming on badly.

"What would be the use of my deceiving you?" she said gently. "I don't think I shall ever marry. I'm sure I could never make you—or anyone else—happy. Won't you let me be your friend?"

"Friend!" he echoed bitterly. "I know what it is; I'm poor. I've got no money bags to lay at your feet. You're like all the Jewish girls after all. But I only ask you to wait; I shall have plenty of money by and by. Who knows what more luck my father might drop in for? There are lots of rich religious cranks. And then I'll work hard, honor bright I will."

"Pray be reasonable," said Esther quietly. "You know you are talking at random. Yesterday this time you had no idea of such a thing. Today you are all on fire. Tomorrow you will forget all about it."

"Never! Never!" he cried. "Haven't I remembered you all these years? They talk of man's faithlessness and woman's faithfulness. It seems to me, it's all the other way. Women are a deceptive lot."

"You know you have no right whatever to talk like that to me," said Esther, her sympathy beginning to pass over into annoyance. "Tomorrow you will be sorry. Hadn't you better go before you give yourself—and me—more cause for regret?"

"Ho, you're sending me away, are you?" he said in angry surprise.

"I am certainly suggesting it as the wisest course."

"Oh, don't give me any of your fine phrases!" he said brutally. "I see what it is—I've made a mistake. You're a stuck-up, conceited little thing. You think because you live in a grand house nobody is good enough for you. But what are you after all? a *Schnorrer*—that's all. A *Schnorrer* living on the charity of strangers. If I mix with grand folks, it is as an independent man and an equal. But you, rather than marry anyone who mightn't be able to give you carriages and footmen, you prefer to remain a *Schnorrer*."

Esther was white and her lips trembled. "Now I must ask you to go," she said.

"All right, don't flurry yourself!" he said savagely. "You don't impress me with your airs. Try them on people who don't know what you were—a *Schnorrer's* daughter. Yes, your father was always a *Schnorrer* and you are his child. It's in the blood. Ha! Ha! Ha! Moses Ansell's daughter! Moses Ansell's daughter—a peddler, who went about the country with brass jewelry and stood in the Lane with lemons and *schnorred* half-crowns of my father. You took jolly good care to ship him off to America, but 'pon my honor, you can't expect others to forget him as quickly as you. It's a rich joke, you refusing me. You're not fit for me to wipe my shoes on. My mother never cared for me to go to your garret; she said I must mix with my equals and goodness knew what disease I might pick up in the dirt; 'pon my honor the old girl was right."

"She *was* right," Esther was stung into retorting. "You must mix only with your equals. Please leave the room now or else I shall."

ISRAEL ZANGWILL

His face changed. His frenzy gave way to a momentary shock of consternation as he realized what he had done.

"No, no, Esther. I was mad, I didn't know what I was saying. I didn't mean it. Forget it."

"I cannot. It was quite true," she said bitterly. "I am only a *Schnorrer's* daughter. Well, are you going or must I?"

He muttered something inarticulate, then seized his hat sulkily and went to the door without looking at her.

"You have forgotten something," she said.

He turned; her forefinger pointed to the bouquet on the table. He had a fresh access of rage at the sight of it, jerked it contemptuously to the floor with a sweep of his hat and stamped upon it. Then he rushed from the room and an instant after she heard the hall door slam.

She sank against the table sobbing nervously. It was her first proposal! A *Schnorrer* and the daughter of a *Schnorrer*. Yes, that-was what she was. And she had even repaid her benefactors with deception! What hopes could she yet cherish? In literature she was a failure; the critics gave her few gleams of encouragement, while all her acquaintances from Raphael downwards would turn and rend her, should she dare declare herself. Nay, she was ashamed of herself for the mischief she had wrought. No one in the world cared for her; she was quite alone. The only man in whose breast she could excite love or the semblance of it was a contemptible cad. And who was she, that she should venture to hope for love? She figured herself as an item in a catalogue; "a little, ugly, low-spirited, absolutely penniless young woman, subject to nervous headaches." Her sobs were interrupted by a ghastly burst of self-mockery. Yes, Levi was right. She ought to think herself lucky to get him. Again, she asked herself what had existence to offer her. Gradually her sobs ceased; she remembered tonight would be *Seder* night, and her thoughts, so violently turned Ghetto-wards, went back to that night, soon after poor Benjamin's death, when she sat before the garret fire striving to picture the larger life of the future. Well, this was the future.

VIII

THE ENDS OF A GENERATION

The same evening Leonard James sat in the stalls of the Colosseum Music Hall, sipping champagne and smoking a cheroot. He had not been to his chambers (which were only round the corner) since the hapless interview with Esther, wandering about in the streets and the clubs in a spirit compounded of outraged dignity, remorse and recklessness. All men must dine; and dinner at the *Flamingo Club* soothed his wounded soul and left only the recklessness, which is a sensation not lacking in agreeableness. Through the rosy mists of the Burgundy there began to surge up other faces than that cold pallid little face which had hovered before him all the afternoon like a tantalizing phantom; at the Chartreuse stage he began to wonder what hallucination, what aberration of sense had overcome him, that he should have been stirred to his depths and distressed so hugely. Warmer faces were these that swam before him, faces fuller of the joy of life. The devil take all stuck-up little saints!

About eleven o'clock, when the great ballet of *Venetia* was over, Leonard hurried round to the stage-door, saluted the door-keeper with a friendly smile and a sixpence, and sent in his card to Miss Gladys Wynne, on the chance that she might have no supper engagement. Miss Wynne was only a humble *coryphée*, but the admirers of her talent were numerous, and Leonard counted himself fortunate in that she was able to afford him the privilege of her society tonight. She came out to him in a red fur-lined cloak, for the air was keen. She was a majestic being with a florid complexion not entirely artificial, big blue eyes and teeth of that whiteness which is the practical equivalent of a sense of humor in evoking the possessor's smiles. They drove to a restaurant a few hundred yards distant, for Miss Wynne detested using her feet except to dance with. It was a fashionable restaurant, where the prices obligingly rose after ten, to accommodate the purses of the supper-*clientèle*. Miss Wynne always drank champagne, except when alone, and in politeness Leonard had to imbibe more of this frothy compound. He knew he would have to pay for the day's extravagance by a week of comparative abstemiousness, but recklessness generally meant magnificence with him. They occupied a cosy little corner behind a screen, and Miss Wynne bubbled over with laughter like an animated champagne bottle. One or two of his acquaintances espied him and winked genially, and Leonard had the satisfaction of feeling that he was not dissipating his money without purchasing enhanced reputation. He had not felt in gayer spirits for months than when, with Gladys Wynne on his arm and a cigarette in his mouth, he sauntered out of the brilliantly-lit restaurant into the feverish dusk of the midnight street, shot with points of fire.

"Hansom, sir!"

"*Levi!*"

A great cry of anguish rent the air—Leonard's cheeks burned. Involuntarily he looked round. Then his heart stood still. There, a few yards from him, rooted to the pavement, with stony staring face, was Reb Shemuel. The old man wore an unbrushed high hat and an uncouth unbuttoned overcoat. His hair and beard were quite white now, and the strong countenance lined with countless wrinkles was distorted with pain and astonishment. He looked a cross between an ancient prophet and a shabby street lunatic. The unprecedented absence of the son from the *Seder* ceremonial had filled the Reb's household with the gravest alarm. Nothing short of death or mortal sickness could be keeping the boy away. It was long before the Reb could bring himself to commence the *Hagadah* without his son to ask the time-honored opening question; and when he did he paused every minute to listen to footsteps or the voice of the wind without. The joyous holiness of the Festival was troubled, a black cloud overshadowed the shining table-cloth, at supper the food choked him. But *Seder* was over and yet no sign of the missing guest; no word of explanation. In poignant anxiety, the old man walked the three miles that lay between him and tidings of the beloved son. At his chambers he learned that their occupant had not been in all day. Another thing he learned there, too; for the *Mezuzah* which he had fixed up on the door-post when his boy moved in had been taken down, and it filled his mind with a dread suspicion that Levi had not been eating at the *kosher* restaurant in Hatton Garden, as he had faithfully vowed to do. But even this terrible thought was swallowed up in the fear that some accident had happened to him. He haunted the house for an hour, filling up the intervals of fruitless inquiry with little random walks round the neighborhood, determined not to return home to his wife without news of their child. The restless life of the great twinkling streets was almost a novelty to him; it was rarely his perambulations in London extended outside the Ghetto, and the radius of his life was proportionately narrow,—with the intensity that narrowness forces on a big soul. The streets dazzled him, he looked blinkingly hither and thither in the despairing hope of finding his boy. His lips moved in silent prayer; he raised his eyes beseechingly to the cold glittering heavens. Then, all at once—as the clocks pointed to midnight—he found him. Found him coming out of an unclean place, where he had violated the Passover. Found him—fit climax of horror—with the "strange woman" of *The Proverbs*, for whom the faithful Jew has a hereditary hatred.

His son—his. Reb Shemuel's! He, the servant of the Most High, the teacher of the Faith to reverential thousands, had brought a son into the world to profane the Name! Verily his gray hairs would go down with sorrow to a speedy grave! And the sin was half his own; he had weakly abandoned his boy in the midst of a great city. For one awful instant, that seemed an eternity, the old man and the young faced each other across the chasm which divided their lives. To the son the shock was scarcely less violent than to the father. The *Seder*, which the day's unwonted excitement had clean swept out of his mind, recurred to him in a flash, and by the light of it he understood the puzzle of his father's appearance. The thought of explaining rushed up only to be dismissed. The door of the restaurant had not yet ceased swinging behind him— there was too much to explain. He felt that all was over between him and his father. It was unpleasant, terrible even, for it meant the annihilation of his resources. But though he still had an almost physical fear of the old man, far more terrible even than the presence of his father was the presence of Miss Gladys Wynne. To explain, to brazen it out, either course was equally impossible. He was not a brave man, but at that moment he felt death were preferable to allowing her to be the witness of such a scene as must ensue. His resolution was taken within a few brief seconds of the tragic rencontre. With wonderful self-possession, he nodded to the cabman who had put the question, and whose vehicle was drawn up opposite the restaurant. Hastily he helped the unconscious Gladys into the hansom. He was putting his foot on the step himself when Reb Shemuel's paralysis relaxed suddenly. Outraged by this final pollution of the Festival, he ran forward and laid his hand on Levi's shoulder. His face was ashen, his heart thumped painfully; the hand on Levi's cloak shook as with palsy.

Levi winced; the old awe was upon him. Through a blinding whirl

ISRAEL ZANGWILL

he saw Gladys staring wonderingly at the queer-looking intruder. He gathered all his mental strength together with a mighty effort, shook off the great trembling hand and leaped into the hansom.

"Drive on!" came in strange guttural tones from his parched throat.

The driver lashed the horse; a rough jostled the old man aside and slammed the door to; Leonard mechanically threw him a coin; the hansom glided away.

"Who was that, Leonard?" said Miss Wynne, curiously.

"Nobody; only an old Jew who supplies me with cash."

Gladys laughed merrily—a rippling, musical laugh.

She knew the sort of person.

IX

THE FLAG FLUTTERS

The *Flag of Judah*, price one penny, largest circulation of any Jewish organ, continued to flutter, defying the battle, the breeze and its communal contemporaries. At Passover there had been an illusive augmentation of advertisements proclaiming the virtues of unleavened everything. With the end of the Festival, most of these fell out, staying as short a time as the daffodils. Raphael was in despair at the meagre attenuated appearance of the erst prosperous-looking pages. The weekly loss on the paper weighed upon his conscience.

"We shall never succeed," said the sub-editor, shaking his romantic hair, "till we run it for the Upper Ten. These ten people can make the paper, just as they are now killing it by refusing their countenance."

"But they must surely reckon with us sooner or later," said Raphael.

"It will he a long reckoning. I fear: you take my advice and put in more butter. It'll be *kosher* butter, coming from us." The little Bohemian laughed as heartily as his eyeglass permitted.

"No; we must stick to our guns. After all, we have had some very good things lately. Those articles of Pinchas's are not bad either."

"They're so beastly egotistical. Still his theories are ingenious and far more interesting than those terribly dull long letters of Henry Goldsmith, which you will put in."

Raphael flushed a little and began to walk up and down the new and superior sanctum with his ungainly strides, puffing furiously at his pipe The appearance of the room was less bare; the floor was carpeted with old newspapers and scraps of letters. A huge picture of an Atlantic Liner, the gift of a Steamship Company, leaned cumbrously against a wall.

"Still, all our literary excellencies," pursued Sampson, "are outweighed by our shortcomings in getting births, marriages and deaths. We are gravelled for lack of that sort of matter What is the use of your elaborate essay on the Septuagint, when the public is dying to hear who's dead?"

"Yes, I am afraid it is so." said Raphael, emitting a huge volume of smoke.

"I'm sure it is so. If you would only give me a freer hand, I feel sure I could work up that column. We can at least make a better show: I would avoid the danger of discovery by shifting the scene to foreign parts. I could marry some people in Born-bay and kill some in Cape Town, redressing the balance by bringing others into existence at Cairo and Cincinnati. Our contemporaries would score off us in local interest, but we should take the shine out of them in cosmopolitanism."

"No, no; remember that *Meshumad*" said Raphael, smiling.

"He was real; if you had allowed me to invent a corpse, we should have been saved that *contretemps*. We have one 'death' this week fortunately, and I am sure to fish out another in the daily papers. But we haven't had a 'birth' for three weeks running; it's just ruining our reputation. Everybody knows that the orthodox are a fertile lot, and it looks as if we hadn't got the support even of our own party. Ta ra ra ta! Now you must really let me have a 'birth.' I give you my word, nobody'll suspect it isn't genuine. Come now. How's this?" He scribbled on a piece of paper and handed it to Raphael, who read:

"Birth, on the 15th inst. at 17 East Stuart Lane, Kennington, the wife of Joseph Samuels of a son."

"There!" said Sampson proudly, "Who would believe the little beggar had no existence? Nobody lives in Kennington, and that East Stuart Lane is a master-stroke. You might suspect Stuart Lane, but nobody would ever dream there's no such place as *East* Stuart Lane. Don't say the little chap must die. I begin to take quite a paternal interest in him. May I announce him? Don't be too scrupulous. Who'll be a penny the worse for it?" He began to chirp, with bird-like trills of melody.

Raphael hesitated: his moral fibre had been weakened. It is impossible to touch print and not be denied.

Suddenly Sampson ceased to whistle and smote his head with his chubby fist. "Ass that I am!" he exclaimed.

"What new reasons have you discovered to think so?" said Raphael.

"Why, we dare not create boys. We shall be found out; boys must be circumcised and some of the periphrastically styled 'Initiators into the Abrahamic Covenant' may spot us. It was a girl that Mrs. Joseph Samuels was guilty of." He amended the sex.

Raphael laughed heartily. "Put it by; there's another day yet; we shall see."

"Very well," said Sampson resignedly. "Perhaps by tomorrow we shall be in luck and able to sing 'unto us a child is born, unto us a son is given.' By the way, did you see the letter complaining of our using that quotation, on the ground it was from the New Testament?"

"Yes," said Raphael smiling. "Of course the man doesn't know his Old Testament, but I trace his misconception to his having heard Handel's Messiah. I wonder he doesn't find fault with the Morning Service for containing the Lord's Prayer, or with Moses for saying 'Thou shalt love thy neighbor as thyself.'"

"Still, that's the sort of man newspapers have to cater for," said the sub-editor. "And we don't. We have cut down our Provincial Notes to a column. My idea would be to make two pages of them, not cutting out any of the people's names and leaving in more of the adjectives. Every man's name we mention means at least one copy sold. Why can't we drag in a couple of thousand names every week?"

"That would make our circulation altogether nominal," laughed Raphael, not taking the suggestion seriously.

Little Sampson was not only the Mephistopheles of the office, debauching his editor's guileless mind with all the wily ways of the old journalistic hand; he was of real use in protecting Raphael against the thousand and one pitfalls that make the editorial chair as perilous to the occupant as Sweeney Todd's; against the people who tried to get libels inserted as news or as advertisements, against the self-puffers and the axe-grinders. He also taught Raphael how to commence interesting correspondence and how to close awkward. The *Flag* played a part in many violent discussions. Little Sampson was great in inventing communal crises, and in getting the public to believe it was excited. He also won a great victory over the other party every three weeks; Raphael did not wish to have so many of these victories, but little Sampson pointed out that if he did not have them, the rival newspaper would annex them. One of the earliest sensations of the *Flag* was a correspondence exposing the misdeeds of some communal officials; but in the end the very persons who made the allegations ate humble pie. Evidently official pressure had been brought to bear, for red tape rampant might have been the heraldic device of Jewish officialdom. In no department did Jews exhibit more strikingly their marvellous powers of assimilation to their neighbors.

Among the discussions which rent the body politic was the question of building a huge synagogue for the poor. The *Flag* said it would only concentrate them, and its word prevailed. There were also the grave questions of English and harmoniums in the synagogue, of the confirmation of girls and their utilization in the choir. The Rabbinate, whose grave difficulties in reconciling all parties to its rule, were augmented by the existence of the *Flag*, pronounced it heinous

ISRAEL ZANGWILL

to introduce English excerpts into the liturgy; if, however, they were not read from the central platform, they were legitimate; harmoniums were permissible, but only during special services; and an organization of mixed voices was allowable, but not a mixed choir; children might be confirmed, but the word "confirmation" should be avoided. Poor Rabbinate! The politics of the little community were extremely complex. What with rabid zealots yearning for the piety of the good old times, spiritually-minded ministers working with uncomfortable earnestness for a larger Judaism, radicals dropping out, moderates clamoring for quiet, and schismatics organizing new and tiresome movements, the Rabbinate could scarcely do aught else than emit sonorous platitudes and remain in office.

And beneath all these surface ruffles was the steady silent drift of the new generation away from the old landmarks. The synagogue did not attract; it spoke Hebrew to those whose mother-tongue was English; its appeal was made through channels which conveyed nothing to them; it was out of touch with their real lives; its liturgy prayed for the restoration of sacrifices which they did not want and for the welfare of Babylonian colleges that had ceased to exist. The old generation merely believed its beliefs; if the new as much as professed them, it was only by virtue of the old home associations and the inertia of indifference. Practically, it was without religion. The Reform Synagogue, though a centre of culture and prosperity, was cold, crude and devoid of magnetism. Half a century of stagnant reform and restless dissolution had left Orthodoxy still the Established Doxy. For, as Orthodoxy evaporated in England, it was replaced by fresh streams from Russia, to be evaporated and replaced in turn, England acting as an automatic distillery. Thus the Rabbinate still reigned, though it scarcely governed either the East End or the West. For the East End formed a Federation of the smaller synagogues to oppose the dominance of the United Synagogue, importing a minister of superior orthodoxy from the Continent, and the *Flag* had powerful leaders on the great struggle between plutocracy and democracy, and the voice of Mr. Henry Goldsmith was heard on behalf of Whitechapel. And the West, in so far as it had spiritual aspirations, fed them on non-Jewish literature and the higher thought of the age. The finer spirits, indeed, were groping for a purpose and a destiny, doubtful even, if the racial isolation they perpetuated were not an anachronism. While the community had been battling for civil and religious liberty, there had been a unifying, almost spiritualizing, influence in the sense of common injustice, and the question *cui bono* had been postponed. Drowning men do not ask if life is worth living. Later, the Russian persecutions came to interfere again with national introspection, sending a powerful wave of racial sympathy round the earth. In England a backwash of the wave left the Asmonean Society, wherein, for the first time in history, Jews gathered with nothing in common save blood—artists, lawyers, writers, doctors—men who in pre-emancipation times might have become Christians like Heine, but who now formed an effective protest against the popular conceptions of the Jew, and a valuable antidote to the disproportionate notoriety achieved by less creditable types. At the Asmonean Society, brilliant freelances, each thinking himself a solitary exception to a race of bigots, met one another in mutual astonishment. Raphael alienated several readers by uncompromising approval of this characteristically modern movement. Another symptom of the new intensity of national brotherhood was the attempt towards amalgamating the Spanish and German communities, but brotherhood broke down under the disparity of revenue, the rich Spanish sect displaying once again the exclusiveness which has marked its history.

Amid these internal problems, the unspeakable immigrant was an added thorn. Very often the victim of Continental persecution was assisted on to America, but the idea that he was hurtful to native labor rankled in the minds of Englishmen, and the Jewish leaders were anxious to remove it, all but proving him a boon. In despair, it was sought to 'anglicize him by discourses in Yiddish. With the Poor Alien question was connected the return to Palestine. The Holy Land League still pinned its faith to Zion, and the *Flag* was with it to the extent of preferring the ancient father-land, as the scene of agricultural experiments, to the South American soils selected by other schemes. It was generally felt that the redemption of Judaism lay largely in a return to the land, after several centuries of less primitive and more degrading occupations. When South America was chosen, Strelitski was the first to counsel the League to co-operate in the experiment, on the principle that half a loaf is better than no bread. But, for the orthodox the difficulties of regeneration by the spade were enhanced by the Sabbatical Year Institute of the Pentateuch, ordaining that land must lie fallow in the seventh year. It happened that this septennial holiday was just going on, and the faithful Palestine farmers were starving in voluntary martyrdom. The *Flag* raised a subscription for their benefit.

ISRAEL ZANGWILL

Raphael wished to head the list with twenty pounds, but on the advice of little Sampson he broke it up into a variety of small amounts, spread over several weeks, and attached to imaginary names and initials. Seeing so many other readers contributing, few readers felt called upon to tax themselves. The *Flag* received the ornate thanks of a pleiad of Palestine Rabbis for its contribution of twenty-five guineas, two of which were from Mr. Henry Goldsmith. Gideon, the member for Whitechapel, remained callous to the sufferings of his brethren in the Holy Land. In daily contact with so many diverse interests, Raphael's mind widened as imperceptibly as the body grows. He learned the manners of many men and committees—admired the genuine goodness of some of the Jewish philanthropists and the fluent oratory of all; even while he realized the pettiness of their outlook and their reluctance to face facts. They were timorous, with a dread of decisive action and definitive speech, suggesting the differential, deprecatory corporeal wrigglings of the mediaeval few. They seemed to keep strict ward over the technical privileges of the different bodies they belonged to, and in their capacity of members of the Fiddle-de-dee to quarrel with themselves as members of the Fiddle-de-dum, and to pass votes of condolence or congratulation twice over as members of both. But the more he saw of his race the more he marvelled at the omnipresent ability, being tempted at times to allow truth to the view that Judaism was a successful sociological experiment, the moral and physical training of a chosen race whose very dietary had been religiously regulated.

And even the revelations of the seamy side of human character which thrust themselves upon the most purblind of editors were blessings in disguise. The office of the *Flag* was a forcing-house for Raphael; many latent thoughts developed into extraordinary maturity. A month of the *Flag* was equal to a year of experience in the outside world. And not even little Sampson himself was keener to appreciate the humors of the office when no principle was involved; though what made the sub-editor roar with laughter often made the editor miserable for the day. For compensation, Raphael had felicities from which little Sampson was cut off; gladdened by revelations of earnestness and piety in letters that were merely bad English to the sub-editor.

A thing that set them both laughing occurred on the top of their conversation about the reader who objected to quotations from the Old Testament. A package of four old *Flags* arrived, accompanied by a letter. This was the letter:

DEAR SIR:

"Your man called upon me last night, asking for payment for four advertisements of my Passover groceries. But I have changed my mind about them and do not want them; and therefore beg to return the four numbers sent me You will see I have not opened them or soiled them in anyway, so please cancel the claim in your books.

Yours truly,
ISAAC WOLLBERG

"He evidently thinks the vouchers sent him *are* the advertisements," screamed little Sampson.

"But if he is as ignorant as all that, how could he have written the letter?" asked Raphael.

"Oh, it was probably written for him for twopence by the Shalotten *Shammos*, the begging-letter writer."

"This is almost as funny as Karlkammer!" said Raphael.

Karlkammer had sent in a long essay on the Sabbatical Year question, which Raphael had revised and published with Karlkammer's title at the head and Karlkammer's name at the foot. Yet, owing to the few rearrangements and inversions of sentences, Karlkammer never identified it as his own, and was perpetually calling to inquire when his article would appear. He brought with him fresh manuscripts of the article as originally written. He was not the only caller; Raphael was much pestered by visitors on kindly counsel bent or stern exhortation. The sternest were those who had never yet paid their subscriptions. De Haan also kept up proprietorial rights of interference. In private life Raphael suffered much from pillars of the Montagu Samuels type, who accused him of flippancy, and no communal crisis invented by little Sampson ever equalled the pother and commotion that arose when Raphael incautiously allowed him to burlesque the notorious *Mordecai Josephs* by comically exaggerating its exaggerations. The community took it seriously, as an attack upon the race. Mr. and Mrs. Henry Goldsmith were scandalized, and Raphael had to shield little Sampson by accepting the whole responsibility for its appearance.

"Talking of Karlkammer's article, are you ever going to use up Herman's scientific paper?" asked little Sampson.

"I'm afraid so," said Raphael; "I don't know how we can get out of it. But his eternal *kosher* meat sticks in my throat. We are Jews for the love of God, not to be saved from consumption bacilli. But I won't use it tomorrow; we have Miss Cissy Levine's tale. It's not half bad. What a pity she has the expenses of her books paid! If she had to achieve publication by merit, her style might be less slipshod."

"I wish some rich Jew would pay the expenses of my opera tour," said little Sampson, ruefully. "My style of doing the thing would be improved. The people who are backing me up are awfully stingy, actually buying up battered old helmets for my chorus of Amazons."

Intermittently the question of the sub-editor's departure for the provinces came up: it was only second in frequency to his "victories." About once a month the preparations for the tour were complete, and he would go about in a heyday of jubilant vocalization; then his comic prima-donna would fall ill or elope, his conductor would get drunk, his chorus would strike, and little Sampson would continue to sub-edit *The Flag of Judah*.

Pinchas unceremoniously turned the handle of the door and came in. The sub-editor immediately hurried out to get a cup of tea. Pinchas had fastened upon him the responsibility for the omission of an article last week, and had come to believe that he was in league with rival Continental scholars to keep Melchitsedek Pinchas's effusions out of print, and so little Sampson dared not face the angry savant. Raphael, thus deserted, cowered in his chair. He did not fear death, but he feared Pinchas, and had fallen into the cowardly habit of bribing him lavishly not to fill the paper. Fortunately, the poet was in high feather.

"Don't forget the announcement that I lecture at the Club on Sunday. You see all the efforts of Reb Shemuel, of the Rev. Joseph Strelitski, of the Chief Rabbi, of Ebenezer vid his blue spectacles, of Sampson, of all the phalanx of English Men-of-the-Earth, they all fail. Ab, I am a great man."

"I won't forget," said Raphael wearily. "The announcement is already in print."

"Ah, I love you. You are the best man in the vorld. It is you who have championed me against those who are thirsting for my blood. And now I vill tell you joyful news. There is a maiden coming up to see you—she is asking in the publisher's office—oh such a lovely maiden!"

Pinchas grinned all over his face, and was like to dig his editor in the ribs.

"What maiden?"

"I do not know; but vai-r-r-y beaudiful. Aha, I vill go. Have you not been good to *me*? But vy come not beaudiful maidens to *me*?"

"No, no, you needn't go," said Raphael, getting red.

Pinchas grinned as one who knew better, and struck a match to rekindle a stump of cigar. "No, no, I go write my lecture—oh it vill be a great lecture. You vill announce it in the paper! You vill not leave it out like Sampson left out my article last week." He was at the door now, with his finger alongside his nose.

Raphael shook himself impatiently, and the poet threw the door wide open and disappeared.

For a full minute Raphael dared not look towards the door for fear of seeing the poet's cajoling head framed in the opening. When he did, he was transfixed to see Esther Ansell's there, regarding him pensively.

His heart beat painfully at the shock; the room seemed flooded with sunlight.

"May I come in?" she said, smiling.

X

ESTHER DEFIES THE UNIVERSE

E sther wore a neat black mantle, and looked taller and more womanly than usual in a pretty bonnet and a spotted veil. There was a flush of color in her cheeks, her eyes sparkled. She had walked in cold sunny weather from the British Museum (where she was still supposed to be), and the wind had blown loose a little wisp of hair over the small shell-like ear. In her left hand she held a roll of manuscript. It contained her criticisms of the May Exhibitions. Whereby hung a tale.

In the dark days that followed the scene with Levi, Esther's resolution had gradually formed. The position had become untenable. She could no longer remain a *Schnorrer*; abusing the bounty of her benefactors into the bargain. She must leave the Goldsmiths, and at once. That was imperative; the second step could be thought over when she had taken the first. And yet she postponed taking the first. Once she drifted out of her present sphere, she could not answer for the future, could not be certain, for instance, that she would be able to redeem her promise to Raphael to sit in judgment upon the Academy and other picture galleries that bloomed in May. At any rate, once she had severed connection with the Goldsmith circle, she would not care to renew it, even in the case of Raphael. No, it was best to get this last duty off her shoulders, then to say farewell to him and all the other human constituents of her brief period of partial sunshine. Besides, the personal delivery of the precious manuscript would afford her the opportunity of this farewell to him. With his social remissness, it was unlikely he would call soon upon the Goldsmiths, and she now restricted her friendship with Addie to receiving Addie's visits, so as to prepare for its dissolution. Addie amused her by reading extracts from Sidney's letters, for the brilliant young artist had suddenly gone off to Norway the morning after the *début* of the new Hamlet. Esther felt that it might be as well if she stayed on to see how the drama of these two lives developed. These things she told herself in the reaction from the first impulse of instant flight.

Raphael put down his pipe at the sight of her and a frank smile of welcome shone upon his flushed face.

"This is so kind of you!" he said; "who would have thought of seeing you here? I am so glad. I hope you are well. You look better." He was wringing her little gloved hand violently as he spoke.

"I feel better, too, thank you. The air is so exhilarating. I'm glad to see you're still in the land of the living. Addie has told me of your debauches of work."

"Addie is foolish. I never felt better. Come inside. Don't be afraid of walking on the papers. They're all old."

"I always heard literary people were untidy," said Esther smiling. "*You* must be a regular genius."

"Well, you see we don't have many ladies coming here," said Raphael deprecatingly, "though we have plenty of old women."

"It's evident you don't. Else some of them would go down on their hands and knees and never get up till this litter was tidied up a bit."

"Never mind that now, Miss Ansell. Sit down, won't you? You must be tired. Take the editorial chair. Allow me a minute." He removed some books from it.

"Is that the way you sit on the books sent in for review?" She sat down. "Dear me! It's quite comfortable. You men like comfort, even the most self-sacrificing. But where is your fighting-editor? It would be awkward if an aggrieved reader came in and mistook me for the editor, wouldn't it? It isn't safe for me to remain in this chair."

"Oh, yes it is! We've tackled our aggrieved readers for today," he assured her.

She looked curiously round. "Please pick up your pipe. It's going out. I don't mind smoke, indeed I don't. Even if I did, I should be prepared to pay the penalty of bearding an editor in his den."

Raphael resumed his pipe gratefully.

"I wonder though you don't set the place on fire," Esther rattled on, "with all this mass of inflammable matter about."

"It is very dry, most of it," he admitted, with a smile.

"Why don't you have a real fire? It must be quite cold sitting here all day. What's that great ugly picture over there?"

"That steamer! It's an advertisement."

"Heavens! What a decoration. I should like to have the criticism of that picture. I've brought you those picture-galleries, you know; that's what I've come for."

"Thank you! That's very good of you. I'll send it to the printers at once." He took the roll and placed it in a pigeon-hole, without taking his eyes off her face.

"Why don't you throw that awful staring thing away?" she asked, contemplating the steamer with a morbid fascination, "and sweep away the old papers, and have a few little water-colors hung up and put a vase of flowers on your desk. I wish I had the control of the office for a week."

"I wish you had," he said gallantly. "I can't find time to think of those things. I am sure you are brightening it up already."

The little blush on her cheek deepened. Compliment was unwonted with him; and indeed, he spoke as he felt. The sight of her seated so strangely and unexpectedly in his own humdrum sanctum; the imaginary picture of her beautifying it and evolving harmony out of the chaos with artistic touches of her dainty hands, filled him with pleasant, tender thoughts, such as he had scarce known before. The commonplace editorial chair seemed to have undergone consecration and poetic transformation. Surely the sunshine that streamed through the dusty window would forever rest on it henceforwards. And yet the whole thing appeared fantastic and unreal.

"I hope you are speaking the truth," replied Esther with a little laugh. "You need brightening, you old dry-as-dust philanthropist, sitting poring over stupid manuscripts when you ought to be in the country enjoying the sunshine." She spoke in airy accents, with an undercurrent of astonishment at her attack of high spirits on an occasion she had designed to be harrowing.

"Why, I haven't *looked* at your manuscript yet," he retorted gaily, but as he spoke there flashed upon him a delectable vision of blue sea and waving pines with one fair wood-nymph flitting through the trees, luring him on from this musty cell of never-ending work to unknown ecstasies of youth and joyousness. The leafy avenues were bathed in sacred sunlight, and a low magic music thrilled through the quiet air. It was but the dream of a second—the dingy walls closed round him again, the great ugly steamer, that never went anywhere, sailed on. But the wood-nymph did not vanish; the sunbeam was still on the editorial chair, lighting up the little face with a celestial halo. And when she spoke again, it was as if the music that filled the visionary glades was a reality, too.

"It's all very well your treating reproof as a jest," she said, more gravely. "Can't you see that it's false economy to risk a break-down even if you use yourself purely for others? You're looking far from well. You are overtaxing human strength. Come now, admit my sermon is just. Remember I speak not as a Pharisee, but as one who made the mistake herself—a fellow-sinner." She turned her dark eyes reproachfully upon him.

"I—I—don't sleep very well," he admitted, "but otherwise I assure you I feel all right."

It was the second time she had manifested concern for his health. The blood coursed deliciously in his veins; a thrill ran through his whole form. The gentle anxious face seemed to grow angelic. Could she really care if his health gave way? Again he felt a rash of self-pity that filled his eyes with tears. He was grateful to her for sharing his sense of the empty cheerlessness of his existence. He wondered why it had seemed so full and cheery just before.

"And you used to sleep so well," said Esther, slily, remembering Addie's domestic revelations. "My stupid manuscript should come in useful."

"Oh, forgive my stupid joke!" he said remorsefully.

"Forgive mine!" she answered. "Sleeplessness is too terrible to joke about. Again I speak as one who knows."

"Oh, I'm sorry to hear that!" he said, his egoistic tenderness instantly transformed to compassionate solicitude.

"Never mind me; I am a woman and can take care of myself. Why don't you go over to Norway and join Mr. Graham?"

"That's quite out of the question," he said, puffing furiously at his pipe. "I can't leave the paper."

"Oh, men always say that. Haven't you let your pipe go out? I don't see any smoke."

He started and laughed. "Yes, there's no more tobacco in it." He laid it down.

"No, I insist on your going on or else I shall feel uncomfortable. Where's your pouch?"

He felt all over his pockets. "It must be on the table."

She rummaged among the mass of papers. "Ha! There are your scissors'" she said scornfully, turning them up. She found the pouch in time and handed it to him. "I ought to have the management of this office for a day," she remarked again.

"Well, fill my pipe for me," he said, with an audacious inspiration. He felt an unreasoning impulse to touch her hand, to smooth her soft cheek with his fingers and press her eyelids down over her dancing eyes. She filled the pipe, full measure and running over; he took it by the stem, her warm gloved fingers grazing his chilly bare hand and suffusing him with a delicious thrill.

"Now you must crown your work," he said. "The matches are somewhere about."

She hunted again, interpolating exclamations of reproof at the risk of fire.

"They're safety matches, I think," he said. They proved to be wax vestas. She gave him a liquid glance of mute reproach that filled him with bliss as overbrimmingly as his pipe had been filled with bird's eye; then she struck a match, protecting the flame scientifically in the hollow of her little hand. Raphael had never imagined a wax vesta could be struck so charmingly. She tip-toed to reach the bowl in his mouth, but he bent his tall form and felt her breath upon his face. The volumes of smoke curled up triumphantly, and Esther's serious countenance relaxed in a smile of satisfaction. She resumed the conversation where it had been broken off by the idyllic interlude of the pipe.

"But if you can't leave London, there's plenty of recreation to be had in town. I'll wager you haven't yet been to see *Hamlet* in lieu of the night you disappointed us."

"Disappointed myself, you mean," he said with a retrospective consciousness of folly. "No, to tell the truth, I haven't been out at all lately. Life is so short."

"Then, why waste it?"

"Oh come, I can't admit I waste it," he said, with a gentle smile that filled her with a penetrating emotion. "You mustn't take such material views of life." Almost in a whisper he quoted: "To him that hath the kingdom of God all things shall be added," and went on: "Socialism is at least as important as Shakspeare."

"Socialism," she repeated. "Are you a Socialist, then?"

"Of a kind," he answered. "Haven't you detected the cloven hoof in my leaders? I'm not violent, you know; don't be alarmed. But I have been doing a little mild propagandism lately in the evenings; land nationalization and a few other things which would bring the world more into harmony with the Law of Moses."

"What! do you find Socialism, too, in orthodox Judaism?"

"It requires no seeking."

"Well, you're almost as bad as my father, who found everything in the Talmud. At this rate you will certainly convert me soon; or at least I shall, like M. Jourdain, discover I've been orthodox all my life without knowing it."

"I hope so," he said gravely. "But have you Socialistic sympathies?"

She hesitated. As a girl she had felt the crude Socialism which is the unreasoned instinct of ambitious poverty, the individual revolt mistaking itself for hatred of the general injustice. When the higher sphere has welcomed the Socialist, he sees he was but the exception to a contented class. Esther had gone through the second phase and was in the throes of the third, to which only the few attain.

"I used to be a red-hot Socialist once," she said. "Today I doubt whether too much stress is not laid on material conditions. High thinking is compatible with the plainest living. 'The soul is its own place and can make a heaven of hell, a hell of heaven.' Let the people who wish to build themselves lordly treasure-houses do so, if they can afford it, but let us not degrade our ideals by envying them."

The conversation had drifted into seriousness. Raphael's thoughts reverted to their normal intellectual cast, but he still watched with pleasure the play of her mobile features as she expounded her opinions.

"Ah, yes, that is a nice abstract theory," he said. "But what if the mechanism of competitive society works so that thousands don't even get the plainest living? You should just see the sights I have seen, then you would understand why for sometime the improvement of the material condition of the masses must be the great problem. Of course, you won't suspect me of underrating the moral and religious considerations."

Esther smiled almost Imperceptibly. The idea of Raphael, who could not see two inches before his nose, telling *her* to examine the spectacle of human misery would have been distinctly amusing, even if her early life had been passed among the same scenes as his. It seemed a part of the irony of things and the paradox of fate that Raphael, who had never known cold or hunger, should be so keenly sensitive to the sufferings of others, while she who had known both had come to regard them with philosophical tolerance. Perhaps she was destined ere long to renew her acquaintance with them. Well, that would test her theories at any rate.

"Who is taking material views of life now?" she asked.

"It is by perfect obedience to the Mosaic Law that the kingdom of God is to be brought about on earth," he answered. "And in spirit, orthodox Judaism is undoubtedly akin to Socialism." His enthusiasm

ISRAEL ZANGWILL

set him pacing the room as usual, his arms working like the sails of a windmill.

Esther shook her head. "Well, give me Shakspeare," she said. "I had rather see *Hamlet* than a world of perfect prigs." She laughed at the oddity of her own comparison and added, still smiling: "Once upon a time I used to think Shakspeare a fraud. But that was merely because he was an institution. It is a real treat to find one superstition that will stand analysis."

"Perhaps you will find the Bible turn out like that," he said hopefully.

"I *have* found it. Within the last few months I have read it right through again—Old and New. It is full of sublime truths, noble apophthegms, endless touches of nature, and great poetry. Our tiny race may well be proud of having given humanity its greatest as well as its most widely circulated books. Why can't Judaism take a natural view of things and an honest pride in its genuine history, instead of building its synagogues on shifting sand?"

"In Germany, later in America, the reconstruction of Judaism has been attempted in every possible way; inspiration has been sought not only in literature, but in archaeology, and even in anthropology; it is these which have proved the shifting sand. You see your scepticism is not even original." He smiled a little, serene in the largeness of his faith. His complacency grated upon her. She jumped up. "We always seem to get into religion, you and I," she said. "I wonder why. It is certain we shall never agree. Mosaism is magnificent, no doubt, but I cannot help feeling Mr. Graham is right when he points out its limitations. Where would the art of the world be if the second Commandment had been obeyed? Is there any such thing as an absolute system of morality? How is it the Chinese have got on all these years without religion? Why should the Jews claim the patent in those moral ideas which you find just as well in all the great writers of antiquity? Why—?" she stopped suddenly, seeing his smile had broadened.

"Which of all these objections am I to answer?" he asked merrily. "Some I'm sure you don't mean."

"I mean all those you can't answer. So please don't try. After all, you're not a professional explainer of the universe, that I should heckle you thus."

"Oh, but I set up to be," he protested.

"No, you don't. You haven't called me a blasphemer once. I'd better go before you become really professional. I shall be late for dinner."

"What nonsense! It is only four o'clock," he pleaded, consulting an old-fashioned silver watch.

"As late as that!" said Esther in horrified tones. "Goodbye! Take care to go through my 'copy' in case any heresies have filtered into it."

"Your copy? Did you give it me?" he inquired.

"Of course I did. You took it from me. Where did you put it? Oh, I hope you haven't mixed it up with those papers. It'll be a terrible task to find it," cried Esther excitedly.

"I wonder if I could have put it in the pigeon-hole for 'copy,'" he said. "Yes! what luck!"

Esther laughed heartily. "You seem tremendously surprised to find anything in its right place."

The moment of solemn parting had come, yet she found herself laughing on. Perhaps she was glad to find the farewell easier than she had foreseen, it had certainly been made easier by the theological passage of arms, which brought out all her latent antagonism to the prejudiced young pietist. Her hostility gave rather a scornful ring to the laugh, which ended with a suspicion of hysteria.

"What a lot of stuff you've written," he said. "I shall never be able to get this into one number."

"I didn't intend you should. It's to be used in instalments, if it's good enough. I did it all in advance, because I'm going away."

"Going away!" he cried, arresting himself in the midst of an inhalation of smoke. "Where?"

"I don't know," she said wearily.

He looked alarm and interrogation.

"I am going to leave the Goldsmiths," she said. "I haven't decided exactly what to do next."

"I hope you haven't quarrelled with them."

"No, no, not at all. In fact they don't even know I am going. I only tell you in confidence. Please don't say anything to anybody. Goodbye. I may not come across you again. So this may be a last goodbye." She extended her hand; he took it mechanically.

"I have no right to pry into your confidence," he said anxiously, "but you make me very uneasy." He did not let go her hand, the warm touch quickened his sympathy. He felt he could not part with her and let her drift into Heaven knew what. "Won't you tell me your trouble?" he went on. "I am sure it is some trouble. Perhaps I can help you. I should be so glad if you would give me the opportunity."

The tears struggled to her eyes, but she did not speak. They stood in silence, with their hands still clasped, feeling very near to each other, and yet still so far apart.

"Cannot you trust me?" he asked. "I know you are unhappy, but I had hoped you had grown cheerfuller of late. You told me so much at our first meeting, surely you might trust me yet a little farther."

"I have told you enough," she said at last "I cannot any longer eat the bread of charity; I must go away and try to earn my own living."

"But what will you do?"

"What do other girls do? Teaching, needlework, anything. Remember, I'm an experienced teacher and a graduate to boot." Her pathetic smile lit up the face with tremulous tenderness.

"But you would be quite alone in the world," he said, solicitude vibrating in every syllable.

"I am used to being quite alone in the world."

The phrase threw a flash of light along the backward vista of her life with the Goldsmiths, and filled his soul with pity and yearning.

"But suppose you fail?"

"If I fail—" she repeated, and rounded off the sentence with a shrug. It was the apathetic, indifferent shrug of Moses Ansell; only his was the shrug of faith in Providence, hers of despair. It filled Raphael's heart with deadly cold and his soul with sinister forebodings. The pathos of her position seemed to him intolerable.

"No, no, this must not be!" he cried, and his hand gripped hers fiercely, as if he were afraid of her being dragged away by main force. He was terribly agitated; his whole being seemed to be undergoing profound and novel emotions. Their eyes met; in one and the same instant the knowledge broke upon her that she loved him, and that if she chose to play the woman he was hers, and life a Paradisian dream. The sweetness of the thought intoxicated her, thrilled her veins with fire. But the next instant she was chilled as by a gray cold fog. The realities of things came back, a whirl of self-contemptuous thoughts blent with a hopeless sense of the harshness of life. Who was she to aspire to such a match? Had her earlier day-dream left her no wiser than that? The *Schnorrer's* daughter setting her cap at the wealthy Oxford man, forsooth! What would people say? And what would they say if they knew how she had sought him out in his busy seclusion to pitch a tale of woe and move him by his tenderness of heart to a pity he mistook momentarily for love? The image of Levi came back suddenly; she quivered, reading herself through his eyes. And yet would not his crude view be right? Suppress the consciousness as she would in her maiden breast, had she not been urged hither by an irresistible impulse? Knowing what she felt now, she could not realize she had been ignorant of it when she set out. She was a deceitful, scheming little thing. Angry with herself, she averted her gaze from the eyes that hungered for her, though they were yet unlit by self-consciousness; she loosed her hand from his, and as if the cessation of the contact restored her self-respect, some of her anger passed unreasonably towards him.

"What right, have you to say it must not be?" she inquired haughtily. "Do you think I can't take care of myself, that I need anyone to protect me or to help me?"

"No—I—I—only mean—" he stammered in infinite distress, feeling himself somehow a blundering brute.

"Remember I am not like the girls you are used to meet. I have known the worst that life can offer. I can stand alone, yes, and face the whole world. Perhaps you don't know that I wrote *Mordecai Josephs*, the book you burlesqued so mercilessly!"

"*You* wrote it!"

"Yes, I. I am Edward Armitage. Did those initials never strike you? I wrote it and I glory in it. Though all Jewry cry out 'The picture is false,' I say it is true. So now you know the truth. Proclaim it to all Hyde Park and Maida Vale, tell it to all your narrow-minded friends and acquaintances, and let them turn and rend me. I can live without them or their praise. Too long they have cramped my soul. Now at last I am going to cut myself free. From them and from you and all your petty prejudices and interests. Goodbye, forever."

She went out abruptly, leaving the room dark and Raphael shaken and dumbfounded; she went down the stairs and into the keen bright air, with a fierce exultation at her heart, an intoxicating sense of freedom and defiance. It was over. She had vindicated herself to herself and to the imaginary critics. The last link that bound her to Jewry was snapped; it was impossible it could ever be reforged. Raphael knew her in her true colors at last. She seemed to herself a Spinoza the race had cast out.

The editor of *The Flag of Judah* stood for some minutes as if petrified; then he turned suddenly to the litter on his table and rummaged among it feverishly. At last, as with a happy recollection, he opened a drawer. What he sought was there. He started reading *Mordecai Josephs*, forgetting to close the drawer. Passage after passage suffused his eyes

ISRAEL ZANGWILL

with tears; a soft magic hovered about the nervous sentences; he read her eager little soul in every line. Now he understood. How blind he had been! How could he have missed seeing? Esther stared at him from every page. She was the heroine of her own book; yes, and the hero, too, for he was but another side of herself translated into the masculine. The whole book was Esther, the whole Esther and nothing but Esther, for even the satirical descriptions were but the revolt of Esther's soul against mean and evil things. He turned to the great love-scene of the book, and read on and on, fascinated, without getting further than the chapter.

XI

Going Home

No need to delay longer; every need for instant flight. Esther had found courage to confess her crime against the community to Raphael; there was no seething of the blood to nerve her to face Mrs. Henry Goldsmith. She retired to her room soon after dinner on the plea (which was not a pretext) of a headache. Then she wrote:

Dear Mrs. Goldsmith:

"When you read this, I shall have left your house, never to return. It would be idle to attempt to explain my reasons. I could not hope to make you see through my eyes. Suffice it to say that I cannot any longer endure a life of dependence, and that I feel I have abused your favor by writing that Jewish novel of which you disapprove so vehemently. I never intended to keep the secret from you, after publication. I thought the book would succeed and you would be pleased; at the same time I dimly felt that you might object to certain things and ask to have them altered, and I have always wanted to write my own ideas, and not other people's. With my temperament, I see now that it was a mistake to fetter myself by obligations to anybody, but the mistake was made in my girlhood when I knew little of the world and perhaps less of myself. Nevertheless, I wish you to believe, dear Mrs. Goldsmith, that all the blame for the unhappy situation which has arisen I put upon my own shoulders, and that I have nothing for you but the greatest affection and gratitude for all the kindnesses I have received at your hands. I beg you not to think that I make the slightest reproach against you; on the contrary, I shall always henceforth reproach myself with the thought that I have made you so poor a return for your generosity and incessant thoughtfulness. But the sphere in which you move is too high for me; I cannot assimilate with it and I return, not without gladness, to the humble sphere whence you took me. With kindest regards and best wishes,

"I am,

Yours ever gratefully,
ESTHER ANSELL

There were tears in Esther's eyes when she finished, and she was penetrated with admiration of her own generosity in so freely admitting Mrs. Goldsmith's and in allowing that her patron got nothing out of the bargain. She was doubtful whether the sentence about the high sphere was satirical or serious. People do not know what they mean almost as often as they do not say it.

Esther put the letter into an envelope and placed it on the open writing-desk she kept on her dressing-table. She then packed a few toilette essentials in a little bag, together with some American photographs of her brother and sisters in various stages of adolescence. She was determined to go back empty-handed as she came, and was reluctant to carry off the few sovereigns of pocket-money in her purse, and hunted up a little gold locket she had received, while yet a teacher, in celebration of the marriage of a communal magnate's daughter. Thrown aside seven years ago, it now bade fair to be the corner-stone of the temple; she had meditated pledging it and living on the proceeds till she found work, but when she realized its puny pretensions to cozen pawnbrokers, it flashed upon her that she could always repay Mrs. Goldsmith the few pounds she was taking away. In a drawer there was a heap of manuscript carefully locked away; she took it and looked through it hurriedly, contemptuously. Some of it was music, some poetry, the bulk prose. At last she threw it suddenly on the bright fire which good Mary O'Reilly had providentially provided in her room; then, as it flared up, stricken with remorse, she tried to pluck the sheets from the flames; only by scorching her fingers and raising blisters did she succeed, and then, with scornful resignation, she instantly threw them back again, warming her feverish hands merrily at the bonfire. Rapidly looking through all her drawers, lest perchance in some stray manuscript she should leave her soul naked behind her, she came upon a forgotten faded rose. The faint fragrance was charged with strange memories of Sidney. The handsome young artist had given it her in the earlier days of their acquaintanceship. To Esther tonight it seemed to belong to a period infinitely more remote than her childhood. When the shrivelled rose had been further crumpled into a little ball and then picked to bits, it only remained to inquire where to go; what to do she could settle when there. She tried to collect her thoughts. Alas! it was not so easy as collecting her luggage. For a long time she crouched on the fender and looked into the fire, seeing in it only fragmentary pictures of the last seven years—bits of scenery, great Cathedral interiors arousing mysterious yearnings, petty incidents of travel, moments with Sidney, drawing-room episodes, strange passionate scenes with herself as single performer, long silent watches of study and aspiration, like the souls of the burned manuscripts made visible. Even that very afternoon's scene with Raphael was part of the "old unhappy far-off things" that could only live henceforwards in fantastic arcades of glowing coal, out of all relation to future realities. Her new-born love for Raphael appeared as ancient and as arid as the girlish ambitions that had seemed on the point of blossoming when she was transplanted from the Ghetto. That, too, was in the flames, and should remain there.

At last she started up with a confused sense of wasted time and began to undress mechanically, trying to concentrate her thoughts the while on the problem that faced her. But they wandered back to her first night in the fine house, when a separate bedroom was a new experience and she was afraid to sleep alone, though turned fifteen. But she was more afraid of appearing a great baby, and so no one in the world ever knew what the imaginative little creature had lived down.

In the middle of brushing her hair she ran to the door and locked it, from a sudden dread that she might oversleep herself and someone would come in and see the letter on the writing-desk. She had not solved the problem even by the time she got into bed; the fire opposite the foot was burning down, but there was a red glow penetrating the dimness. She had forgotten to draw the blind, and she saw the clear stars shining peacefully in the sky. She looked and looked at them and they led her thoughts away from the problem once more. She seemed to be lying in Victoria Park, looking up with innocent mystic rapture and restfulness at the brooding blue sky. The blood-and-thunder boys' story she had borrowed from Solomon had fallen from her hand and lay unheeded on the grass. Solomon was tossing a ball to Rachel, which he had acquired by a colossal accumulation of buttons, and Isaac and Sarah were rolling and wrangling on the grass. Oh, why had she deserted them? What were they doing now, without her mother-care, out and away beyond the great seas? For weeks together, the thought of them had not once crossed her mind; tonight she stretched her arms involuntarily towards her loved ones, not towards the shadowy figures of reality, scarcely less phantasmal than the dead Benjamin, but towards the childish figures of the past. What happy times they had had together in the dear old garret!

In her strange half-waking hallucination, her outstretched arms were clasped round little Sarah. She was putting her to bed and the tiny thing was repeating after her, in broken Hebrew, the children's night-prayer: "Suffer me to lie down in peace, and let me rise up in peace. Hear O Israel, the Lord our God, the Lord is one," with its unauthorized appendix in baby English: "Dod teep me, and mate me a dood dirl, orways."

She woke to full consciousness with a start; her arms chilled, her face wet. But the problem was solved.

She would go back to them, back to her true home, where loving faces waited to welcome her, where hearts were open and life was simple and the weary brain could find rest from the stress and struggle of obstinate questionings of destiny. Life was so simple at bottom; it was she that was so perversely complex. She would go back to her father whose naïve devout face swam glorified upon a sea of tears; yea, and back to her father's primitive faith like a tired lost child that spies its home at last. The quaint, monotonous cadence of her father's prayers rang pathetically in her ears; and a great light, the light that Raphael had shown her, seemed to blend mystically with the once meaningless sounds. Yea, all things were from Him who created light and darkness, good and evil; she felt her cares falling from her, her soul absorbing itself in the sense of a Divine Love, awful, profound, immeasurable, underlying and transcending all things, incomprehensibly satisfying the soul and justifying and explaining the universe. The infinite fret and fume of life seemed like the petulance of an infant in the presence of this restful tenderness diffused through the great spaces. How holy the stars seemed up there in the quiet sky, like so many Sabbath lights shedding visible consecration and blessing!

Yes, she would go back to her loved ones, back from this dainty room, with its white laces and perfumed draperies, back if need be to a Ghetto garret. And in the ecstasy of her abandonment of all worldly things, a great peace fell upon her soul.

In the morning the nostalgia of the Ghetto was still upon her, blent with a passion of martyrdom that made her yearn for a lower social depth than was really necessary. But the more human aspects of the situation were paramount in the gray chillness of a bleak May dawn. Her resolution to cross the Atlantic forthwith seemed a little hasty, and though she did not flinch from it, she was not sorry to remember that she had not money enough for the journey. She must perforce stay in London till she had earned it; meantime she would go back to the districts and the people she knew so well, and accustom herself again to the old ways, the old simplicities of existence.

She dressed herself in her plainest apparel, though she could not help her spring bonnet being pretty. She hesitated between a hat and a bonnet, but decided that her solitary position demanded as womanly an appearance as possible. Do what she would, she could not prevent herself looking exquisitely refined, and the excitement of adventure had lent that touch of color to her face which made it fascinating. About seven o'clock she left her room noiselessly and descended the stairs cautiously, holding her little black bag in her hand.

"Och, be the holy mother, Miss Esther, phwat a turn you gave me," said Mary O'Reilly, emerging unexpectedly from the dining-room and meeting her at the foot of the stairs. "Phwat's the matther?"

"I'm going out, Mary," she said, her heart beating violently.

"Sure an' it's rale purty ye look, Miss Esther; but it's divil a bit the marnin' for a walk, it looks a raw kind of a day, as if the weather was sorry for bein' so bright yisterday."

"Oh, but I must go, Mary."

"Ah, the saints bliss your kind heart!" said Mary, catching sight of the bag. "Sure, then, it's a charity irrand you're bent on. I mind me how my blissed old masther, Mr. Goldsmith's father, *Olov Hasholom*, who's gone to glory, used to walk to *Shool* in all winds and weathers; sometimes it was five o'clock of a winter's marnin' and I used to get up and make him an iligant cup of coffee before he wint to *Selichoth*; he niver would take milk and sugar in it, becaz that would be atin' belike, poor dear old ginthleman. Ah the Holy Vargin be kind to him!"

"And may she be kind to you, Mary," said Esther. And she impulsively pressed her lips to the old woman's seamed and wrinkled cheek, to the astonishment of the guardian of Judaism. Virtue was its own reward, for Esther profited by the moment of the loquacious creature's breathlessness to escape. She opened the hall door and passed into the silent streets, whose cold pavements seemed to reflect the bleak stony tints of the sky.

ISRAEL ZANGWILL

For the first few minutes she walked hastily, almost at a run. Then her pace slackened; she told herself there was no hurry, and she shook her head when a cabman interrogated her. The omnibuses were not running yet. When they commenced, she would take one to Whitechapel. The signs of awakening labor stirred her with new emotions; the early milkman with his cans, casual artisans with their tools, a grimy sweep, a work-girl with a paper lunch-package, an apprentice whistling. Great sleeping houses lined her path like gorged monsters drowsing voluptuously. The world she was leaving behind her grew alien and repulsive, her heart went out to the patient world of toil. What had she been doing all these years, amid her books and her music and her rose-leaves, aloof from realities?

The first 'bus overtook her half-way and bore her back to the Ghetto.

The Ghetto was all astir, for it was half-past eight of a work-a-day morning. But Esther had not walked a hundred yards before her breast was heavy with inauspicious emotions. The well-known street she had entered was strangely broadened. Instead of the dirty picturesque houses rose an appalling series of artisans' dwellings, monotonous brick barracks, whose dead, dull prose weighed upon the spirits. But, as in revenge, other streets, unaltered, seemed incredibly narrow. Was it possible it could have taken even her childish feet six strides to cross them, as she plainly remembered? And they seemed so unspeakably sordid and squalid. Could she ever really have walked them with light heart, unconscious of the ugliness? Did the gray atmosphere that overhung them ever lift, or was it their natural and appropriate mantle? Surely the sun could never shine upon these slimy pavements, kissing them to warmth and life.

Great magic shops where all things were to be had; peppermints and cotton, china-faced dolls and lemons, had dwindled into the front windows of tiny private dwelling-houses; the black-wigged crones, the greasy shambling men, were uglier and greasier than she had ever conceived them. They seemed caricatures of humanity; scarecrows in battered hats or draggled skirts. But gradually, as the scene grew upon her, she perceived that in spite of the "model dwellings" builder, it was essentially unchanged. No vestige of improvement had come over Wentworth Street: the narrow noisy market street, where serried barrows flanked the reeking roadway exactly as of old, and where Esther trod on mud and refuse and babies. Babies! They were everywhere; at the breasts of unwashed women, on the knees of grandfathers smoking pipes, playing under the barrows, sprawling in the gutters and the alleys. All the babies' faces were sickly and dirty with pathetic, childish prettinesses asserting themselves against the neglect and the sallowness. One female mite in a dingy tattered frock sat in an orange-box, surveying the bustling scene with a preternaturally grave expression, and realizing literally Esther's early conception of the theatre. There was a sense of blankness in the wanderer's heart, of unfamiliarity in the midst of familiarity. What had she in common with all this mean wretchedness, with this semi-barbarous breed of beings? The more she looked, the more her heart sank. There was no flaunting vice, no rowdiness, no drunkenness, only the squalor of an oriental city without its quaintness and color. She studied the posters and the shop-windows, and caught old snatches of gossip from the groups in the butchers' shops—all seemed as of yore. And yet here and there the hand of Time had traced new inscriptions. For Baruch Emanuel the hand of Time had written a new placard. It was a mixture of German, bad English and Cockneyese, phonetically spelt in Hebrew letters:

Mens Solen Und Eelen, 2/6
Lydies Deeto, 1/6
Kindersche Deeto, 1/6
Hier wird gemacht
Aller Hant Sleepers
Fur Trebbelers
Zu De Billigsten Preissen.

Baruch Emanuel had prospered since the days when he wanted "lasters and riveters" without being able to afford them. He no longer gratuitously advertised *Mordecai Schwartz* in envious emulation, for he had several establishments and owned five two-story houses, and was treasurer of his little synagogue, and spoke of Socialists as an inferior variety of Atheists. Not that all this bourgeoning was to be counted to leather, for Baruch had developed enterprises in all directions, having all the versatility of Moses Ansell without his catholic capacity for failure.

The hand of Time had also constructed a "working-men's Métropole" almost opposite Baruch Emanuel's shop, and papered its outside walls with moral pictorial posters, headed, "Where have you been to,

Thomas Brown?" "Mike and his moke," and so on. Here, single-bedded cabins could be had as low as fourpence a night. From the journals in a tobacconist's window Esther gathered that the reading-public had increased, for there were importations from New York, both in jargon and in pure Hebrew, and from a large poster in Yiddish and English, announcing a public meeting, she learned of the existence of an off-shoot of the Holy Land League—"The Flowers of Zion Society—established by East-End youths for the study of Hebrew and the propagation of the Jewish National Idea." Side by side with this, as if in ironic illustration of the other side of the life of the Ghetto, was a seeming royal proclamation headed VR., informing the public that by order of the Secretary of State for War a sale of wrought-and cast-iron, zinc, canvas, tools and leather would take place at the Royal Arsenal, Woolwich.

As she wandered on, the great school-bell began to ring; involuntarily, she quickened her step and joined the chattering children's procession. She could have fancied the last ten years a dream. Were they, indeed, other children, or were they not the same that jostled her when she picked her way through this very slush in her clumsy masculine boots? Surely those little girls in lilac print frocks were her classmates! It was hard to realize that Time's wheel had been whirling on, fashioning her to a woman; that, while she had been living and learning and seeing the manners of men and cities, the Ghetto, unaffected by her experiences, had gone on in the same narrow rut. A new generation of children had arisen to suffer and sport in room of the old, and that was all. The thought overwhelmed her, gave her a new and poignant sense of brute, blind forces; she seemed to catch in this familiar scene of childhood the secret of the gray atmosphere of her spirit, it was here she had, all insensibly, absorbed those heavy vapors that formed the background of her being, a permanent sombre canvas behind all the iridescent colors of joyous emotion. *What* had she in common with all this mean wretchedness? Why, everything. This it was with which her soul had intangible affinities, not the glory of sun and sea and forest, "the palms and temples of the South."

The heavy vibrations of the bell ceased; the street cleared; Esther turned back and walked instinctively homewards—to Royal Street. Her soul was full of the sense of the futility of life; yet the sight of the great shabby house could still give her a chill. Outside the door a wizened old woman with a chronic sniff had established a stall for wizened old apples, but Esther passed her by heedless of her stare, and ascended the two miry steps that led to the mud-carpeted passage.

The apple-woman took her for a philanthropist paying a surprise visit to one of the families of the house, and resented her as a spy. She was discussing the meanness of the thing with the pickled-herring dealer next door, while Esther was mounting the dark stairs with the confidence of old habit. She was making automatically for the garret, like a somnambulist, with no definite object—morbidly drawn towards the old home. The unchanging musty smells that clung to the staircase flew to greet her nostrils, and at once a host of sleeping memories started to life, besieging her and pressing upon her on every side. After a tumultuous intolerable moment a childish figure seemed to break from the gloom ahead—the figure of a little girl with a grave face and candid eyes, a dutiful, obedient shabby little girl, so anxious to please her schoolmistress, so full of craving to learn and to be good, and to be loved by God, so audaciously ambitious of becoming a teacher, and so confident of being a good Jewess always. Satchel in hand, the little girl sped up the stairs swiftly, despite her cumbrous, slatternly boots, and Esther, holding her bag, followed her more slowly, as if she feared to contaminate her by the touch of one so weary-worldly-wise, so full of revolt and despair.

All at once Esther sidled timidly towards the balustrade, with an instinctive movement, holding her bag out protectingly. The figure vanished, and Esther awoke to the knowledge that "Bobby" was not at his post. Then with a flash came the recollection of Bobby's mistress—the pale, unfortunate young seamstress she had so unconscionably neglected. She wondered if she were alive or dead. A waft of sickly odors surged from below; Esther felt a deadly faintness coming over her; she had walked far, and nothing had yet passed her lips since yesterday's dinner, and at this moment, too, an overwhelming terrifying feeling of loneliness pressed like an icy hand upon her heart. She felt that in another instant she must swoon, there, upon the foul landing. She sank against the door, beating passionately at the panels. It was opened from within; she had just strength enough to clutch the door-post so as not to fall. A thin, careworn woman swam uncertainly before her eyes. Esther could not recognize her, but the plain iron bed, almost corresponding in area with that of the room, was as of old, and so was the little round table with a tea-pot and a cup and saucer, and half a loaf standing out amid a litter of sewing, as if the owner had been interrupted in the middle of breakfast. Stay—what was that journal resting against the half-loaf as for perusal during the meal? Was it not the *London Journal*? Again she looked, but with more confidence, at the woman's face. A wave of curiosity, of astonishment at the stylishly dressed visitor, passed over it, but in the curves of the mouth, in the movement of the eyebrows, Esther renewed indescribably subtle memories.

"Debby!" she cried hysterically. A great flood of joy swamped her soul. She was not alone in the world, after all! Dutch Debby uttered a little startled scream. "I've come back, Debby, I've come back," and the next moment the brilliant girl-graduate fell fainting into the seamstress's arms.

XII

A Sheaf of Sequels

Within half an hour Esther was smiling pallidly and drinking tea out of Debby's own cup, to Debby's unlimited satisfaction. Debby had no spare cup, but she had a spare chair without a back, and Esther was of course seated on the other. Her bonnet and cloak were on the bed.

"And where is Bobby?" inquired the young lady visitor.

Debby's joyous face clouded.

"Bobby is dead," she said softly. "He died four years ago, come next *Shevuos*."

"I'm so sorry," said Esther, pausing in her tea-drinking with a pang of genuine emotion. "At first I was afraid of him, but that was before I knew him."

"There never beat a kinder heart on God's earth," said Debby, emphatically. "He wouldn't hurt a fly."

Esther had often seen him snapping at flies, but she could not smile.

"I buried him secretly in the back yard," Debby confessed. "See! there, where the paving stone is loose."

Esther gratified her by looking through the little back window into the sloppy enclosure where washing hung. She noticed a cat sauntering quietly over the spot without any of the satisfaction it might have felt had it known it was walking over the grave of an hereditary enemy.

"So I don't feel as if he was far away," said Debby. "I can always look out and picture him squatting above the stone instead of beneath it."

"But didn't you get another?"

"Oh, how can you talk so heartlessly?"

"Forgive me, dear; of course you couldn't replace him. And haven't you had any other friends?"

"Who would make friends with me, Miss Ansell?" Debby asked quietly.

"I shall 'make out friends' with you, Debby, if you call me that," said Esther, half laughing, half crying. "What was it we used to say in school? I forget, but I know we used to wet our little fingers in our mouths and jerk them abruptly toward the other party. That's what I shall have to do with you."

"Oh well, Esther, don't be cross. But you do look such a real lady. I always said you would grow up clever, didn't I, though?"

"You did, dear, you did. I can never forgive myself for not having looked you up."

"Oh, but you had so much to do, I have no doubt," said Debby magnanimously, though she was not a little curious to hear all Esther's wonderful adventures and to gather more about the reasons of the girl's mysterious return than had yet been vouchsafed her. All she had dared to ask was about the family in America.

"Still, it was wrong of me," said Esther, in a tone that brooked no protest. "Suppose you had been in want and I could have helped you?"

"Oh, but you know I never take any help," said Debby stiffly.

"I didn't know that," said Esther, touched. "Have you never taken soup at the Kitchen?"

"I wouldn't dream of such a thing. Do you ever remember me going to the Board of Guardians? I wouldn't go there to be bullied, not if I was starving. It's only the cadgers who don't want it who get relief. But, thank God, in the worst seasons I have always been able to earn a crust and a cup of tea. You see I am only a small family," concluded Debby with a sad smile, "and the less one has to do with other people the better."

Esther started slightly, feeling a strange new kinship with this lonely soul.

"But surely you would have taken help of me," she said. Debby shook her head obstinately.

"Well, I'm not so proud," said Esther with a tremulous smile, "for see, I have come to take help of you."

Then the tears welled forth and Debby with an impulsive movement pressed the little sobbing form against her faded bodice bristling with pin-heads. Esther recovered herself in a moment and drank some more tea.

"Are the same people living here?" she said.

"Not altogether. The Belcovitches have gone up in the world. They live on the first floor now."

"Not much of a rise that," said Esther smiling, for the Belcovitches had always lived on the third floor.

"Oh, they could have gone to a better street altogether," explained Debby, "only Mr. Belcovitch didn't like the expense of a van."

"Then, Sugarman the *Shadchan* must have moved, too," said Esther. "He used to have the first floor."

"Yes, he's got the third now. You see, people get tired of living in the same place. Then Ebenezer, who became very famous through writing a book (so he told me), went to live by himself, so they didn't want to be so grand. The back apartment at the top of the house you used once to inhabit,"—Debby put it as delicately as she could—"is vacant. The last family had the brokers in."

"Are the Belcovitches all well? I remember Fanny married and went to Manchester before I left here."

"Oh yes, they are all well."

"What? Even Mrs. Belcovitch?"

"She still takes medicine, but she seems just as strong as ever."

"Becky married yet?"

"Oh no, but she has won two breach of promise cases."

"She must be getting old."

"She is a fine young woman, but the young men are afraid of her now."

"Then they don't sit on the stairs in the morning anymore?"

"No, young men seem so much less romantic now-a-days," said Debby, sighing. "Besides there's one flight less now and half the stairs face the street door. The next flight was so private."

"I suppose I shall look in and see them all," said Esther, smiling. "But tell me. Is Mrs. Simons living here still?"

"No."

"Where, then? I should like to see her. She was so very kind to little Sarah, you know. Nearly all our fried fish came from her."

"She is dead. She died of cancer. She suffered a great deal."

"Oh!" Esther put her cup down and sat back with face grown white.

"I am afraid to ask about anyone else," she said at last. "I suppose the Sons of the Covenant are getting on all right; *they* can't be dead, at least not all of them."

"They have split up," said Debby gravely, "into two communities. Mr. Belcovitch and the Shalotten *Shammos* quarrelled about the sale of the *Mitzvahs* at the Rejoicing of the Law two years ago. As far as I could gather, the carrying of the smallest scroll of the Law was knocked down to the Shalotten *Shammos*, for eighteenpence, but Mr. Belcovitch, who had gone outside a moment, said he had bought up the privilege in advance to present to Daniel Hyams, who was a visitor, and whose old father had just died in Jerusalem. There was nearly a free fight in the *Shool*. So the Shalotten *Shammos* seceded with nineteen followers and their wives and set up a rival *Chevrah* round the corner. The other twenty-five still come here. The deserters tried to take Greenberg the *Chazan* with them, but Greenberg wanted a stipulation that they wouldn't engage an extra Reader to do his work during the High Festivals; he even offered to do it cheaper if they would let him do all the work, but they wouldn't consent. As a compromise, they proposed to replace him only on the Day of Atonement, as his voice was not agreeable enough for that. But Greenberg was obstinate. Now I believe there is a movement for the Sons of the Covenant to connect their *Chevrah* with the Federation of minor synagogues, but Mr. Belcovitch says he won't join the Federation unless the term 'minor' is omitted. He is a great politician now."

"Ah, I dare say he reads *The Flag of Judah*," said Esther, laughing, though Debby recounted all this history quite seriously. "Do you ever see that paper?"

"I never heard of it before," said Debby simply. "Why should I waste money on new papers when I can always forget the *London journal* sufficiently?" Perhaps Mr. Belcovitch buys it: I have seen him with a Yiddish paper. The 'hands' say that instead of breaking off suddenly in the middle of a speech, as of old, he sometimes stops pressing for five minutes together to denounce Gideon, the member for Whitechapel, and to say that Mr. Henry Goldsmith is the only possible saviour of Judaism in the House of Commons."

"Ah, then he does read *The flag of Judah*! His English must have improved."

"I was glad to hear him say that," added Debby, when she had finished struggling with the fit of coughing brought on by too much monologue, "because I thought it must be the husband of the lady who was so good to you. I never forgot her name."

Esther took up the *London Journal* to hide her reddening cheeks.

"Oh, read some of it aloud," cried Dutch Debby. "It'll be like old times."

Esther hesitated, a little ashamed of such childish behavior. But, deciding to fall in for a moment with the poor woman's humor, and glad to change the subject, she read: "Soft scents steeped the dainty conservatory in delicious drowsiness. Reclining on a blue silk couch, her wonderful beauty rather revealed than concealed by the soft clinging draperies she wore, Rosaline smiled bewitchingly at the poor young peer, who could not pluck up courage to utter the words of flame that were scorching his lips. The moon silvered the tropical palms, and from the brilliant ball-room were wafted the sweet penetrating strains of the 'Blue Danube' waltz—"

Dutch Debby heaved a great sigh of rapture.

"And you have seen such sights!" she said in awed admiration.

"I have been in brilliant ball-rooms and moonlit conservatories," said Esther evasively. She did not care to rob Dutch Debby of her ideals by explaining that high life was not all passion and palm-trees.

"I am so glad," said Debby affectionately. "I have often wished to myself, only a make-believe wish, you know, not a real wish, if you understand what I mean, for of course I know it's impossible. I sometimes sit at that window before going to bed and look at the moon as it silvers the swaying clothes-props, and I can easily imagine they are great tropical palms, especially when an organ is playing round the corner. Sometimes the moon shines straight down on Bobby's tombstone, and then I am glad. Ah, now you're smiling. I know you think me a crazy old thing."

"Indeed, indeed, dear, I think you're the darlingest creature in the world," and Esther jumped up and kissed her to hide her emotion. "But I mustn't waste your time," she said briskly. "I know you have your sewing to do. It's too long to tell you my story now; suffice it to say (as the *London Journal* says) that I am going to take a lodging in the neighborhood. Oh, dear, don't make those great eyes! I want to live in the East End."

"You want to live here like a Princess in disguise. I see."

"No you don't, you romantic old darling. I want to live here like everybody else. I'm going to earn my own living."

"Oh, but you can never live by yourself."

"Why not? Now from romantic you become conventional. *You've* lived by yourself."

"Oh, but I'm different," said Debby, flushing.

"Nonsense, I'm just as good as you. But if you think it improper," here Esther had a sudden idea, "come and live with me."

"What, be your chaperon!" cried Debby in responsive excitement; then her voice dropped again. "Oh, no, how could I?"

"Yes, yes, you must," said Esther eagerly.

Debby's obstinate shake of the head repelled the idea. "I couldn't

ISRAEL ZANGWILL

leave Bobby," she said. After a pause, she asked timidly: "Why not stay here?"

"Don't be ridiculous," Esther answered. Then she examined the bed. "Two couldn't sleep here," she said.

"Oh yes, they could," said Debby, thoughtfully bisecting the blanket with her hand. "And the bed's quite clean or I wouldn't venture to ask you. Maybe it's not so soft as you've been used to."

Esther pondered; she was fatigued and she had undergone too many poignant emotions already to relish the hunt for a lodging. It was really lucky this haven offered itself. "I'll stay for tonight, anyhow," she announced, while Debby's face lit up as with a bonfire of joy. "Tomorrow we'll discuss matters further. And now, dear, can I help you with your sewing?"

"No, Esther, thank you kindly. You see there's only enough for one," said Debby apologetically. "Tomorrow there may be more. Besides you were never as clever with your needle as your pen. You always used to lose marks for needlework, and don't you remember how you herring-boned the tucks of those petticoats instead of feather-stitching them? Ha, ha, ha! I have often laughed at the recollection."

"Oh, that was only absence of mind," said Esther, tossing her head in affected indignation. "If my work isn't good enough for you, I think I'll go down and help Becky with her machine." She put on her bonnet, and, not without curiosity, descended a flight, of stairs and knocked at a door which, from the steady whirr going on behind it, she judged to be that of the work-room.

"Art thou a man or a woman?" came in Yiddish the well-remembered tones of the valetudinarian lady.

"A woman!" answered Esther in German. She was glad she learned German; it would be the best substitute for Yiddish in her new-old life.

"*Herein!*" said Mrs. Belcovitch, with sentry-like brevity.

Esther turned the handle, and her surprise was not diminished when she found herself not in the work-room, but in the invalid's bedroom. She almost stumbled over the pail of fresh water, the supply of which was always kept there. A coarse bouncing full-figured young woman, with frizzly black hair, paused, with her foot on the treadle of her machine, to stare at the newcomer. Mrs. Belcovitch, attired in a skirt and a night-cap, stopped aghast in the act of combing out her wig, which hung over an edge of the back of a chair, that served as a barber's block. Like the apple-woman, she fancied the apparition a lady philanthropist—and though she had long ceased to take charity, the old instincts leaped out under the sudden shock.

"Becky, quick rub my leg with liniment, the thick one," she whispered in Yiddish.

"It's only me, Esther Ansell!" cried the visitor.

"What! Esther!" cried Mrs. Belcovitch. "*Gott in Himmel!*" and, throwing down the comb, she fell in excess of emotion upon Esther's neck. "I have so often wanted to see you," cried the sickly-looking little woman who hadn't altered a wrinkle. "Often have I said to my Becky, where is little Esther?—gold one sees and silver one sees, but Esther sees one not. Is it not so, Becky? Oh, how fine you look! Why, I mistook you for a lady! You are married—not? Ah well, you'll find wooers as thick as the street dogs. And how goes it with the father and the family in America?"

"Excellently," answered Esther. "How are you, Becky?"

Becky murmured something, and the two young women shook hands. Esther had an olden awe of Becky, and Becky was now a little impressed by Esther.

"I suppose Mr. Weingott is getting a good living now in Manchester?" Esther remarked cheerfully to Mrs. Belcovitch.

"No, he has a hard struggle," answered his mother-in-law, "but I have seven grandchildren, God be thanked, and I expect an eighth. If my poor lambkin had been alive now, she would have been a great-grandmother. My eldest grandchild, Hertzel, has a talent for the fiddle. A gentleman is paying for his lessons, God be thanked. I suppose you have heard I won four pounds on the lotter*ee*. You see I have not tried thirty years for nothing! If I only had my health, I should have little to grumble at. Yes, four pounds, and what think you I have bought with it? You shall see it inside. A cupboard with glass doors, such as we left behind in Poland, and we have hung the shelves with pink paper and made loops for silver forks to rest in—it makes me feel as if I had just cut off my tresses. But then I look on my Becky and I remember that— go thou inside, Becky, my life! Thou makest it too hard for him. Give him a word while I speak with Esther."

Becky made a grimace and shrugged her shoulders, but disappeared through the door that led to the real workshop.

"A fine maid!" said the mother, her eyes following the girl with pride. "No wonder she is so hard to please. She vexes him so that he eats out his heart. He comes every morning with a bag of cakes or an orange or a fat Dutch herring, and now she has moved her machine to my bedroom, where he can't follow her, the unhappy youth."

"Who is it now?" inquired Esther in amusement.

"Shosshi Shmendrik."

"Shosshi Shmendrik! Wasn't that the young man who married the Widow Finkelstein?"

"Yes—a very honorable and seemly youth. But she preferred her first husband," said Mrs. Belcovitch laughing, "and followed him only four years after Shosshi's marriage. Shosshi has now all her money—a very seemly and honorable youth."

"But will it come to anything?"

"It is already settled. Becky gave in two days ago. After all, she will not always be young. The *Tanaim* will be held next Sunday. Perhaps you would like to come and see the betrothal contract signed. The Kovna *Maggid* will be here, and there will be rum and cakes to the heart's desire. Becky has Shosshi in great affection; they are just suited. Only she likes to tease, poor little thing. And then she is so shy. Go in and see them, and the cupboard with glass doors."

Esther pushed open the door, and Mrs. Belcovitch resumed her loving manipulation of the wig.

The Belcovitch workshop was another of the landmarks of the past that had undergone no change, despite the cupboard with glass doors and the slight difference in the shape of the room. The paper roses still bloomed in the corners of the mirror, the cotton-labels still adorned the wall around it. The master's new umbrella still stood unopened in a corner. The "hands" were other, but then Mr. Belcovitch's hands were always changing. He never employed "union-men," and his hirelings never stayed with him longer than they could help. One of the present batch, a bent, middle-aged man, with a deeply-lined face, was Simon Wolf, long since thrown over by the labor party he had created, and fallen lower and lower till he returned to the Belcovitch workshop whence he sprang. Wolf, who had a wife and six children, was grateful to Mr. Belcovitch in a dumb, sullen way, remembering how that capitalist had figured in his red rhetoric, though it was an extra pang of martyrdom to have to listen deferentially to Belcovitch's numerous political and economical fallacies. He would have preferred the curter dogmatism of earlier days. Shosshi Shmendrik was chatting quite gaily with Becky, and held her finger-tips cavalierly in his coarse fist, without obvious objection on her part. His face was still pimply, but it had lost its painful shyness and its readiness to blush without provocation. His bearing, too, was less clumsy and uncouth. Evidently, to love the Widow Finkelstein had been a liberal education to him. Becky had broken the news of Esther's arrival to her father, as was evident from the odor of turpentine emanating from the opened bottle of rum on the central table. Mr. Belcovitch, whose hair was gray now, but who seemed to have as much stamina as ever, held out his left hand (the right was wielding the pressing-iron) without moving another muscle.

"*Nu*, it gladdens me to see you are better off than of old," he said gravely in Yiddish.

"Thank you. I am glad to see you looking so fresh and healthy," replied Esther in German.

"You were taken away to be educated, was it not?"

"Yes."

"And how many tongues do you know?"

"Four or five," said Esther, smiling.

"Four or five!" repeated Mr. Belcovitch, so impressed that he stopped pressing. "Then you can aspire to be a clerk! I know several firms where they have young women now."

"Don't be ridiculous, father," interposed Becky. "Clerks aren't so grand now-a-days as they used to be. Very likely she would turn up her nose at a clerkship."

"I'm sure I wouldn't," said Esther.

"There! thou hearest!" said Mr. Belcovitch, with angry satisfaction. "It is thou who hast too many flies in thy nostrils. Thou wouldst throw over Shosshi if thou hadst thine own way. Thou art the only person in the world who listens not to me. Abroad my word decides great matters. Three times has my name been printed in *The Flag of Judah*. Little Esther had not such a father as thou, but never did she make mock of him."

"Of course, everybody's better than me," said Becky petulantly, as she snatched her fingers away from Shosshi.

"No, thou art better than the whole world," protested Shosshi Shmendrik, feeling for the fingers.

"Who spoke to thee?" demanded Belcovitch, incensed.

"Who spoke to thee?" echoed Becky. And when Shosshi, with empurpled pimples, cowered before both, father and daughter felt allies again, and peace was re-established at Shosshi's expense. But Esther's curiosity was satisfied. She seemed to see the whole future of this domestic group: Belcovitch accumulating gold-pieces and

Mrs. Belcovitch medicine-bottles till they died, and the lucky but henpecked Shosshi gathering up half the treasure on behalf of the buxom Becky. Refusing the glass of rum, she escaped.

The dinner which Debby (under protest) did not pay for, consisted of viands from the beloved old cook-shop, the potatoes and rice of childhood being supplemented by a square piece of baked meat, likewise knives and forks. Esther was anxious to experience again the magic taste and savor of the once coveted delicacies. Alas! the preliminary sniff failed to make her mouth water, the first bite betrayed the inferiority of the potatoes used. Even so the unattainable tart of infancy mocks the moneyed but dyspeptic adult. But she concealed her disillusionment bravely.

"Do you know," said Debby, pausing in her voluptuous scouring of the gravy-lined plate with a bit of bread, "I can hardly believe my eyes. It seems a dream that you are sitting at dinner with me. Pinch me, will you?"

"You have been pinched enough," said Esther sadly. Which shows that one can pun with a heavy heart. This is one of the things Shakspeare knew and Dr. Johnson didn't.

In the afternoon, Esther went round to Zachariah Square. She did not meet any of the old faces as she walked through the Ghetto, though a little crowd that blocked her way at one point turned out to be merely spectators of an epileptic performance by Meckisch. Esther turned away, in amused disgust. She wondered whether Mrs. Meckisch still flaunted it in satins and heavy necklaces, or whether Meckisch had divorced her, or survived her, or something equally inconsiderate. Hard by the old Ruins (which she found "ruined" by a railway) Esther was almost run over by an iron hoop driven by a boy with a long swarthy face that irresistibly recalled Malka's.

"Is your grandmother in town?" she said at a venture.

"Y—e—s," said the driver wonderingly. "She is over in her own house."

Esther did not hasten towards it.

"Your name's Ezekiel, isn't it?"

"Yes," replied the boy; and then Esther was sure it was the Redeemed Son of whom her father had told her.

"Are your mother and father well?"

"Father's away travelling." Ezekiel's tone was a little impatient, his feet shuffled uneasily, itching to chase the flying hoop.

"How's your aunt—your aunt—I forget her name."

"Aunt Leah. She's gone to Liverpool."

"What for?"

"She lives there; she has opened a branch store of granma's business. Who are you?" concluded Ezekiel candidly.

"You won't remember me," said Esther. "Tell me, your aunt is called Mrs. Levine, isn't she?"

"Oh yes, but," with a shade of contempt, "she hasn't got any children."

"How many brothers and sisters have *you* got?" said Esther with a little laugh.

"Heaps. Oh, but you won't see them if you go in; they're in school, most of 'em."

"And why aren't you at school?"

The Redeemed Son became scarlet. "I've got a bad leg," ran mechanically off his tongue. Then, administering a savage thwack to his hoop, he set out in pursuit of it. "It's no good calling on mother," he yelled back, turning his head unexpectedly. "She ain't in."

Esther walked into the Square, where the same big-headed babies were still rocking in swings suspended from the lintels, and where the same ruddy-faced septuagenarians sat smoking short pipes and playing nap on trays in the sun. From several doorways came the reek of fish frying. The houses looked ineffably petty and shabby. Esther wondered how she could ever have conceived this a region of opulence; still more how she could ever have located Malka and her family on the very outskirt of the semi-divine classes. But the semi-divine persons themselves had long since shrunk and dwindled.

She found Malka brooding over the fire; on the side-table was the clothes-brush. The great events of a crowded decade of European history had left Malka's domestic interior untouched. The fall of dynasties, philosophies and religions had not shaken one china dog from its place; she had not turned a hair of her wig; the black silk bodice might have been the same; the gold chain at her bosom was. Time had written a few more lines on the tan-colored equine face, but his influence had been only skin deep. Everybody grows old: few people grow. Malka was of the majority.

It was only with difficulty that she recollected Esther, and she was visibly impressed by the young lady's appearance.

"It's very good of you to come and see an old woman," she said in her mixed dialect, which skipped irresponsibly from English to Yiddish

ISRAEL ZANGWILL

and back again. "It's more than my own *Kinder* do. I wonder they let you come across and see me."

"I haven't been to see them yet," Esther interrupted.

"Ah, that explains it," said Malka with satisfaction. "They'd have told you, 'Don't go and see the old woman, she's *meshuggah*, she ought to be in the asylum.' I bring children into the world and buy them husbands and businesses and bed-clothes, and this is my profit. The other day my Milly—the impudent-face! I would have boxed her ears if she hadn't been suckling Nathaniel. Let her tell me again that ink isn't good for the ring-worm, and my five fingers shall leave a mark on her face worse than any of Gabriel's ring-worms. But I have washed my hands of her; she can go her way and I'll go mine. I've taken an oath I'll have nothing to do with her and her children—no, not if I live a thousand years. It's all through Milly's ignorance she has had such heavy losses."

"What! Mr. Phillips's business been doing badly? I'm so sorry."

"No, no! my family never does bad business. It's my Milly's children. She lost two. As for my Leah, God bless her, she's been more unfortunate still; I always said that old beggar-woman had the Evil Eye! I sent her to Liverpool with her Sam."

"I know," murmured Esther.

"But she is a good daughter. I wish I had a thousand such. She writes to me every week and my little Ezekiel writes back; English they learn them in that heathen school," Malka interrupted herself sarcastically, "and it was I who had to learn him to begin a letter properly with 'I write you these few lines hoping to find you in good health as, thank God, it leaves me at present;' he used to begin anyhow—"

She came to a stop, having tangled the thread of her discourse and bethought herself of offering Esther a peppermint. But Esther refused and bethought herself of inquiring after Mr. Birnbaum.

"My Michael is quite well, thank God," said Malka, "though he is still pig-headed in business matters! He buys so badly, you know; gives a hundred pounds for what's not worth twenty."

"But you said business was all right?"

"Ah, that's different. Of course he sells at a good profit,—thank God. If I wanted to provoke Providence I could keep my carriage like any of your grand West-End ladies. But that doesn't make him a good buyer. And the worst of it is he always thinks he has got a bargain. He won't listen to reason, at all," said Malka, shaking her head dolefully. "He might be a child of mine, instead of my husband. If God didn't send him such luck and blessing, we might come to want bread, coal, and meat tickets ourselves, instead of giving them away. Do you know I found out that Mrs. Isaacs, across the square, only speculates her guinea in the drawings to give away the tickets she wins to her poor relations, so that she gets all the credit of charity and her name in the papers, while saving the money she'd have to give to her poor relations all the same! Nobody can say I give my tickets to my poor relations. You should just see how much my Michael vows away at *Shool*—he's been *Parnass* for the last twelve years straight off; all the members respect him so much; it isn't often you see a business man with such fear of Heaven. Wait! my Ezekiel will be *Barmitzvah* in a few years; then you shall see what I will do for that *Shool*. You shall see what an example of *Yiddshkeit* I will give to a *link* generation. Mrs. Benjamin, of the Ruins, purified her knives and forks for Passover by sticking them between the boards of the floor. Would you believe she didn't make them red hot first? I gave her a bit of my mind. She said she forgot. But not she! She's no cat's head. She's a regular Christian, that's what she is. I shouldn't wonder if she becomes one like that blackguard, David Brandon; I always told my Milly he was not the sort of person to allow across the threshold. It was Sam Levine who brought him. You see what comes of having the son of a proselyte in the family! Some say Reb Shemuel's daughter narrowly escaped being engaged to him. But that story has a beard already. I suppose it's the sight of you brings up *Olov Hashotom* times. Well, and how *are* you?" she concluded abruptly, becoming suddenly conscious of imperfect courtesy.

"Oh, I'm very well, thank you," said Esther.

"Ah, that's right. You're looking very well, *imbeshreer*. Quite a grand lady. I always knew you'd be one some day. There was your poor mother, peace be upon him! She went and married your father, though I warned her he was a *Schnorrer* and only wanted her because she had a rich family; he'd have sent you out with matches if I hadn't stopped it. I remember saying to him, 'That little Esther has Aristotle's head—let her learn all she can, as sure as I stand here she will grow up to be a lady; I shall have no need to be ashamed of owning her for a cousin.' He was not so pig-headed as your mother, and you see the result."

She surveyed the result with an affectionate smile, feeling genuinely proud of her share in its production. "If my Ezekiel were only a few years older," she added musingly.

"Oh, but I am not a great lady," said Esther, hastening to disclaim false pretensions to the hand of the hero of the hoop, "I've left the Goldsmiths and come back to live in the East End."

"What!" said Malka. "Left the West End!" Her swarthy face grew darker; the skin about her black eyebrows was wrinkled with wrath.

"Are you *Meshuggah*?" she asked after an awful silence. "Or have you, perhaps, saved up a tidy sum of money?"

Esther flushed and shook her head.

"There's no use coming to me. I'm not a rich woman, far from it; and I have been blessed with *Kinder* who are helpless without me. It's as I always said to your father. 'Méshe,' I said, 'you're a *Schnorrer* and your children'll grow up *Schnorrers*.'"

Esther turned white, but the dwindling of Malka's semi-divinity had diminished the old woman's power of annoying her.

"I want to earn my own living," she said, with a smile that was almost contemptuous. "Do you call that being a *Schnorrer*?"

"Don't argue with me. You're just like your poor mother, peace be upon him!" cried the irate old woman. "You God's fool! You were provided for in life and you have no right to come upon the family."

"But isn't it *Schnorring* to be dependent on strangers?" inquired Esther with bitter amusement.

"Don't stand there with your impudence-face!" cried Malka, her eyes blazing fire. "You know as well as I do that a *Schnorrer* is a person you give sixpences to. When a rich family takes in a motherless girl like you and clothes her and feeds her, why it's mocking Heaven to run away and want to earn your own living. Earn your living. Pooh! What living can you earn, you with your gloves? You're all by yourself in the world now; your father can't help you anymore. He did enough for you when you were little, keeping you at school when you ought to have been out selling matches. You'll starve and come to me, that's what you'll do."

"I may starve, but I'll never come to you," said Esther, now really irritated by the truth in Malka's words. What living, indeed, could she earn! She turned her back haughtily on the old woman; not without a recollection of a similar scene in her childhood. History was repeating itself on a smaller scale than seemed consistent with its dignity. When she got outside she saw Milly in conversation with a young lady at the door of her little house, diagonally opposite. Milly had noticed the strange visitor to her mother, for the rival camps carried on a system of espionage from behind their respective gauze blinds, and she had come to the door to catch a better glimpse of her when she left. Esther was passing through Zachariah Square without any intention of recognizing Milly. The daughter's flaccid personality was not so attractive as the mother's; besides, a visit to her might be construed into a mean revenge on the old woman. But, as if in response to a remark of Milly's, the young lady turned her face to look at Esther, and then Esther saw that it was Hannah Jacobs. She felt hot and uncomfortable, and half reluctant to renew acquaintance with Levi's family, but with another impulse she crossed over to the group, and went through the inevitable formulae. Then, refusing Milly's warm-hearted invitation to have a cup of tea, she shook hands and walked away.

"Wait a minute, Miss Ansell," said Hannah. "I'll come with you."

Milly gave her a shilling, with a facetious grimace, and she rejoined Esther.

"I'm collecting money for a poor family of *Greeners* just landed," she said. "They had a few roubles, but they fell among the usual sharks at the docks, and the cabman took all the rest of their money to drive them to the Lane. I left them all crying and rocking themselves to and fro in the street while I ran round to collect a little to get them a lodging."

"Poor things!" said Esther.

"Ah, I can see you've been away from the Jews," said Hannah smiling. "In the olden days you would have said *Achi-nebbich*."

"Should I?" said Esther, smiling in return and beginning to like Hannah. She had seen very little of her in those olden days, for Hannah had been an adult and well-to-do as long as Esther could remember; it seemed amusing now to walk side by side with her in perfect equality and apparently little younger. For Hannah's appearance had not aged perceptibly, which was perhaps why Esther recognized her at once. She had not become angular like her mother, nor coarse and stout like other mothers. She remained slim and graceful, with a virginal charm of expression. But the pretty face had gained in refinement; it looked earnest, almost spiritual, telling of suffering and patience, not unblent with peace.

Esther silently extracted half-a-crown from her purse and handed it to Hannah.

"I didn't mean to ask you, indeed I didn't," said Hannah.

"Oh, I am glad you told me," said Esther tremulously.

The idea of *her* giving charity, after the account of herself she had just heard, seemed ironical enough. She wished the transfer of the coin

ISRAEL ZANGWILL

had taken place within eyeshot of Malka; then dismissed the thought as unworthy.

"You'll come in and have a cup of tea with us, won't you, after we've lodged the *Greeners*?" said Hannah. "Now don't say no. It'll brighten up my father to see 'Reb Moshe's little girl.'"

Esther tacitly assented.

"I heard of all of you recently," she said, when they had hurried on a little further. "I met your brother at the theatre."

Hannah's face lit up.

"How long was that ago?" she said anxiously.

"I remember exactly. It was the night before the first *Seder* night."

"Was he well?"

"Perfectly."

"Oh, I am so glad."

She told Esther of Levi's strange failure to appear at the annual family festival. "My father went out to look for him. Our anxiety was intolerable. He did not return until half-past one in the morning. He was in a terrible state. 'Well,' we asked, 'have you seen him?' 'I have seen him,' he answered. 'He is dead.'"

Esther grew pallid. Was this the sequel to the strange episode in Mr. Henry Goldsmith's library?

"Of course he wasn't really dead," pursued Hannah to Esther's relief. "My father would hardly speak a word more, but we gathered he had seen him doing something very dreadful, and that henceforth Levi would be dead to him. Since then we dare not speak his name. Please don't refer to him at tea. I went to his rooms on the sly a few days afterwards, but he had left them, and since then I haven't been able to hear anything of him. Sometimes I fancy he's gone off to the Cape."

"More likely to the provinces with a band of strolling players. He told me he thought of throwing up the law for the boards, and I know you cannot make a beginning in London."

"Do you think that's it?" said Hannah, looking relieved in her turn.

"I feel sure that's the explanation, if he's not in London. But what in Heaven's name can your father have seen him doing?"

"Nothing very dreadful, depend upon it," said Hannah, a slight shade of bitterness crossing her wistful features. "I know he's inclined to be wild, and he should never have been allowed to get the bit between his teeth, but I dare say it was only some ceremonial crime Levi was caught committing."

"Certainly. That would be it," said Esther. "He confessed to me that he was very *link*. Judging by your tone, you seem rather inclined that way yourself," she said, smiling and a little surprised.

"Do I? I don't know," said Hannah, simply. "Sometimes I think I'm very *froom*."

"Surely you know what you are?" persisted Esther. Hannah shook her head.

"Well, you know whether you believe in Judaism or not?"

"I don't know what I believe. I do everything a Jewess ought to do, I suppose. And yet—oh, I don't know."

Esther's smile faded; she looked at her companion with fresh interest. Hannah's face was full of brooding thought, and she had unconsciously come to a standstill. "I wonder whether anybody understands herself," she said reflectively. "Do you?"

Esther flushed at the abrupt question without knowing why. "I—I don't know," she stammered.

"No, I don't think anybody does, quite," Hannah answered. "I feel sure I don't. And yet—yes, I do. I must be a good Jewess. I must believe my life."

Somehow the tears came into her eyes; her face had the look of a saint. Esther's eyes met hers in a strange subtle glance. Then their souls were knit. They walked on rapidly.

"Well, I do hope you'll hear from him soon," said Esther.

"It's cruel of him not to write," replied Hannah, knowing she meant Levi; "he might easily send me a line in a disguised hand. But then, as Miriam Hyams always says, brothers are so selfish."

"Oh, how is Miss Hyams? I used to be in her class."

"I could guess that from your still calling her Miss," said Hannah with a gentle smile.

"Why, is she married?"

"No, no; I don't mean that. She still lives with her brother and his wife; he married Sugarman the *Shadchan's* daughter, you know."

"Bessie, wasn't it?"

"Yes; they are a devoted couple, and I suspect Miriam is a little jealous; but she seems to enjoy herself anyway. I don't think there is a piece at the theatres she can't tell you about, and she makes Daniel take her to all the dances going."

"Is she still as pretty?" asked Esther. "I know all her girls used to rave over her and throw her in the faces of girls with ugly teachers. She certainly knew how to dress."

ISRAEL ZANGWILL

"She dresses better than ever," said Hannah evasively.

"That sounds ominous," observed Esther, laughingly.

"Oh, she's good-looking enough! Her nose seems to have turned up more; but perhaps that's an optical illusion; she talks so sarcastically now-a-days that I seem to see it." Hannah smiled a little. "She doesn't think much of Jewish young men. By the way, are you engaged yet, Esther?"

"What an idea!" murmured Esther, blushing beneath her spotted veil.

"Well, you're very young," said Hannah, glancing down at the smaller figure with a sweet matronly smile.

"I shall never marry," Esther said in low tones.

"Don't be ridiculous, Esther! There's no happiness for a woman without it. You needn't talk like Miriam Hyams—at least not yet. Oh yes, I know what you're thinking—"

"No, I'm not," faintly protested Esther.

"Yes, you are," said Hannah, smiling at the paradoxical denial. "But who'd have *me*? Ah, here are the *Greeners!*" and her smile softened to angelic tenderness.

It was a frowzy, unsightly group that sat on the pavement, surrounded by a semi-sympathetic crowd—the father in a long grimy coat, the mother covered, as to her head, with a shawl, which also contained the baby. But the elders were naively childish and the children uncannily elderly; and something in Esther's breast seemed to stir with a strange sense of kinship. The race instinct awoke to consciousness of itself. Dulled by contact with cultured Jews, transformed almost to repulsion by the spectacle of the coarsely prosperous, it leaped into life at the appeal of squalor and misery. In the morning the Ghetto had simply chilled her; her heart had turned to it as to a haven, and the reality was dismal. Now that the first ugliness had worn off, she felt her heart warming. Her eyes moistened. She thrilled from head to foot with the sense of a mission—of a niche in the temple of human service which she had been predestined to fill. Who could comprehend as she these stunted souls, limited in all save suffering? Happiness was not for her; but service remained. Penetrated by the new emotion, she seemed to herself to have found the key to Hannah's holy calm.

With the money now in hand, the two girls sought a lodging for the poor waifs. Esther suddenly remembered the empty back garret in No. 1 Royal Street, and here, after due negotiations with the pickled-herring dealer next door, the family was installed. Esther's emotions at the sight of the old place were poignant; happily the bustle of installation, of laying down a couple of mattresses, of borrowing Dutch Debby's tea-things, and of getting ready a meal, allayed their intensity. That little figure with the masculine boots showed itself but by fits and flashes. But the strangeness of the episode formed the undercurrent of all her thoughts; it seemed to carry to a climax the irony of her initial gift to Hannah.

Escaping from the blessings of the *Greeners*, she accompanied her new friend to Reb Shemuel's. She was shocked to see the change in the venerable old man; he looked quite broken up. But he was chivalrous as of yore: the vein of quiet humor was still there, though his voice was charged with gentle melancholy. The Rebbitzin's nose had grown sharper than ever; her soul seemed to have fed on vinegar. Even in the presence of a stranger the Rebbitzin could not quite conceal her dominant thought. It hardly needed a woman to divine how it fretted Mrs. Jacobs that Hannah was an old maid; it needed a woman like Esther to divine that Hannah's renunciation was voluntary, though even Esther could not divine her history nor understand that her mother's daily nagging was the greater because the pettier part of her martyrdom.

THEY ALL JUMBLED THEMSELVES INTO grotesque combinations, the things of today and the things of endless yesterdays, as Esther slept in the narrow little bed next to Dutch Debby, who squeezed herself into the wall, pretending to revel in exuberant spaciousness. It was long before she could get to sleep. The excitement of the day had brought on her headache; she was depressed by restriking the courses of so many narrow lives; the glow of her new-found mission had already faded in the thought that she was herself a pauper, and she wished she had let the dead past lie in its halo, not peered into the crude face of reality. But at bottom she felt a subtle melancholy joy in understanding herself at last, despite Hannah's scepticism; in penetrating the secret of her pessimism, in knowing herself a Child of the Ghetto.

And yet Pesach Weingott played the fiddle merrily enough when she went to Becky's engagement-party in her dreams, and galoped with Shoshi Shmendrik, disregarding the terrible eyes of the bride to be: when Hannah, wearing an aureole like a bridal veil, paired off with Meckisch, frothing at the mouth with soap, and Mrs. Belcovitch, whirling a medicine-bottle, went down the middle on a pair of huge stilts, one a thick one and one a thin one, while Malka spun round like a teetotum, throwing Ezekiel in long clothes through a hoop; what time Moses Ansell waltzed superbly with the dazzling Addie Leon, quite cutting out Levi and Miriam Hyams, and Raphael awkwardly twisted the Widow Finkelstein, to the evident delight of Sugarman the *Shadchan*, who had effected the introduction. It was wonderful how agile they all were, and how dexterously they avoided treading on her brother Benjamin, who lay unconcernedly in the centre of the floor, taking assiduous notes in a little copy-book for incorporation in a great novel, while Mrs. Henry Goldsmith stooped down to pat his brown hair patronizingly.

Esther thought it very proper of the grateful *Greeners* to go about offering the dancers rum from Dutch Debby's tea-kettle, and very selfish of Sidney to stand in a corner, refusing to join in the dance and making cynical remarks about the whole thing for the amusement of the earnest little figure she had met on the stairs.

XIII

THE DEAD MONKEY AGAIN

Esther woke early, little refreshed. The mattress was hard, and in her restricted allowance of space she had to deny herself the luxury of tossing and turning lest she should arouse Debby. To open one's eyes on a new day is not pleasant when situations have to be faced. Esther felt this disagreeable duty could no longer be shirked. Malka's words rang in her ears. How, indeed, could she earn a living? Literature had failed her; with journalism she had no point of contact save *The Flag of Judah*, and that journal was out of the question. Teaching—the last resort of the hopeless—alone remained. Maybe even in the Ghetto there were parents who wanted their children to learn the piano, and who would find Esther's mediocre digital ability good enough. She might teach as of old in an elementary school. But she would not go back to her own— all the human nature in her revolted at the thought of exposing herself to the sympathy of her former colleagues. Nothing was to be gained by lying sleepless in bed, gazing at the discolored wallpaper and the forlorn furniture. She slipped out gently and dressed herself, the absence of any apparatus for a bath making her heart heavier with reminders of the realities of poverty. It was not easy to avert her thoughts from her dainty bedroom of yesterday. But she succeeded; the cheerlessness of the little chamber turned her thoughts backwards to the years of girlhood, and when she had finished dressing she almost mechanically lit the fire and put the kettle to boil. Her childish dexterity returned, unimpaired by disuse. When Debby awoke, she awoke to a cup of tea ready for her to drink in bed—an unprecedented luxury, which she received with infinite consternation and pleasure.

"Why, it's like the duchesses who have lady's-maids," she said, "and read French novels before getting up." To complete the picture, her hand dived underneath the bed and extracted a *London Journal*, at the risk of upsetting the tea. "But it's you who ought to be in bed, not me."

"I've been a sluggard too often," laughed Esther, catching the contagion of good spirits from Debby's radiant delight. Perhaps the capacity for simple pleasures would come back to her, too.

At breakfast they discussed the situation.

ISRAEL ZANGWILL

"I'm afraid the bed's too small," said Esther, when Debby kindly suggested a continuance of hospitality.

"Perhaps I took up too much room," said the hostess.

"No, dear; you took up too little. We should have to have a wider bed and, as it is, the bed is almost as big as the room."

"There's the back garret overhead! It's bigger, and it looks on the back yard just as well. I wouldn't mind moving there," said Debby, "though I wouldn't let old Guggenheim know that I value the view of the back yard, or else he'd raise the rent."

"You forget the *Greeners* who moved in yesterday."

"Oh, so I do!" answered Debby with a sigh.

"Strange," said Esther, musingly, "that I should have shut myself out of my old home."

The postman's knuckles rapping at the door interrupted her reflections. In Royal Street the poor postmen had to mount to each room separately; fortunately, the tenants got few letters. Debby was intensely surprised to get one.

"It isn't for me at all," she cried, at last, after a protracted examination of the envelope; "it's for you, care of me."

"But that's stranger still." said Esther. "Nobody in the world knows my address."

The mystery was not lessened by the contents. There was simply a blank sheet of paper, and when this was unfolded a half-sovereign rolled out. The postmark was Houndsditch. After puzzling herself in vain, and examining at length the beautiful copy-book penmanship of the address, Esther gave up the enigma. But it reminded her that it would be advisable to apprise her publishers of her departure from the old address, and to ask them to keep any chance letter till she called. She betook herself to their offices, walking. The day was bright, but Esther walked in gloom, scarcely daring to think of her position. She entered the office, apathetically hopeless. The junior partner welcomed her heartily.

"I suppose you've come about your account," he said. "I have been intending to send it you for some months, but we are so busy bringing out new things before the dead summer season comes on." He consulted his books. "Perhaps you would rather not be bothered," he said, "with a formal statement. I have it all clearly here—the book's doing fairly well—let me write you a cheque at once!"

She murmured assent, her cheeks blanching, her heart throbbing with excitement and surprise.

"There you are—sixty-two pounds ten," he said. "Our profits are just one hundred and twenty-five. If you'll endorse it, I'll send a clerk to the bank round the corner and get it cashed for you at once."

The pen scrawled an agitated autograph that would not have been accepted at the foot of a cheque, if Esther had had a banking account of her own.

"But I thought you said the book was a failure," she said.

"So it was," he answered cheerfully, "so it was at first. But gradually, as its nature leaked out, the demand increased. I understand from Mudie's that it was greatly asked for by their Jewish clients. You see, when there's a run on a three-volume book, the profits are pretty fair. I believed in it myself, or I should never have given you such good terms nor printed seven hundred and fifty copies. I shouldn't be surprised if we find ourselves able to bring it out in one-volume form in the autumn. We shall always be happy to consider any further work of yours; something on the same lines, I should recommend."

The recommendation did not convey any definite meaning to her at the moment. Still in a pleasant haze, she stuffed the twelve five-pound notes and the three gold-pieces into her purse, scribbled a receipt, and departed. Afterwards the recommendation rang mockingly in her ears. She felt herself sterile, written out already. As for writing again on the same lines, she wondered what Raphael would think if he knew of the profits she had reaped by bespattering his people. But there! Raphael was a prig like the rest. It was no use worrying about *his* opinions. Affluence had come to her—that was the one important and exhilarating fact. Besides, had not the hypocrites really enjoyed her book? A new wave of emotion swept over her—again she felt strong enough to defy the whole world.

When she got "home," Debby said, "Hannah Jacobs called to see you."

"Oh, indeed, what did she want?"

"I don't know, but from something she said I believe I can guess who sent the half-sovereign."

"Not Reb Shemuel?" said Esther, astonished.

"No, *your* cousin Malka. It seems that she saw Hannah leaving Zachariah Square with you, and so went to her house last night to get your address."

Esther did not know whether to laugh or be angry; she compromised by crying. People were not so bad, after all, nor the fates so hard to her.

It was only a little April shower of tears, and soon she was smiling and running upstairs to give the half-sovereign to the *Greeners*. It would have been ungracious to return it to Malka, and she purchased all the luxury of doing good, including the effusive benedictions of the whole family, on terms usually obtainable only by professional almoners.

Then she told Debby of her luck with the publishers. Profound was Debby's awe at the revelation that Esther was able to write stories equal to those in the *London Journal*. After that, Debby gave up the idea of Esther living or sleeping with her; she would as soon have thought of offering a share of her bed to the authoresses of the tales under it. Debby suffered scarce any pang when her one-night companion transferred herself to Reb Shemuel's.

For it was to suggest this that Hannah had called. The idea was her father's; it came to him when she told him of Esther's strange position. But Esther said she was going to America forthwith, and she only consented on condition of being allowed to pay for her keep during her stay. The haggling was hard, but Esther won. Hannah gave up her room to Esther, and removed her own belongings to Levi's bedroom, which except at Festival seasons had been unused for years, though the bed was always kept ready for him. Latterly the women had had to make the bed from time to time, and air the room, when Reb Shemuel was at synagogue. Esther sent her new address to her brothers and sisters, and made inquiries as to the prospects of educated girls in the States. In reply she learned that Rachel was engaged to be married. Her correspondents were too taken up with this gigantic fact to pay satisfactory attention to her inquiries. The old sense of protecting motherhood came back to Esther when she learned the news. Rachel was only eighteen, but at once Esther felt middle-aged. It seemed of the fitness of things that she should go to America and resume her interrupted maternal duties. Isaac and Sarah were still little more than children, perhaps they had not yet ceased bickering about their birthdays. She knew her little ones would jump for joy, and Isaac still volunteer sleeping accommodation in his new bed, even though the necessity for it had ceased. She cried when she received the cutting from the American Jewish paper; under other circumstances she would have laughed. It was one of a batch headed "Personals," and ran: "Sam Wiseberg, the handsome young drummer, of Cincinnati, has become engaged to Rachel Ansell, the fair eighteen-year-old typewriter and daughter of Moses Ansell, a well-known Chicago Hebrew. Life's sweetest blessings on the pair! The marriage will take place in the Fall." Esther dried her eyes and determined to be present at the ceremony. It is so grateful to the hesitant soul to be presented with a landmark. There was nothing to be gained now by arriving before the marriage; nay, her arrival just in time for it would clench the festivities. Meantime she attached herself to Hannah's charitable leading-strings, alternately attracted to the Children of the Ghetto by their misery, and repulsed by their failings. She seemed to see them now in their true perspective, correcting the vivid impressions of childhood by the insight born of wider knowledge of life. The accretion of pagan superstition was greater than she had recollected. Mothers averted fever by a murmured charm and an expectoration, children in new raiment carried bits of coal or salt in their pockets to ward off the evil-eve. On the other hand, there was more resourcefulness, more pride of independence. Her knowledge of Moses Ansell had misled her into too sweeping a generalization. And she was surprised to realize afresh how much illogical happiness flourished amid penury, ugliness and pain. After school-hours the muggy air vibrated with the joyous laughter of little children, tossing their shuttlecocks, spinning their tops, turning their skipping-ropes, dancing to barrel-organs or circling hand-in-hand in rings to the sound of the merry traditional chants of childhood. Esther often purchased a pennyworth of exquisite pleasure by enriching some sad-eyed urchin. Hannah (whose own scanty surplus was fortunately augmented by an anonymous West-End Reform Jew, who employed her as his agent) had no prepossessions to correct, no pendulum-oscillations to distract her, no sentimental illusions to sustain her. She knew the Ghetto as it was; neither expected gratitude from the poor, nor feared she might "pauperize them," knowing that the poor Jew never exchanges his self-respect for respect for his benefactor, but takes by way of rightful supplement to his income. She did not drive families into trickery, like ladies of the West, by being horrified to find them eating meat. If she presided at a stall at a charitable sale of clothing, she was not disheartened if articles were snatched from under her hand, nor did she refuse loans because borrowers sometimes merely used them to evade the tallyman by getting their jewelry at cash prices. She not only gave alms to the poor, but made them givers, organizing their own farthings into a powerful auxiliary of the institutions which helped them. Hannah's sweet patience soothed Esther, who had no natural aptitude for personal philanthropy; the primitive, ordered pieties of the Reb's household helping to give her calm. Though she accepted the inevitable, and had laughed in melancholy mockery at the exaggerated importance given to love by the novelists (including her cruder self), she dreaded meeting Raphael Leon. It was very unlikely her whereabouts would penetrate to the West; and she rarely went outside of the Ghetto by day, or even walked within it in the evening. In the twilight, unless prostrated by headache, she played on Hannah's disused old-fashioned grand piano. It had one cracked note which nearly always spoiled the melody; she would not have the note repaired, taking a morbid pleasure in a fantastic analogy between the instrument and herself. On Friday nights after the Sabbath-hymns she read *The Flag of Judah*. She was not surprised to find Reb Shemuel beginning to look askance at his favorite paper. She noted a growing tendency in it to insist mainly on the ethical side of Judaism, salvation by works being contrasted with the salvation by spasm of popular Christianity. Once Kingsley's line, "Do noble things, not dream them all day long," was put forth as "Judaism *versus* Christianity in a nut-shell;" and the writer added, "for so thy dreams shall become noble, too." Sometimes she fancied phrases and lines of argument were aimed at her. Was it the editor's way of keeping in touch with her, using his leaders as a medium of communication—a subtly sweet secret known only to him and her? Was it fair to his readers? Then she would remember his joke about the paper being started merely to convert her, and she would laugh. Sometimes he repeated what he already said to her privately, so that she seemed to hear him talking.

Then she would shake her head, and say, "I love you for your blindness, but I have the terrible gift of vision."

XIV

SIDNEY SETTLES DOWN

Mrs. Henry Goldsmith's newest seaside resort had the artistic charm which characterized everything she selected. It was a straggling, hilly, leafy village, full of archaic relics—human as well as architectural—sloping down to a gracefully curved bay, where the blue waves broke in whispers, for on summer days a halcyon calm overhung this magic spot, and the great sea stretched away, unwrinkled, ever young. There were no neutral tones in the colors of this divine picture— the sea was sapphire, the sky amethyst. There were dark-red houses nestling amid foliage, and green-haired monsters of gray stone squatted about on the yellow sand, which was strewn with quaint shells and mimic earth-worms, cunningly wrought by the waves. Half a mile to the east a blue river rippled into the bay. The white bathing tents which Mrs. Goldsmith had pitched stood out picturesquely, in harmonious contrast with the rich boscage that began to climb the hills in the background.

Mrs. Goldsmith's party lived in the Manse; it was pretty numerous, and gradually overflowed into the bedrooms of the neighboring cottages. Mr. Goldsmith only came down on Saturday, returning on Monday. One Friday Mr. Percy Saville, who had been staying for the week, left suddenly for London, and next day the beautiful hostess poured into her husband's projecting ears a tale that made him gnash his projecting teeth, and cut the handsome stockbroker off his visiting-list forever. It was only an indiscreet word that the susceptible stockbroker had spoken—under the poetic influences of the scene. His bedroom came in handy, for Sidney unexpectedly dropped down from Norway, *via* London, on the very Friday. The poetic influences of the scene soon infected the newcomer, too. On the Saturday he was lost for hours, and came up smiling, with Addie on his arm. On the Sunday afternoon the party went boating up the river—a picturesque medley of flannels and parasols. Once landed, Sidney and Addie did not return for tea, prior to re-embarking. While Mr. Montagu Samuels was gallantly handing round the sugar, they were sitting somewhere along the bank, half covered with leaves, like babes in the wood. The sunset burned behind the willows—a fiery rhapsody of crimson and orange. The gay laughter of the picnic-party just reached their ears; otherwise, an almost solemn calm prevailed—not a bird twittered, not a leaf stirred.

"It'll be all over London tomorrow," said Sidney in a despondent tone.

"I'm afraid so," said Addie, with a delicious laugh.

The sweet English meadows over which her humid eyes wandered were studded with simple wild-flowers. Addie vaguely felt the angels had planted such in Eden. Sidney could not take his eyes off his terrestrial angel clad in appropriate white. Confessed love had given the last touch to her intoxicating beauty. She gratified his artistic sense almost completely. But she seemed to satisfy deeper instincts, too. As he looked into her limpid, trustful eyes, he felt he had been a weak fool. An irresistible yearning to tell her all his past and crave forgiveness swept over him.

"Addie," he said, "isn't it funny I should be marrying a Jewish girl, after all?"

He wanted to work round to it like that, to tell her of his engagement to Miss Hannibal at least, and how, on discovering with whom he was really in love, he had got out of it simply by writing to the Wesleyan M.P. that he was a Jew—a fact sufficient to disgust the disciple of Dissent and the claimant champion of religious liberty. But Addie only smiled at the question.

"You smile," he said: "I see you do think it funny."

"That's not why I am smiling."

"Then why are you smiling?" The lovely face piqued him; he kissed the lips quickly with a bird-like peck.

"Oh—I—no, you wouldn't understand."

"That means *you* don't understand. But there! I suppose when a girl is in love, she's not accountable for her expression. All the same, it is strange. You know, Addie dear, I have come to the conclusion that Judaism exercises a strange centrifugal and centripetal effect on its sons—sometimes it repulses them, sometimes it draws them; only it never leaves them neutral. Now, here had I deliberately made up my mind not to marry a Jewess."

"Oh! Why not?" said Addie, pouting.

"Merely because she would be a Jewess. It's a fact."

"And why have you broken your resolution?" she said, looking up naively into his face, so that the scent of her hair thrilled him.

"I don't know." he said frankly, scarcely giving the answer to be expected. "*C'est plus fort que moi*. I've struggled hard, but I'm beaten. Isn't there something of the kind in Esther—in Miss Ansell's book? I know I've read it somewhere—and anything that's beastly subtle I always connect with her."

"Poor Esther!" murmured Addie.

Sidney patted her soft warm hand, and smoothed the finely-curved arm, and did not seem disposed to let the shadow of Esther mar the moment, though he would ever remain grateful to her for the hint which had simultaneously opened his eyes to Addie's affection for him, and to his own answering affection so imperceptibly grown up. The river glided on softly, glorified by the sunset.

"It makes one believe in a dogged destiny," he grumbled, "shaping the ends of the race, and keeping it together, despite all human volition. To think that I should be doomed to fall in love, not only with a Jewess but with a pious Jewess! But clever men always fall in love with conventional women. I wonder what makes you so conventional, Addie."

Addie, still smiling, pressed his hand in silence, and gazed at him in fond admiration.

"Ah, well, since you are so conventional, you may as well kiss me."

Addie's blush deepened, her eyes sparkled ere she lowered them, and subtly fascinating waves of expression passed across the lovely face.

"They'll be wondering what on earth has become of us," she said.

"It shall be nothing on earth—something in heaven," he answered. "Kiss me, or I shall call you unconventional."

She touched his cheek hurriedly with her soft lips.

"A very crude and amateur kiss," he said critically. "However, after all, I have an excuse for marrying you—which all clever Jews who marry conventional Jewesses haven't got—you're a fine model. That is another of the many advantages of my profession. I suppose you'll be a model wife, in the ordinary sense, too. Do you know, my darling, I begin to understand that I could not love you so much if you were not so religious, if you were not so curiously like a Festival Prayer-Book, with gilt edges and a beautiful binding."

"Ah, I am so glad, dear, to hear you say that," said Addie, with the faintest suspicion of implied past disapproval.

"Yes," he said musingly. "It adds the last artistic touch to your relation to me."

"But you will reform!" said Addie, with girlish confidence.

ISRAEL ZANGWILL

"Do you think so? I might commence by becoming a vegetarian— that would prevent me eating forbidden flesh. Have I ever told you my idea that vegetarianism is the first step in a great secret conspiracy for gradually converting the world to Judaism? But I'm afraid I can't be caught as easily as the Gentiles, Addie dear. You see, a Jewish sceptic beats all others. *Corruptio optimi pessima*, probably. Perhaps you would like me to marry in a synagogue?"

"Why, of course! Where else?"

"Heavens!" said Sidney, in comic despair. "I feared it would come to that. I shall become a pillar of the synagogue when I am married, I suppose."

"Well, you'll have to take a seat," said Addie seriously, "because otherwise you can't get buried."

"Gracious, what ghoulish thoughts for an embryo bride! Personally, I have no objection to haunting the Council of the United Synagogue till they give me a decently comfortable grave. But I see what it will be! I shall be whitewashed by the Jewish press, eulogized by platform orators as a shining light in Israel, the brilliant impressionist painter, and all that. I shall pay my synagogue bill and never go. In short, I shall be converted to Philistinism, and die in the odor of respectability. And Judaism will continue to flourish. Oh, Addie, Addie, if I had thought of all that, I should never have asked you to be my wife."

"I am glad you didn't think of it," laughed Addie, ingenuously.

"There! You never will take me seriously!" he grumbled. "Nobody ever takes me seriously—I suppose because I speak the truth. The only time you ever took me seriously in my life was a few minutes ago. So you actually think I'm going to submit to the benedictions of a Rabbi."

"You must," said Addie.

"I'll be blest If I do," he said.

"Of course you will," said Addie, laughing merrily.

"Thanks—I'm glad you appreciate my joke. You perhaps fancy it's yours. However, I'm in earnest. I won't be a respectable high-hatted member of the community—not even for your sake, dear. Why, I might as well go back to my ugly real name, Samuel Abrahams, at once."

"So you might, dear," said Addie boldly, and smiled into his eyes to temper her audacity.

"Ah, well, I think it'll be quite enough if *you* change your name," he said, smiling back.

"It's just as easy for me to change it to Abrahams as to Graham," she said with charming obstinacy.

He contemplated her for some moments in silence, with a whimsical look on his face. Then he looked up at the sky—the brilliant color harmonies were deepening into a more sober magnificence.

"I'll tell you what I will do. Ill join the Asmoneans. There! that's a great concession to your absurd prejudices. But you must make a concession to mine. You know how I hate the Jewish canvassing of engagements. Let us keep ours entirely *entre nous* a fortnight—so that the gossips shall at least get their material stale, and we shall be hardened. I wonder why you're so conventional," he said again, when she had consented without enthusiasm. "You had the advantage of Esther—of Miss Ansell's society."

"Call her Esther if you like; I don't mind," said Addie.

"I wonder Esther didn't convert you," he went on musingly. "But I suppose you had Raphael on your right hand, as some prayer or other says. And so you really don't know what's become of her?"

"Nothing beyond what I wrote to you. Mrs. Goldsmith discovered she had written the nasty book, and sent her packing. I have never liked to broach the subject myself to Mrs. Goldsmith, knowing how unpleasant it must be to her. Raphael's version is that Esther went away of her own accord; but I can't see what grounds he has for judging."

"I would rather trust Raphael's version," said Sidney, with an adumbration of a wink in his left eyelid. "But didn't you look for her?"

"Where? If she's in London, she's swallowed up. If she's gone to another place, it's still more difficult to find her."

"There's the Agony Column!"

"If Esther wanted us to know her address, what can prevent her sending it?" asked Addie, with dignity.

"I'd find her soon enough, if I wanted to," murmured Sidney.

"Yes; but I'm not sure we want to. After all, she cannot be so nice as I thought. She certainly behaved very ungratefully to Mrs. Goldsmith. You see what becomes of wild opinions."

"Addie! Addie!" said Sidney reproachfully, "how *can* you be so conventional?"

"I'm *not* conventional!" protested Addie, provoked at last. "I always liked Esther very much. Even now, nothing would give me greater pleasure than to have her for a bridesmaid. But I can't help feeling she deceived us all."

"Stuff and nonsense!" said Sidney warmly. "An author has a right to be anonymous. Don't you think I'd paint anonymously if I dared? Only, if I didn't put my name to my things no one would buy them. That's another of the advantages of my profession. Once make your name as an artist, and you can get a colossal income by giving up art."

"It was a vulgar book!" persisted Addie, sticking to the point.

"Fiddlesticks! It was an artistic book—bungled."

"Oh, well!" said Addie, as the tears welled from her eyes, "if you're so fond of unconventional girls, you'd better marry them."

"I would," said Sidney, "but for the absurd restriction against polygamy."

Addie got up with an indignant jerk. "You think I'm a child to be played with!"

She turned her back upon him. His face changed instantly; he stood still a moment, admiring the magnificent pose. Then he recaptured her reluctant hand.

"Don't be jealous already, Addie," he said. "It's a healthy sign of affection, is a storm-cloud, but don't you think it's just a wee, tiny, weeny bit too previous?"

A pressure of the hand accompanied each of the little adjectives. Addie sat down again, feeling deliriously happy. She seemed to be lapped in a great drowsy ecstasy of bliss.

The sunset was fading into sombre grays before Sidney broke the silence; then his train of thought revealed itself.

"If you're so down on Esther, I wonder how you can put up with me! How is it?"

Addie did not hear the question.

"You think I'm a very wicked, blasphemous boy," he insisted. "Isn't that the thought deep down in your heart of hearts?"

"I'm sure tea must be over long ago," said Addie anxiously.

"Answer me," said Sidney inexorably.

"Don't bother. Aren't they cooeying for us?"

"Answer me."

"I do believe that was a water-rat. Look! the water is still eddying."

"I'm a very wicked, blasphemous boy. Isn't that the thought deep down in your heart of hearts?"

"You are there, too," she breathed at last, and then Sidney forgot her beauty for an instant, and lost himself in unaccustomed humility. It seemed passing wonderful to him—that he should be the deity of such a spotless shrine. Could any man deserve the trust of this celestial soul?

Suddenly the thought that he had not told her about Miss Hannibal after all, gave him a chilling shock. But he rallied quickly. Was it really worth while to trouble the clear depths of her spirit with his turbid past? No; wiser to inhale the odor of the rose at her bosom, sweeter to surrender himself to the intoxicating perfume of her personality, to the magic of a moment that must fade like the sunset, already grown gray.

So Addie never knew.

XV

FROM SOUL TO SOUL

On the Friday that Percy Saville returned to town, Raphael, in a state of mental prostration modified by tobacco, was sitting in the editorial chair. He was engaged in his pleasing weekly occupation of discovering, from a comparison with the great rival organ, the deficiencies of *The Flag of Judah* in the matter of news, his organization for the collection of which partook of the happy-go-lucky character of little Sampson. Fortunately, today there were no flagrant omissions, no palpable shortcomings such as had once and again thrown the office of the *Flag* into mourning when communal pillars were found dead in the opposition paper.

The arrival of a visitor put an end to the invidious comparison.

"Ah, Strelitski!" cried Raphael, jumping up in glad surprise. "What an age it is since I've seen you!" He shook the black-gloved hand of the fashionable minister heartily; then his face grew rueful with a sudden recollection. "I suppose you have come to scold me for not answering the invitation to speak at the distribution of prizes to your religion class?" he said; "but I *have* been so busy. My conscience has kept up a dull pricking on the subject, though, forever so many weeks. You're such an epitome of all the virtues that you can't understand the sensation, and even I can't understand why one submits to this undercurrent of reproach rather than take the simple step it exhorts one to. But I suppose it's human nature." He puffed at his pipe in humorous sadness.

"I suppose it is," said Strelitski wearily.

"But of course I'll come. You know that, my dear fellow. When my conscience was noisy, the *advocatus diaboli* used to silence it by saying, 'Oh, Strelitski'll take it for granted.' You can never catch the *advocatus diaboli* asleep," concluded Raphael, laughing.

"No," assented Strelitski. But he did not laugh.

"Oh!" said Raphael, his laugh ceasing suddenly and his face growing long. "Perhaps the prize-distribution is over?"

Strelitski's expression seemed so stern that for a second it really occurred to Raphael that he might have missed the great event. But before the words were well out of his mouth he remembered that it was an event that made "copy," and little Sampson would have arranged with him as to the reporting thereof.

"No; it's Sunday week. But I didn't come to talk about my religion class at all," he said pettishly, while a shudder traversed his form. "I came to ask if you know anything about Miss Ansell."

Raphael's heart stood still, then began to beat furiously. The sound of her name always affected him incomprehensibly. He began to stammer, then took his pipe out of his mouth and said more calmly;

"How should I know anything about Miss Ansell?"

"I thought you would," said Strelitski, without much disappointment in his tone.

"Why?"

"Wasn't she your art-critic?"

"Who told you that?"

"Mrs. Henry Goldsmith."

"Oh!" said Raphael.

"I thought she might possibly be writing for you still, and so, as I was passing, I thought I'd drop in and inquire. Hasn't anything been heard of her? Where is she? Perhaps one could help her."

"I'm sorry, I really know nothing, nothing at all," said Raphael gravely. "I wish I did. Is there any particular reason why you want to know?"

As he spoke, a strange suspicion that was half an apprehension came into his head. He had been looking the whole time at Strelitski's face with his usual unobservant gaze, just seeing it was gloomy. Now, as in a sudden flash, he saw it sallow and careworn to the last degree. The eyes were almost feverish, the black curl on the brow was unkempt, and there was a streak or two of gray easily visible against the intense sable. What change had come over him? Why this new-born interest in Esther? Raphael felt a vague unreasoning resentment rising in him, mingled with distress at Strelitski's discomposure.

"No; I don't know that there is any *particular* reason why I want to know," answered his friend slowly. "She was a member of my congregation. I always had a certain interest in her, which has naturally not been diminished by her sudden departure from our midst, and by the knowledge that she was the author of that sensational novel. I think it was cruel of Mrs. Henry Goldsmith to turn her adrift; one must allow for the effervescence of genius."

"Who told you Mrs. Henry Goldsmith turned her adrift?" asked Raphael hotly.

"Mrs. Henry Goldsmith," said Strelitski with a slight accent of wonder.

"Then it's a lie!" Raphael exclaimed, thrusting out his arms in intense agitation. "A mean, cowardly lie! I shall never go to see that woman again, unless it is to let her know what I think of her."

"Ah, then you do know something about Miss Ansell?" said Strelitski, with growing surprise. Raphael in a rage was a new experience. There were those who asserted that anger was not among his gifts.

"Nothing about her life since she left Mrs. Goldsmith; but I saw her before, and she told me it was her intention to cut herself adrift. Nobody knew about her authorship of the book; nobody would have known to this day if she had not chosen to reveal it."

The minister was trembling.

"She cut herself adrift?" he repeated interrogatively. "But why?"

"I will tell you," said Raphael in low tones. "I don't think it will be betraying her confidence to say that she found her position of dependence extremely irksome; it seemed to cripple her soul. Now I see what Mrs. Goldsmith is. I can understand better what life in her society meant for a girl like that."

"And what has become of her?" asked the Russian. His face was agitated, the lips were almost white.

"I do not know," said Raphael, almost in a whisper, his voice failing in a sudden upwelling of tumultuous feeling. The ever-whirling wheel of journalism—that modern realization of the labor of Sisyphus—had carried him round without giving him even time to remember that time was flying. Day had slipped into week and week into month, without his moving an inch from his groove in search of the girl whose unhappiness was yet always at the back of his thoughts. Now he was shaken with astonished self-reproach at his having allowed her to drift perhaps irretrievably beyond his ken.

"She is quite alone in the world, poor thing!" he said after a pause. "She must be earning her own living, somehow. By journalism, perhaps. But she prefers to live her own life. I am afraid it will be a hard one." His voice trembled again. The minister's breast, too, was laboring with emotion that checked his speech, but after a moment utterance came to him—a strange choked utterance, almost blasphemous from those clerical lips.

"By God!" he gasped. "That little girl!"

He turned his back upon his friend and covered his face with his hands, and Raphael saw his shoulders quivering. Then his own vision grew dim. Conjecture, resentment, wonder, self-reproach, were lost in a new and absorbing sense of the pathos of the poor girl's position.

Presently the minister turned round, showing a face that made no pretence of calm.

"That was bravely done," he said brokenly. "To cut herself adrift! She will not sink; strength will be given her even as she gives others strength. If I could only see her and tell her! But she never liked me; she always distrusted me. I was a hollow windbag in her eyes—a thing of shams and cant—she shuddered to look at me. Was it not so? You are a friend of hers, you know what she felt."

"I don't think it was you she disliked," said Raphael in wondering pity. "Only your office."

"Then, by God, she was right!" cried the Russian hoarsely. "It was this—this that made me the target of her scorn." He tore off his white tie madly as he spoke, threw it on the ground, and trampled upon it. "She and I were kindred in suffering; I read it in her eyes, averted as they were at the sight of this accursed thing! You stare at me—you think I have gone mad. Leon, you are not as other men. Can you not guess that this damnable white tie has been choking the life and manhood out of me? But it is over now. Take your pen, Leon, as you are my friend, and write what I shall dictate."

Silenced by the stress of a great soul, half dazed by the strange, unexpected revelation, Raphael seated himself, took his pen, and wrote:

"We understand that the Rev. Joseph Strelitski has resigned his position in the Kensington Synagogue."

Not till he had written it did the full force of the paragraph overwhelm his soul.

"But you will not do this?" he said, looking up almost incredulously at the popular minister.

"I will; the position has become impossible. Leon, do you not understand? I am not what I was when I took it. I have lived, and life is change. Stagnation is death. Surely you can understand, for you, too, have changed. Cannot I read between the lines of your leaders?"

"Cannot you read in them?" said Raphael with a wan smile. "I have modified some opinions, it is true, and developed others; but I have disguised none."

"Not consciously, perhaps, but you do not speak all your thought."

"Perhaps I do not listen to it," said Raphael, half to himself. "But you—whatever your change—you have not lost faith in primaries?"

"No; not in what I consider such."

"Then why give up your platform, your housetop, whence you may do so much good? You are loved, venerated."

Strelitski placed his palms over his ears.

"Don't! don't!" he cried. "Don't you be the *advocatus diaboli*! Do you think I have not told myself all these things a thousand times? Do you think I have not tried every kind of opiate? No, no, be silent if you can say nothing to strengthen me in my resolution: am I not weak enough already? Promise me, give me your hand, swear to me that you will put that paragraph in the paper. Saturday. Sunday, Monday, Tuesday, Wednesday, Thursday—in six days I shall change a hundred times. Swear to me, so that I may leave this room at peace, the long conflict ended. Promise me you will insert it, though I myself should ask you to cancel it."

"But—" began Raphael.

Strelitski turned away impatiently and groaned.

"My God!" he cried hoarsely. "Leon, listen to me," he said, turning round suddenly. "Do you realize what sort of a position you are asking me to keep? Do you realize how it makes me the fief of a Rabbinate that is an anachronism, the bondman of outworn forms, the slave of the *Shulcan Aruch* (a book the Rabbinate would not dare publish in English), the professional panegyrist of the rich? Ours is a generation of whited sepulchres." He had no difficulty about utterance now; the words flowed in a torrent. "How can Judaism—and it alone—escape going through the fire of modern scepticism, from which, if religion emerge at all, it will emerge without its dross? Are not we Jews always the first prey of new ideas, with our alert intellect, our swift receptiveness, our keen critical sense? And if we are not hypocrites, we are indifferent—which is almost worse. Indifference is the only infidelity I recognize, and it is unfortunately as conservative as zeal. Indifference and hypocrisy between them keep orthodoxy alive—while they kill Judaism."

"Oh, I can't quite admit that," said Raphael. "I admit that scepticism is better than stagnation, but I cannot see why orthodoxy is the antithesis to Judaism Purified—and your own sermons are doing something to purify it—orthodoxy—"

"Orthodoxy cannot be purified unless by juggling with words," interrupted Strelitski vehemently. "Orthodoxy is inextricably entangled with ritual observance; and ceremonial religion is of the ancient world, not the modern."

"But our ceremonialism is pregnant with sublime symbolism, and its discipline is most salutary. Ceremony is the casket of religion."

"More often its coffin," said Strelitski drily. "Ceremonial religion is so apt to stiffen in a *rigor mortis*. It is too dangerous an element; it creates hypocrites and Pharisees. All cast-iron laws and dogmas do. Not that I share the Christian sneer at Jewish legalism. Add the Statute Book to the New Testament, and think of the network of laws hampering the feet of the Christian. No; much of our so-called ceremonialism is merely the primitive mix-up of everything with religion in a theocracy. The Mosaic code has been largely embodied in civil law, and superseded by it."

"That is just the flaw of the modern world, to keep life and religion apart," protested Raphael; "to have one set of principles for week-days and another for Sundays; to grind the inexorable mechanism of supply and demand on pagan principles, and make it up out of the poor-box."

Strelitski shook his head.

"We must make broad our platform, not our phylacteries. It is because I am with you in admiring the Rabbis that I would undo much of their work. Theirs was a wonderful statesmanship, and they built wiser than they knew; just as the patient labors of the superstitious zealots who counted every letter of the Law preserved the text unimpaired for the benefit of modern scholarship. The Rabbis constructed a casket, if you will, which kept the jewel safe, though at the cost of concealing its lustre. But the hour has come now to wear the jewel on our breasts before all the world. The Rabbis worked for their time—we must work for ours. Judaism was before the Rabbis. Scientific criticism shows its thoughts widening with the process of the suns—even as its God, Yahweh, broadened from a local patriotic Deity to the ineffable Name. For Judaism was worked out from within—Abraham asked, 'Shall not the Judge of all the earth do right?'—the thunders of Sinai were but the righteous indignation of the developed moral consciousness. In every age our great men have modified and developed Judaism. Why should it not be trimmed into concordance with the culture of the time? Especially when the alternative is death. Yes, death! We babble about petty minutiae of ritual while Judaism is dying! We are like the crew of a sinking ship, holy-stoning the deck instead of being at the pumps. No, I must speak out; I cannot go on salving my conscience by unsigned letters to the press. Away with all this anonymous apostleship!"

He moved about restlessly with animated gestures as he delivered

ISRAEL ZANGWILL

his harangue at tornado speed, speech bursting from him like some dynamic energy which had been accumulating for years, and could no longer be kept in. It was an upheaval of the whole man under the stress of pent forces. Raphael was deeply moved. He scarcely knew how to act in this unique crisis. Dimly he foresaw the stir and pother there would be in the community. Conservative by instinct, apt to see the elements of good in attacked institutions—perhaps, too, a little timid when it came to take action in the tremendous realm of realities—he was loth to help Strelitski to so decisive a step, though his whole heart went out to him in brotherly sympathy.

"Do not act so hastily," he pleaded. "Things are not so black as you see them—you are almost as bad as Miss Ansell. Don't think that I see them rosy: I might have done that three months ago. But don't you—don't all idealists—overlook the quieter phenomena? Is orthodoxy either so inefficacious or so moribund as you fancy? Is there not a steady, perhaps semi-conscious, stream of healthy life, thousands of cheerful, well-ordered households, of people neither perfect nor cultured, but more good than bad? You cannot expect saints and heroes to grow like blackberries."

"Yes; but look what Jews set up to be—God's witnesses!" interrupted Strelitski. "This mediocrity may pass in the rest of the world."

"And does lack of modern lights constitute ignorance?" went on Raphael, disregarding the interruption. He began walking up and down, and thrashing the air with his arms. Hitherto he had remained comparatively quiet, dominated by Strelitski's superior restlessness. "I cannot help thinking there is a profound lesson in the Bible story of the oxen who, unguided, bore safely the Ark of the Covenant. Intellect obscures more than it illumines."

"Oh, Leon, Leon, you'll turn Catholic, soon!" said Strelitski reprovingly.

"Not with a capital C," said Raphael, laughing a little. "But I am so sick of hearing about culture, I say more than I mean. Judaism is so human—that's why I like it. No abstract metaphysics, but a lovable way of living the common life, sanctified by the centuries. Culture is all very well—doesn't the Talmud say the world stands on the breath of the school-children?—but it has become a cant. Too often it saps the moral fibre."

"You have all the old Jewish narrowness," said Strelitski.

"I'd rather have that than the new Parisian narrowness—the cant of decadence. Look at my cousin Sidney. He talks as if the Jew only introduced moral-headache into the world—in face of the corruptions of paganism which are still flagrant all over Asia and Africa and Polynesia—the idol worship, the abominations, the disregard of human life, of truth, of justice."

"But is the civilized world any better? Think of the dishonesty of business, the self-seeking of public life, the infamies and hypocrisies of society, the prostitutions of soul and body! No, the Jew has yet to play a part in history. Supplement his Hebraism by what Hellenic ideals you will, but the Jew's ideals must ever remain the indispensable ones," said Strelitski, becoming exalted again. "Without righteousness a kingdom cannot stand. The world is longing for a broad simple faith that shall look on science as its friend and reason as its inspirer. People are turning in their despair even to table-rappings and Mahatmas. Now, for the first time in history, is the hour of Judaism. Only it must enlarge itself; its platform must be all-inclusive. Judaism is but a specialized form of Hebraism; even if Jews stick to their own special historical and ritual ceremonies, it is only Hebraism—the pure spiritual kernel—that they can offer the world."

"But that is quite the orthodox Jewish idea on the subject," said Raphael.

"Yes, but orthodox ideas have a way of remaining ideas," retorted Strelitski. "Where I am heterodox is in thinking the time has come to work them out. Also in thinking that the monotheism is not the element that needs the most accentuation. The formula of the religion of the future will be a Jewish formula—Character, not Creed. The provincial period of Judaism is over though even its Dark Ages are still lingering on in England. It must become cosmic, universal. Judaism is too timid, too apologetic, too deferential. Doubtless this is the result of persecution, but it does not tend to diminish persecution. We may as well try the other attitude. It is the world the Jewish preacher should address, not a Kensington congregation. Perhaps, when the Kensington congregation sees the world is listening, it will listen, too," he said, with a touch of bitterness.

"But it listens to you now," said Raphael.

"A pleasing illusion which has kept me too long in my false position. With all its love and reverence, do you think it forgets I am its hireling? I may perhaps have a little more prestige than the bulk of my fellows—though even that is partly due to my congregants being rich and fashionable—but at bottom everybody knows I am taken like a house—

on a three years' agreement. And I dare not speak, I cannot, while I wear the badge of office; it would be disloyal; my own congregation would take alarm. The position of a minister is like that of a judicious editor—which, by the way, you are not; he is led, rather than leads. He has to feel his way, to let in light wherever he sees a chink, a cranny. But let them get another man to preach to them the echo of their own voices; there will be no lack of candidates for the salary. For my part, I am sick of this petty jesuitry; in vain I tell myself it is spiritual statesmanship like that of so many Christian clergymen who are silently bringing Christianity back to Judaism."

"But it *is* spiritual statesmanship," asserted Raphael.

"Perhaps. You are wiser, deeper, calmer than I. You are an Englishman, I am a Russian. I am all for action, action, action! In Russia I should have been a Nihilist, not a philosopher. I can only go by my feelings, and I feel choking. When I first came to England, before the horror of Russia wore off, I used to go about breathing in deep breaths of air, exulting in the sense of freedom. Now I am stifling again. Do you not understand? Have you never guessed it? And yet I have often said things to you that should have opened your eyes. I must escape from the house of bondage—must be master of myself, of my word and thought. Oh, the world is so wide, so wide—and we are so narrow! Only gradually did the web mesh itself about me. At first my fetters were flowery bands, for I believed all I taught and could teach all I believed. Insensibly the flowers changed to iron chains, because I was changing as I probed deeper into life and thought, and saw my dreams of influencing English Judaism fading in the harsh daylight of fact. And yet at moments the iron links would soften to flowers again. Do you think there is no sweetness in adulation, in prosperity—no subtle cajolery that soothes the conscience and coaxes the soul to take its pleasure in a world of make-believe? Spiritual statesmanship, forsooth!" He made a gesture of resolution. "No, the Judaism of you English weighs upon my spirits. It is so parochial. Everything turns on finance; the United Synagogue keeps your community orthodox because it has the funds and owns the burying-grounds. Truly a dismal allegory—a creed whose strength lies in its cemeteries. Money is the sole avenue to distinction and to authority; it has its coarse thumb over education, worship, society. In my country—even in your own Ghetto—the Jews do not despise money, but at least piety and learning are the titles to position and honor. Here the scholar is classed with the *Schnorrer*; if an artist or an author is admired, it is for his success. You are right; it is oxen that carry your Ark of the Covenant—fat oxen. You admire them, Leon; you are an Englishman, and cannot stand outside it all. But I am stifling under this weight of moneyed mediocrity, this *régime* of dull respectability. I want the atmosphere of ideas and ideals."

He tore at his high clerical collar as though suffocating literally.

Raphael was too moved to defend English Judaism. Besides, he was used to these jeremiads now—had he not often heard them from Sidney? Had he not read them in Esther's book? Nor was it the first time he had listened to the Russian's tirades, though he had lacked the key to the internal conflict that embittered them.

"But how will you live?" he asked, tacitly accepting the situation. "You will not, I suppose, go over to the Reform Synagogue?"

"That fossil, so proud of its petty reforms half a century ago that it has stood still ever since to admire them! It is a synagogue for snobs—who never go there."

Raphael smiled faintly. It was obvious that Strelitski on the war-path did not pause to weigh his utterances.

"I am glad you are not going over, anyhow. Your congregation would—"

"Crucify me between two money-lenders?"

"Never mind. But how will you live?"'

"How does Miss Ansell live? I can always travel with cigars—I know the line thoroughly." He smiled mournfully. "But probably I shall go to America—the idea has been floating in my mind for months. There Judaism is grander, larger, nobler. There is room for all parties. The dead bones are not worshipped as relics. Free thought has its vent-holes—it is not repressed into hypocrisy as among us. There is care for literature, for national ideals. And one deals with millions, not petty thousands. This English community, with its squabbles about rituals, its four Chief Rabbis all in love with one another, its stupid Sephardim, its narrow-minded Reformers, its fatuous self-importance, its invincible ignorance, is but an ant-hill, a negligible quantity in the future of the faith. Westward the course of Judaism as of empire takes its way—from the Euphrates and Tigris it emigrated to Cordova and Toledo, and the year that saw its expulsion from Spain was the year of the Discovery of America. *Ex Oriente lux.* Perhaps it will return to you here by way of the Occident. Russia and America are the two strongholds of the race, and Russia is pouring her streams into America, where they will be made free men and free thinkers. It is in America, then, that the last great battle of Judaism will be fought out; amid the temples of the New World it will make its last struggle to survive. It is there that the men who have faith in its necessity must be, so that the psychical force conserved at such a cost may not radiate uselessly away. Though Israel has sunk low, like a tree once green and living, and has become petrified and blackened, there is stored-up sunlight in him. Our racial isolation is a mere superstition unless turned to great purposes. We have done nothing *as Jews* for centuries, though our Old Testament has always been an arsenal of texts for the European champions of civil and religious liberty. We have been unconsciously pioneers of modern commerce, diffusers of folk-lore and what not. Cannot we be a conscious force, making for nobler ends? Could we not, for instance, be the link of federation among the nations, acting everywhere in favor of Peace? Could we not be the centre of new sociologic movements in each country, as a few American Jews have been the centre of the Ethical Culture movement?"

"You forget," said Raphael, "that, wherever the old Judaism has not been overlaid by the veneer of Philistine civilization, we are already sociological object-lessons in good fellowship, unpretentious charity, domestic poetry, respect for learning, disrespect for respectability. Our social system is a bequest from the ancient world by which the modern may yet benefit. The demerits you censure in English Judaism are all departures from the old way of living. Why should we not revive or strengthen that, rather than waste ourselves on impracticable novelties? And in your prognostications of the future of the Jews have you not forgotten the all-important factor of Palestine?"

"No; I simply leave it out of count. You know how I have persuaded the Holy Land League to co-operate with the movements for directing the streams of the persecuted towards America. I have alleged with truth that Palestine is impracticable for the moment. I have not said what I have gradually come to think—that the salvation of Judaism is not in the national idea at all. That is the dream of visionaries—and young men," he added with a melancholy smile. "May we not dream nobler dreams than political independence? For, after all, political independence is only a means to an end, not an end in itself, as it might easily become, and as it appears to other nations. To be merely one among the nations—that is not, despite George Eliot, so satisfactory an ideal. The restoration to Palestine, or the acquisition of a national centre, may be a political solution, but it is not a spiritual idea. We must abandon it—it cannot be held consistently with our professed attachment to the countries in which our lot is cast—and we have abandoned it. We have fought and slain one another in the Franco-German war, and in the war of the North and the South. Your whole difficulty with your pauper immigrants arises from your effort to keep two contradictory ideals going at once. As Englishmen, you may have a right to shelter the exile; but not as Jews. Certainly, if the nations cast us out, we could, draw together and form a nation as of yore. But persecution, expulsion, is never simultaneous; our dispersal has saved Judaism, and it may yet save the world. For I prefer the dream that we are divinely dispersed to bless it, wind-sown seeds to fertilize its waste places. To be a nation without a fatherland, yet with a mother-tongue, Hebrew—there is the spiritual originality, the miracle of history. Such has been the real kingdom of Israel in the past—we have been 'sons of the Law' as other men have been sons of France, of Italy, of Germany. Such may our fatherland continue, with 'the higher life' substituted for 'the law'—a kingdom not of space, not measured by the vulgar meteyard of an Alexander, but a great spiritual Republic, as devoid of material form as Israel's God, and congruous with his conception of the Divine. And the conquest of this kingdom needs no violent movement—if Jews only practised what they preach, it would be achieved tomorrow; for all expressions of Judaism, even to the lowest, have common sublimities. And this kingdom—as it has no space, so it has no limits; it must grow till all mankind, are its subjects. The brotherhood of Israel will be the nucleus of the brotherhood of man."

"It is magnificent," said Raphael; "but it is not Judaism. If the Jews have the future you dream of, the future will have no Jews. America is already decimating them with Sunday-Sabbaths and English Prayer-Books. Your Judaism is as eviscerated as the Christianity I found in vogue when I was at Oxford, which might be summed up: There is no God, but Jesus Christ is His Son. George Eliot was right. Men are men, not pure spirit. A fatherland focusses a people. Without it we are but the gypsies of religion. All over the world, at every prayer, every Jew turns towards Jerusalem. We must not give up the dream. The countries we live in can never be more than 'step-fatherlands' to us. Why, if your visions were realized, the prophecy of Genesis, already practically fulfilled, 'Thou shalt spread abroad to the west and to the east, and to the north and to the south; and in thee and in thy seed shall all the families of the earth be blessed,' would be so remarkably consummated that we might reasonably hope to come to our own again according to the promises."

"Well, well," said Strelitski, good-humoredly, "so long as you admit it is not within the range of practical politics now."

"It is your own dream that is premature," retorted Raphael; "at any rate, the cosmic part of it. You are thinking of throwing open the citizenship of your Republic to the world. But today's task is to make its citizens by blood worthier of their privilege."

"You will never do it with the old generation," said Strelitski. "My hope is in the new. Moses led the Jews forty years through the wilderness merely to eliminate the old. Give me young men, and I will move the world."

"You will do nothing by attempting too much," said Raphael; "you will only dissipate your strength. For my part, I shall be content to raise Judaea an inch."

"Go on, then," said Strelitski. "That will give me a barley-corn. But I've wasted too much' of your time, I fear. Goodbye. Remember your promise."

He held out his hand. He had grown quite calm, now his decision was taken.

"Goodbye," said Raphael, shaking it warmly. "I think I shall cable to America, 'Behold, Joseph the dreamer cometh.'"

"Dreams are our life," replied Strelitski. "Lessing was right—aspiration is everything."

"And yet you would rob the orthodox Jew of his dream of Jerusalem! Well, if you must go, don't go without your tie," said Raphael, picking it up, and feeling a stolid, practical Englishman in presence of this enthusiast. "It is dreadfully dirty, but you must wear it a little longer."

"Only till the New Year, which is bearing down upon us," said Strelitski, thrusting it into his pocket. "Cost what it may, I shall no longer countenance the ritual and ceremonial of the season of Repentance. Goodbye again. If you should be writing to Miss Ansell, I should like her to know how much I owe her."

"But I tell you I don't know her address," said Raphael, his uneasiness reawakening.

"Surely you can write to her publishers?"

And the door closed upon the Russian dreamer, leaving the practical Englishman dumbfounded at his never having thought of this simple expedient. But before he could adopt it the door was thrown open again by Pinchas, who had got out of the habit of knocking through Raphael being too polite to reprimand him. The poet, tottered in, dropped wearily into a chair, and buried his face in his hands, letting an extinct cigar-stump slip through his fingers on to the literature that carpeted the floor.

"What is the matter?" inquired Raphael in alarm.

"I am miserable—vairy miserable."

"Has anything happened?"

"Nothing. But I have been thinking vat have I come to after all these years, all these vanderings. Nothing! Vat vill be my end? Oh. I am so unhappy."

"But you are better off than you ever were in your life. You no longer live amid the squalor of the Ghetto; you are clean and well dressed: you yourself admit that you can afford to give charity now. That looks as if you'd come to something—not nothing."

"Yes," said the poet, looking up eagerly, "and I am famous through the vorld. *Metatoron's Flames* vill shine eternally." His head drooped again. "I have all I vant, and you are the best man in the vorld. But I am the most miserable."

"Nonsense! cheer up," said Raphael.

"I can never cheer up anymore. I vill shoot myself. I have realized the emptiness of life. Fame, money, love—all is Dead Sea fruit."

His shoulders heaved convulsively; he was sobbing. Raphael stood by helpless, his respect for Pinchas as a poet and for himself as a practical Englishman returning. He pondered over the strange fate that had thrown him among three geniuses—a male idealist, a female pessimist, and a poet who seemed to belong to both sexes and categories. And yet there was not one of the three to whom he seemed able to be of real service. A letter brought in by the office-boy rudely snapped the thread of reflection. It contained three enclosures. The first was an epistle; the hand was the hand of Mr. Goldsmith, but the voice was the voice of his beautiful spouse.

DEAR MR. LEON:

"I have perceived many symptoms lately of your growing divergency from the ideas with which *The Flag of Judah* was started. It is obvious that you find yourself unable to emphasize the olden features of our faith—the questions of *kosher* meat, etc.—as forcibly as our readers desire. You no doubt cherish ideals which are neither practical nor within the grasp of the masses to whom we appeal. I fully appreciate the delicacy that makes you reluctant—in the dearth of genius and Hebrew learning—to saddle me with the task of finding a substitute, but I feel it is time for me to restore your peace of mind even at the expense of my own. I have been thinking that, with your kind occasional supervision, it might be possible for Mr. Pinchas, of whom you have always spoken so highly, to undertake the duties of editorship, Mr. Sampson remaining sub-editor as before. Of course I count on you to continue your purely scholarly articles, and to impress upon the two gentlemen who will now have direct relations with me my wish to remain in the background.

Yours sincerely,

HENRY GOLDSMITH

"P.S.—On second thoughts I beg to enclose a cheque for four guineas, which will serve instead of a formal month's notice, and will enable you to accept at once my wife's invitation, likewise enclosed herewith. Your sister seconds Mrs. Goldsmith in the hope that you will do so. Our tenancy of the Manse only lasts a few weeks longer, for of course we return for the New Year holidays."

This was the last straw. It was not so much the dismissal that staggered him, but to be called a genius and an idealist himself—to have his own orthodoxy impugned—just at this moment, was a rough shock.

"Pinchas!" he said, recovering himself. Pinchas would not look up. His face was still hidden in his hands. "Pinchas, listen! You are appointed editor of the paper, instead of me. You are to edit the next number."

Pinchas's head shot up like a catapult. He bounded to his feet, then bent down again to Raphael's coat-tail and kissed it passionately.

"Ah, my benefactor, my benefactor!" he cried, in a joyous frenzy. "Now vill I give it to English Judaism. She is in my power. Oh, my benefactor!"

"No, no," said Raphael, disengaging himself. "I have nothing to do with it."

"But de paper—she is yours!" said the poet, forgetting his English in his excitement.

"No, I am only the editor. I have been dismissed, and you are appointed instead of me."

Pinchas dropped back into his chair like a lump of lead. He hung his head again and folded his arms.

"Then they get not me for editor," he said moodily.

"Nonsense, why not?" said Raphael, flushing.

"Vat you think me?" Pinchas asked indignantly. "Do you think I have a stone for a heart like Gideon M.P. or your English stockbrokers and Rabbis? No, you shall go on being editor. They think you are not able enough, not orthodox enough—they vant me—but do not fear. I shall not accept."

"But then what will become of the next number?" remonstrated Raphael, touched. "I must not edit it."

"Vat you care? Let her die!" cried Pinchas, in gloomy complacency. "You have made her; vy should she survive you? It is not right another should valk in your shoes—least of all, *I*."

"But I don't mind—I don't mind a bit," Raphael assured him. Pinchas shook his head obstinately. "If the paper dies, Sampson will have nothing to live upon," Raphael reminded him.

"True, vairy true," said the poet, patently beginning to yield. "That alters things. Ve cannot let Sampson starve."

"No, you see!" said Raphael. "So you must keep it alive."

"Yes, but," said Pinchas, getting up thoughtfully, "Sampson is going off soon on tour vith his comic opera. He vill not need the *Flag*."

"Oh, well, edit it till then."

"Be it so," said the poet resignedly. "Till Sampson's comic-opera tour."

"Till Sampson's comic-opera tour," repeated Raphael contentedly.

ISRAEL ZANGWILL

XVI

Love's Temptation

Raphael walked out of the office, a free man. Mountains of responsibility seemed to roll off his shoulders. His Messianic emotions were conscious of no laceration at the failure of this episode of his life; they were merged in greater. What a fool he had been to waste so much time, to make no effort to find the lonely girl! Surely, Esther must have expected him, if only as a friend, to give some sign that he did not share in the popular execration. Perchance she had already left London or the country, only to be found again by protracted knightly quest! He felt grateful to Providence for setting him free for her salvation. He made at once for the publishers' and asked for her address. The junior partner knew of no such person. In vain Raphael reminded him that they had published *Mordecai Josephs*. That was by Mr. Edward Armitage. Raphael accepted the convention, and demanded this gentleman's address instead. That, too, was refused, but all letters would be forwarded. Was Mr. Armitage in England? All letters would be forwarded. Upon that the junior partner stood, inexpugnable.

Raphael went out, not uncomforted. He would write to her at once. He got letter-paper at the nearest restaurant and wrote, "Dear Miss Ansell." The rest was a blank. He had not the least idea how to renew the relationship after what seemed an eternity of silence. He stared helplessly round the mirrored walls, seeing mainly his own helpless stare. The placard "Smoking not permitted till 8 P.M.," gave him a sudden shock. He felt for his pipe, and ultimately found it stuck, half full of charred bird's eye, in his breast-pocket. He had apparently not been smoking for some hours. That completed his perturbation. He felt he had undergone too much that day to be in a fit state to write a judicious letter. He would go home and rest a bit, and write the letter—very diplomatically—in the evening. When he got home, he found to his astonishment it was Friday evening, when letter-writing is of the devil. Habit carried him to synagogue, where he sang the Sabbath hymn, "Come, my beloved, to meet the bride," with strange sweet tears and a complete indifference to its sacred allegorical signification. Next afternoon he haunted the publishers' doorstep with the brilliant idea that Mr. Armitage sometimes crossed it. In this hope, he did *not* write the letter; his phrases, he felt, would be better for the inspiration of that gentleman's presence. Meanwhile he had ample time to mature them, to review the situation in every possible light, to figure Esther under the most poetical images, to see his future alternately radiant and sombre. Four long summer days of espionage only left him with a heartache, and a specialist knowledge of the sort of persons who visit publishers. A temptation to bribe the office-boy he resisted as unworthy.

Not only had he not written that letter, but Mr. Henry Goldsmith's edict and Mrs. Henry Goldsmith's invitation were still unacknowledged. On Thursday morning a letter from Addie indirectly reminded him both of his remissness to her hostess, and of the existence of *The Flag of Judah*. He remembered it was the day of going to press; a vision of the difficulties of the day flashed vividly upon his consciousness; he wondered if his ex-lieutenants were finding new ones. The smell of the machine-room was in his nostrils; it co-operated with the appeal of his good-nature to draw him to his successor's help. Virtue proved its own reward. Arriving at eleven o'clock, he found little Sampson in great excitement, with the fountain of melody dried up on his lips.—

"Thank God!" he cried. "I thought you'd come when you heard the news."

"What news?"

"Gideon the member for Whitechapel's dead. Died suddenly, early this morning."

"How shocking!" said Raphael, growing white.

"Yes, isn't it?" said little Sampson. "If he had died yesterday, I shouldn't have minded it so much, while tomorrow would have given us a clear week. He hasn't even been ill," he grumbled. "I've had to send Pinchas to the Museum in a deuce of a hurry, to find out about his early life. I'm awfully upset about it, and what makes it worse is a telegram from Goldsmith, ordering a page obituary at least with black rules, besides a leader. It's simply sickening. The proofs are awful enough as it is— my blessed editor has been writing four columns of his autobiography in his most original English, and he wants to leave out all the news part to make room for 'em. In one way Gideon's death is a boon; even Pinchas'll see his stuff must be crowded out. It's frightful having to edit your editor. Why wasn't he made sub?"

"That would have been just as trying for you," said Raphael with a melancholy smile. He took up a galley-proof and began to correct it. To his surprise he came upon his own paragraph about Strelitski's resignation: it caused him fresh emotion. This great spiritual crisis had quite slipped his memory, so egoistic are the best of us at times. "Please be careful that Pinchas's autobiography does not crowd that out," he said.

Pinchas arrived late, when little Sampson was almost in despair. "It is all right." he shouted, waving a roll of manuscript. "I have him from the cradle—the stupid stockbroker, the Man-of-the-Earth, who sent me back my poesie, and vould not let me teach his boy Judaism. And vhile I had the inspiration I wrote the leader also in the Museum—it is here—oh, vairy beautiful! Listen to the first sentence. 'The Angel of Death has passed again over Judaea; he has flown off vith our visest and our best, but the black shadow of his ving vill long rest upon the House of Israel.' And the end is vordy of the beginning. He is dead: but he lives forever enshrined in the noble tribute to his genius in *Metatoron's Flames*."

Little Sampson seized the "copy" and darted with it to the composing-room, where Raphael was busy giving directions. By his joyful face Raphael saw the crisis was over. Little Sampson handed the manuscript to the foreman, then drawing a deep breath of relief, he began to hum a sprightly march.

"I say, you're a nice chap!" he grumbled, cutting himself short with a staccato that was not in the music.

"What have I done?" asked Raphael.

"Done? You've got me into a nice mess. The guvnor—the new guvnor, the old guvnor, it seems—called the other day to fix things with me and Pinchas. He asked me if I was satisfied to go on at the same screw. I said he might make it two pound ten. 'What, more than double?' says he. 'No, only nine shillings extra,' says I, 'and for that I'll throw in some foreign telegrams the late editor never cared for.' And then it came out that he only knew of a sovereign, and fancied I was trying it on."

"Oh, I'm so sorry," said Raphael, in deep scarlet distress.

"You must have been paying a guinea out of your own pocket!" said little Sampson sharply.

Raphael's confusion increased. "I—I—didn't want it myself," he faltered. "You see, it was paid me just for form, and you really did the work. Which reminds me I have a cheque of yours now," he ended boldly. "That'll make it right for the coming month, anyhow."

He hunted out Goldsmith's final cheque, and tendered it sheepishly.

"Oh no, I can't take it now," said little Sampson. He folded his arms, and drew his cloak around him like a toga. No August sun ever divested little Sampson of his cloak.

"Has Goldsmith agreed to your terms, then?" inquired Raphael timidly.

"Oh no, not he. But—"

"Then I must go on paying the difference," said Raphael decisively. "I am responsible to you that you get the salary you're used to; it's my fault that things are changed, and I must pay the penalty," He crammed the cheque forcibly into the pocket of the toga.

"Well, if you put it in that way," said little Sampson, "I won't say I couldn't do with it. But only as a loan, mind."

"All right," murmured Raphael.

"And you'll take it back when my comic opera goes on tour. You won't back out?"

"No."

"Give us your hand on it," said little Sampson huskily. Raphael gave him his hand, and little Sampson swung it up and down like a baton.

"Hang it all! and that man calls himself a Jew!" he thought. Aloud he said: "When my comic opera goes on tour."

They returned to the editorial den, where they found Pinchas raging, a telegram in his hand.

"Ah, the Man-of-the-Earth!" he cried. "All my beautiful peroration he spoils." He crumpled up the telegram and threw it pettishly at little Sampson, then greeted Raphael with effusive joy and hilarity. Little Sampson read the telegram. It ran as follows:

"Last sentence of Gideon leader. 'It is too early yet in this moment of grief to speculate as to his successor in the constituency. But, difficult as it will be to replace him, we may find some solace in the thought that it will not be impossible. The spirit of the illustrious dead would itself rejoice to acknowledge the special qualifications of one whose name will at once rise to every lip as that of a brother Jew whose sincere piety and genuine public spirit mark him out as the one worthy substitute in the representation of a district embracing so many of our poor Jewish brethren. Is it too much to hope that he will be induced to stand?' Goldsmith."

"That's a cut above Henry," murmured little Sampson, who knew nearly everything, save the facts he had to supply to the public. "He wired to the wife, and it's hers. Well, it saves him from writing his own puffs, anyhow. I suppose Goldsmith's only the signature, not intended to be the last word on the subject. Wants touching up, though; can't have 'spirit' twice within four lines. How lucky for him Leon is just off the box seat! That queer beggar would never have submitted to any dictation anymore than the boss would have dared show his hand so openly."

While the sub-editor mused thus, a remark dropped from the editor's lips, which turned Raphael whiter than the news of the death of Gideon had done.

"Yes, and in the middle of writing I look up and see the maiden—oh, vairy beautiful! How she gives it to English Judaism sharp in that book—the stupid heads,—the Men-of-the-Earth! I could kiss her for it, only I have never been introduced. Gideon, he is there! Ho! ho!" he sniggered, with purely intellectual appreciation of the pungency.

"What maiden? What are you talking about?" asked Raphael, his breath coming painfully.

"Your maiden," said Pinchas, surveying him with affectionate roguishness. "The maiden that came to see you here. She was reading; I walk by and see it is about America."

"At the British Museum?" gasped Raphael. A thousand hammers beat "Fool!" upon his brain. Why had he not thought of so likely a place for a *littérateur*?

He rushed out of the office and into a hansom. He put his pipe out in anticipation. In seven minutes he was at the gates, just in time—heaven be thanked!—to meet her abstractedly descending the steps. His heart gave a great leap of joy. He studied the pensive little countenance for an instant before it became aware of him; its sadness shot a pang of reproach through him. Then a great light, as of wonder and joy, came into the dark eyes, and glorified the pale, passionate face. But it was only a flash that faded, leaving the cheeks more pallid than before, the lips quivering.

"Mr. Leon!" she muttered.

He raised his hat, then held out a trembling hand that closed upon hers with a grip that hurt her.

"I'm so glad to see you again!" he said, with unconcealed enthusiasm. "I have been meaning to write to you for days—care of your publishers. I wonder if you will ever forgive me!"

"You had nothing to write to me," she said, striving to speak coldly.

"Oh yes, I had!" he protested.

She shook her head.

"Our journalistic relations are over—there were no others."

"Oh!" he said reproachfully, feeling his heart grow chill. "Surely we were friends?"

She did not answer.

"I wanted to write and tell you how much," he began desperately, then stammered, and ended—"how much I liked *Mordecai Josephs*."

This time the reproachful "Oh!" came from her lips. "I thought better of you," she said. "You didn't say that in *The Flag of Judah*; writing it privately to me wouldn't do me any good in any case."

He felt miserable; from the crude standpoint of facts, there was no answer to give. He gave none.

"I suppose it is all about now?" she went on, seeing him silent.

"Pretty well," he answered, understanding the question. Then, with an indignant accent, he said, "Mrs. Goldsmith tells everybody she found it out; and sent you away."

"I am glad she says that," she remarked enigmatically. "And, naturally, everybody detests me?"

"Not everybody," he began threateningly.

"Don't let us stand on the steps," she interrupted. "People will be looking at us." They moved slowly downwards, and into the hot, bustling streets. "Why are you not at the *Flag*? I thought this was your busy day." She did not add, "And so I ventured to the Museum, knowing there was no chance of your turning up;" but such was the fact.

"I am not the editor any longer," he replied.

"Not?" She almost came to a stop. "So much for my critical faculty; I could have sworn to your hand in every number."

"Your critical faculty equals your creative," he began.

"Journalism has taught you sarcasm."

"No, no! please do not be so unkind. I spoke in earnestness. I have only just been dismissed."

"Dismissed!" she echoed incredulously. "I thought the *Flag* was your own?"

He grew troubled. "I bought it—but for another. We—he—has dispensed with my services."

"Oh, how shameful!"

The latent sympathy of her indignation cheered him again.

"I am not sorry," he said. "I'm afraid I really was outgrowing its original platform."

"What?" she asked, with a note of mockery in her voice. "You have left off being orthodox?"

"I don't say that, it seems to me, rather, that I have come to understand I never was orthodox in the sense that the orthodox understand the word. I had never come into contact with them before. I never realized how unfair orthodox writers are to Judaism. But I do not abate one word of what I have ever said or written, except, of course, on questions of scholarship, which are always open to revision."

"But what is to become of me—of my conversion?" she said, with mock piteousness.

"You need no conversion!" he answered passionately, abandoning without a twinge all those criteria of Judaism for which he had fought with Strelitski. "You are a Jewess not only in blood, but in spirit. Deny it as you may, you have all the Jewish ideals,—they are implied in your attack on our society."

She shook her head obstinately.

"You read all that into me, as you read your modern thought into the old naïve books."

"I read what is in you. Your soul is in the right, whatever your brain says." He went on, almost to echo Strelitski's words, "Selfishness is the only real atheism; aspiration, unselfishness, the only real religion. In the language of our Hillel, this is the text of the Law; the rest is commentary. You and I are at one in believing that, despite all and after all, the world turns on righteousness, on justice"—his voice became a whisper—"on love."

The old thrill went through her, as when first they met. Once again the universe seemed bathed in holy joy. But she shook off the spell almost angrily. Her face was definitely set towards the life of the New World. Why should he disturb her anew?

"Ah, well, I'm glad you allow me a little goodness," she said sarcastically. "It is quite evident how you have drifted from orthodoxy. Strange result of *The Flag of Judah*! Started to convert me, it has ended by alienating you—its editor—from the true faith. Oh, the irony of circumstance! But don't look so glum. It has fulfilled its mission all the same; it *has* converted me—I will confess it to you." Her face grew grave, her tones earnest "So I haven't an atom of sympathy with your broader attitude. I am full of longing for the old impossible Judaism."

His face took on a look of anxious solicitude. He was uncertain whether she spoke ironically or seriously. Only one thing was certain—

that she was slipping from him again. She seemed so complex, paradoxical, elusive—and yet growing every moment more dear and desirable.

"Where are you living?" he asked abruptly. "It doesn't matter where," she answered. "I sail for America in three weeks."

The world seemed suddenly empty. It was hopeless, then—she was almost in his grasp, yet he could not hold her. Some greater force was sweeping her into strange alien solitudes. A storm of protest raged in his heart—all he had meant to say to her rose to his lips, but he only said, "Must you go?"

"I must. My little sister marries. I have timed my visit so as to arrive just for the wedding—like a fairy godmother." She smiled wistfully.

"Then you will live with your people, I suppose?"

"I suppose so. I dare say I shall become quite good again. Ah, your new Judaisms will never appeal like the old, with all its imperfections. They will never keep the race together through shine and shade as that did. They do but stave off the inevitable dissolution. It is beautiful—that old childlike faith in the pillar of cloud by day and the pillar of fire by night, that patient waiting through the centuries for the Messiah who even to you, I dare say, is a mere symbol." Again the wistful look lit up her eyes. "That's what you rich people will never understand—it doesn't seem to go with dinners in seven courses, somehow."

"Oh, but I do understand," he protested. "It's what I told Strelitski, who is all for intellect in religion. He is going to America, too," he said, with a sudden pang of jealous apprehension.

"On a holiday?"

"No; he is going to resign his ministry here."

"What! Has he got a better offer from America?"

"Still so cruel to him," he said reprovingly. "He is resigning for conscience' sake."

"After all these years?" she queried sarcastically.

"Miss Ansell, you wrong him! He was not happy in his position. You were right so far. But he cannot endure his shackles any longer. And it is you who have inspired him to break them."

"I?" she exclaimed, startled.

"Yes, I told him why you had left Mrs. Henry Goldsmith's—it seemed to act like an electrical stimulus. Then and there he made me write a paragraph announcing his resignation. It will appear tomorrow."

Esther's eyes filled with soft light. She walked on in silence; then, noticing she had automatically walked too much in the direction of her place of concealment, she came to an abrupt stop.

"We must part here," she said. "If I ever come across my old shepherd in America, I will be nicer to him. It is really quite heroic of him—you must have exaggerated my own petty sacrifice alarmingly if it really supplied him with inspiration. What is he going to do in America?"

"To preach a universal Judaism. He is a born idealist; his ideas have always such a magnificent sweep. Years ago he wanted all the Jews to return to Palestine."

Esther smiled faintly, not at Strelitski, but at Raphael's calling another man an idealist. She had never yet done justice to the strain of common-sense that saved him from being a great man; he and the new Strelitski were of one breed to her.

"He will make Jews no happier and Christians no wiser," she said sceptically. "The great populations will sweep on, as little affected by the Jews as this crowd by you and me. The world will not go back on itself—rather will Christianity transform itself and take the credit. We are such a handful of outsiders. Judaism—old or new—is a forlorn hope."

"The forlorn hope will yet save the world," he answered quietly, "but it has first to be saved to the world."

"Be happy in your hope," she said gently. "Goodbye." She held out her little hand. He had no option but to take it.

"But we are not going to part like this," he said desperately. "I shall see you again before you go to America?"

"No, why should you?"

"Because I love you," rose to his lips. But the avowal seemed too plump. He prevaricated by retorting, "Why should I not?"

"Because I fear you," was in her heart, but nothing rose to her lips. He looked into her eyes to read an answer there, but she dropped them. He saw his opportunity.

"Why should I not?" he repeated.

"Your time is valuable," she said faintly.

"I could not spend it better than with you," he answered boldly.

"Please don't insist," she said in distress.

"But I shall; I am your friend. So far as I know, you are lonely. If you are bent upon going away, why deny me the pleasure of the society I am about to lose forever?"

"Oh, how can you call it a pleasure—such poor melancholy company as I am!"

"Such poor melancholy company that I came expressly to seek it, for someone told me you were at the Museum. Such poor melancholy company that if I am robbed of it life will be a blank."

He had not let go her hand; his tones were low and passionate; the heedless traffic of the sultry London street was all about them.

Esther trembled from head to foot; she could not look at him. There was no mistaking his meaning now; her breast was a whirl of delicious pain.

But in proportion as the happiness at her beck and call dazzled her, so she recoiled from it. Bent on self-effacement, attuned to the peace of despair, she almost resented the solicitation to be happy; she had suffered so much that she had grown to think suffering her natural element, out of which she could not breathe; she was almost in love with misery. And in so sad a world was there not something ignoble about happiness, a selfish aloofness from the life of humanity? And, illogically blent with this questioning, and strengthening her recoil, was an obstinate conviction that there could never be happiness for her, a being of ignominious birth, without roots in life, futile, shadowy, out of relation to the tangible solidities of ordinary existence. To offer her a warm fireside seemed to be to tempt her to be false to something—she knew not what. Perhaps it was because the warm fireside was in the circle she had quitted, and her heart was yet bitter against it, finding no palliative even in the thought of a triumphant return. She did not belong to it; she was not of Raphael's world. But she felt grateful to the point of tears for his incomprehensible love for a plain, penniless, low-born girl. Surely, it was only his chivalry. Other men had not found her attractive. Sidney had not; Levi only fancied himself in love. And yet beneath all her humility was a sense of being loved for the best in her, for the hidden qualities Raphael alone had the insight to divine. She could never think so meanly of herself or of humanity again. He had helped and strengthened her for her lonely future; the remembrance of him would always be an inspiration, and a reminder of the nobler side of human nature.

All this contradictory medley of thought and feeling occupied but a few seconds of consciousness. She answered him without any perceptible pause, lightly enough.

"Really, Mr. Leon, I don't expect *you* to say such things. Why should we be so conventional, you and I? How can your life be a blank, with Judaism yet to be saved?"

ISRAEL ZANGWILL

"Who am I to save Judaism? I want to save you," he said passionately.

"What a descent! For heaven's sake, stick to your earlier ambition!"

"No, the two are one to me. Somehow you seem to stand for Judaism, too. I cannot disentwine my hopes; I have come to conceive your life as an allegory of Judaism, the offspring of a great and tragic past with the germs of a rich blossoming, yet wasting with an inward canker, I have grown to think of its future as somehow bound up with yours. I want to see your eyes laughing, the shadows lifted from your brow; I want to see you face life courageously, not in passionate revolt nor in passionless despair, but in faith and hope and the joy that springs from them. I want you to seek peace, not in a despairing surrender of the intellect to the faith of childhood, but in that faith intellectually justified. And while I want to help you, and to fill your life with the sunshine it needs, I want you to help me, to inspire me when I falter, to complete my life, to make me happier than I had ever dreamed. Be my wife, Esther. Let me save you from yourself."

"Let me save you from yourself, Raphael. Is it wise to wed with the gray spirit of the Ghetto that doubts itself?"

And like a spirit she glided from his grasp and disappeared in the crowd.

XVII

THE PRODIGAL SON

The New Year dawned upon the Ghetto, heralded by a month of special matins and the long-sustained note of the ram's horn. It was in the midst of the Ten Days of Repentance which find their awful climax in the Day of Atonement that a strange letter for Hannah came to startle the breakfast-table at Reb Shemuel's. Hannah read it with growing pallor and perturbation.

"What is the matter, my dear?" asked the Reb, anxiously.

"Oh, father," she cried, "read this! Bad news of Levi."

A spasm of pain contorted the old man's furrowed countenance.

"Mention not his name!" he said harshly "He is dead."

"He may be by now!" Hannah exclaimed agitatedly. "You were right, Esther. He did join a strolling company, and now he is laid up with typhoid in the hospital in Stockbridge. One of his friends writes to tell us. He must have caught it in one of those insanitary dressing-rooms we were reading about."

Esther trembled all over. The scene in the garret when the fatal telegram came announcing Benjamin's illness had never faded from her mind. She had an instant conviction that it was all over with poor Levi.

"My poor lamb!" cried the Rebbitzin, the coffee-cup dropping from her nerveless hand.

"Simcha," said Reb Shemuel sternly, "calm thyself; we have no son to lose. The Holy One—blessed be He!—hath taken him from us. The Lord giveth, and the Lord taketh. Blessed be the name of the Lord."

Hannah rose. Her face was white and resolute. She moved towards the door.

"Whither goest thou?" inquired her father in German.

"I am going to my room, to put on my hat and jacket," replied Hannah quietly.

"Whither goest thou?" repeated Reb Shemuel.

"To Stockbridge. Mother, you and I must go at once."

The Reb sprang to his feet. His brow was dark; his eyes gleamed with anger and pain.

"Sit down and finish thy breakfast," he said.

"How can I eat? Levi is dying," said Hannah, in low, firm tones. "Will you come, mother, or must I go alone?"

The Rebbitzin began to wring her hands and weep. Esther stole gently to Hannah's side and pressed the poor girl's hand. "You and I will go," her clasp said.

"Hannah!" said Reb Shemuel. "What madness is this? Dost thou think thy mother will obey thee rather than her husband?"

"Levi is dying. It is our duty to go to him." Hannah's gentle face was rigid. But there was exaltation rather than defiance in the eyes.

"It is not the duty of women," said Reb Shemuel harshly. "I will go to Stockbridge. If he dies (God have mercy upon his soul!) I will see that he is buried among his own people. Thou knowest women go not to funerals." He reseated himself at the table, pushing aside his scarcely touched meal, and began saying the grace. Dominated by his will and by old habit, the three trembling women remained in reverential silence.

"The Lord will give strength to His people; the Lord will bless His people with Peace," concluded the old man in unfaltering accents. He rose from the table and strode to the door, stern and erect "Thou wilt remain here, Hannah, and thou, Simcha," he said. In the passage his shoulders relaxed their stiffness, so that the long snow-white beard drooped upon his breast. The three women looked at one another.

"Mother," said Hannah, passionately breaking the silence, "are you going to stay here while Levi is dying in a strange town?"

"My husband wills it," said the Rebbitzin, sobbing. "Levi is a sinner in Israel. Thy father will not see him; he will not go to him till he is dead."

"Oh yes, surely he will," said Esther. "But be comforted. Levi is young and strong. Let us hope he will pull through."

"No, no!" moaned the Rebbitzin. "He will die, and my husband will but read the psalms at his death-bed. He will not forgive him; he will not speak to him of his mother and sister."

"Let *me* go. I will give him your messages," said Esther.

"No, no," interrupted Hannah. "What are you to him? Why should you risk infection for our sakes?"

"Go, Hannah, but secretly," said the Rebbitzin in a wailing whisper. "Let not thy father see thee till thou arrive; then he will not send thee back. Tell Levi that I—oh, my poor child, my poor lamb!" Sobs overpowered her speech.

"No, mother," said Hannah quietly, "thou and I shall go. I will tell father we are accompanying him."

She left the room, while the Rebbitzin fell weeping and terrified into a chair, and Esther vainly endeavored to soothe her. The Reb was changing his coat when Hannah knocked at the door and called "Father."

"Speak not to me, Hannah," answered the Reb, roughly. "It is useless." Then, as if repentant of his tone, he threw open the door, and passed his great trembling hand lovingly over her hair. "Thou art a good daughter," he said tenderly. "Forget that thou hast had a brother."

"But how can I forget?" she answered him in his own idiom. "Why should I forget? What hath he done?"

He ceased to smooth her hair—his voice grew sad and stern.

"He hath profaned the Name. He hath lived like a heathen; he dieth like a heathen now. His blasphemy was a by-word in the congregation. I alone knew it not till last Passover. He hath brought down my gray hairs in sorrow to the grave."

"Yes, father, I know," said Hannah, more gently. "But he is not all to blame!"

"Thou meanest that I am not guiltless; that I should have kept him at my side?" said the Reb, his voice faltering a little.

"No, father, not that! Levi could not always be a baby. He had to walk alone some day."

"Yes, and did I not teach him to walk alone?" asked the Reb eagerly. "My God, thou canst not say I did not teach him Thy Law, day and night." He uplifted his eyes in anguished appeal.

"Yes, but he is not all to blame," she repeated. "Thy teaching did not reach his soul; he is of another generation, the air is different, his life was cast amid conditions for which the Law doth not allow."

"Hannah!" Reb Shemuel's accents became harsh and chiding again. "What sayest thou? The Law of Moses is eternal; it will never be changed. Levi knew God's commandments, but he followed the desire of his own heart and his own eyes. If God's Word were obeyed, he should have been stoned with stones. But Heaven itself hath punished him; he will die, for it is ordained that whosoever is stubborn and disobedient, that soul shall surely be cut off from among his people. 'Keep My commandments, that thy days may be long in the land,' God Himself hath said it. Is it not written: 'Rejoice, O young man, in thy youth, and let thy heart cheer thee in the days of thy youth, and walk in the ways of thine heart and in the sight of thine eyes; but know thou that for all these things the Lord will bring thee into judgment'? But thou, my Hannah," he started caressing her hair again, "art a good Jewish maiden. Between Levi and thee there is naught in common. His touch would profane thee. Sadden not thy innocent eyes with the sight of his end. Think of him as one who died in boyhood. My God! why didst thou not take him then?" He turned away, stifling a sob.

"Father," she put her hand on his shoulder, "we will go with thee to Stockbridge—I and the mother."

He faced her again, stern and rigid.

"Cease thy entreaties. I will go alone."

"No, we will all go."

"Hannah," he said, his voice tremulous with pain and astonishment, "dost thou, too, set light by thy father?"

"Yes," she cried, and there was no answering tremor in her voice. "Now thou knowest! I am not a good Jewish maiden. Levi and I are brother and sister. His touch profane me, forsooth!" She laughed bitterly.

"Thou wilt take this journey though I forbid thee?" he cried in acrid accents, still mingled with surprise.

"Yes; would I had taken the journey thou wouldst have forbidden ten years ago!"

"What journey? thou talkest madness."

"I talk truth. Thou hast forgotten David Brandon; I have not. Ten years last Passover I arranged to fly with him, to marry him, in defiance of the Law and thee."

A new pallor overspread the Reb's countenance, already ashen. He trembled and almost fell backwards.

"But thou didst not?" he whispered hoarsely.

"I did not, I know not why," she said sullenly; "else thou wouldst never have seen me again. It may be I respected thy religion, although thou didst not dream what was in my mind. But thy religion shall not keep me from this journey."

The Reb had hidden his face in his hands. His lips were moving; was it in grateful prayer, in self-reproach, or merely in nervous trembling? Hannah never knew. Presently the Reb's arms dropped, great tears rolled down towards the white beard. When he spoke, his tones were hushed as with awe.

"This man—tell me, my daughter, thou lovest him still?"

She shrugged her shoulders with a gesture of reckless despair.

"What does it matter? My life is but a shadow."

The Reb took her to his breast, though she remained stony to his touch, and laid his wet face against her burning cheeks.

"My child, my poor Hannah; I thought God had sent thee peace ten years ago; that He had rewarded thee for thy obedience to His Law."

She drew her face away from his.

"It was not His Law; it was a miserable juggling with texts. Thou alone interpretedst God's law thus. No one knew of the matter."

He could not argue; the breast against which he held her was shaken by a tempest of grief, which swept away all save human remorse, human love.

"My daughter," he sobbed, "I have ruined thy life!" After an agonized pause, he said: "Tell me, Hannah, is there nothing I can do to make atonement to thee?"

"Only one thing, father," she articulated chokingly; "forgive Levi."

There was a moment of solemn silence. Then the Reb spake.

"Tell thy mother to put on her things and take what she needs for the journey. Perchance we may be away for days."

They mingled their tears in sweet reconciliation. Presently, the Reb said:

"Go now to thy mother, and see also that the boy's room be made ready as of old. Perchance God will hear my prayer, and he will yet be restored to us."

A new peace fell upon Hannah's soul. "My sacrifice was not in vain after all," she thought, with a throb of happiness that was almost exultation.

But Levi never came back. The news of his death arrived on the eve of *Yom Kippur*, the Day of Atonement, in a letter to Esther who had been left in charge of the house.

"He died quietly at the end," Hannah wrote, "happy in the consciousness of father's forgiveness, and leaning trustfully upon his interposition with Heaven; but he had delirious moments, during which he raved painfully. The poor boy was in great fear of death, moaning prayers that he might be spared till after *Yom Kippur*, when he would be cleansed of sin, and babbling about serpents that would twine themselves round his arm and brow, like the phylacteries he had not worn. He made father repeat his 'Verse' to him over and over again, so that he might remember his name when the angel of the grave asked it; and borrowed father's phylacteries, the headpiece of which was much

ISRAEL ZANGWILL

too large for him with his shaven crown. When he had them on, and the *Talith* round him, he grew easier, and began murmuring the death-bed prayers with father. One of them runs: 'O may my death be an atonement for all the sins, iniquities and transgressions of which I have been guilty against Thee!' I trust it may be so indeed. It seems so hard for a young man full of life and high spirits to be cut down, while the wretched are left alive. Your name was often on his lips. I was glad to learn he thought so much of you. 'Be sure to give Esther my love,' he said almost with his last breath, 'and ask her to forgive me.' I know not if you have anything to forgive, or whether this was delirium. He looks quite calm now—but oh! so worn. They have closed the eyes. The beard he shocked father so by shaving off, has sprouted scrubbily during his illness. On the dead face it seems a mockery, like the *Talith* and phylacteries that have not been removed."

A phrase of Leonard James vibrated in Esther's ears: "If the chappies could see me!"

XVIII

Hopes and Dreams

The morning of the Great White Fast broke bleak and gray. Esther, alone in the house save for the servant, wandered from room to room in dull misery. The day before had been almost a feast-day in the Ghetto—everybody providing for the morrow. Esther had scarcely eaten anything. Nevertheless she was fasting, and would fast for over twenty-four hours, till the night fell. She knew not why. Her record was unbroken, and instinct resented a breach now. She had always fasted—even the Henry Goldsmiths fasted, and greater than the Henry Goldsmiths! Q.C.'s fasted, and peers, and prize-fighters and actors. And yet Esther, like many far more pious persons, did not think of her sins for a moment. She thought of everything but them—of the bereaved family in that strange provincial town; of her own family in that strange distant land. Well, she would soon be with them now. Her passage was booked—a steerage passage it was, not because she could not afford cabin fare, but from her morbid impulse to identify herself with poverty. The same impulse led her to choose a vessel in which a party of Jewish pauper immigrants was being shipped farther West. She thought also of Dutch Debby, with whom she had spent the previous evening; and of Raphael Leon, who had sent her, *via* the publishers, a letter which she could not trust herself to answer cruelly, and which she deemed it most prudent to leave unanswered. Uncertain of her powers of resistance, she scarcely ventured outside the house for fear of his stumbling across her. Happily, everyday diminished the chance of her whereabouts leaking out through some unsuspected channel.

About noon, her restlessness carried her into the streets. There was a festal solemnity about the air. Women and children, not at synagogue, showed themselves at the doors, pranked in their best. Indifferently pious young men sought relief from the ennui of the day-long service in lounging about for a breath of fresh air; some even strolled towards the Strand, and turned into the National Gallery, satisfied to reappear for the twilight service. On all sides came the fervent roar of prayer which indicated a synagogue or a *Chevrah*, the number of places of worship having been indefinitely increased to accommodate those who made their appearance for this occasion only.

Everywhere friends and neighbors were asking one another how they were bearing the fast, exhibiting their white tongues and generally comparing symptoms, the physical aspects of the Day of Atonement more or less completely diverting attention from the spiritual. Smelling-salts passed from hand to hand, and men explained to one another that, but for the deprivation of their cigars, they could endure *Yom Kippur* with complacency.

Esther passed the Ghetto school, within which free services were going on even in the playground, poor Russians and Poles, fanatically observant, fore-gathering with lax fishmongers and welshers; and without which hulking young men hovered uneasily, feeling too out of tune with religion to go in, too conscious of the terrors of the day to stay entirely away. From the interior came from sunrise to nightfall a throbbing thunder of supplication, now pealing in passionate outcry, now subsiding to a low rumble. The sounds of prayer that pervaded the Ghetto, and burst upon her at every turn, wrought upon Esther strangely; all her soul went out in sympathy with these yearning outbursts; she stopped every now and then to listen, as in those far-off days when the Sons of the Covenant drew her with their melancholy cadences.

At last, moved by an irresistible instinct, she crossed the threshold of a large *Chevrah* she had known in her girlhood, mounted the stairs and entered the female compartment without hostile challenge. The reek of many breaths and candles nearly drove her back, but she pressed forwards towards a remembered window, through a crowd of be-wigged women, shaking their bodies fervently to and fro.

This room had no connection with the men's; it was simply the room above part of theirs, and the declamations of the unseen cantor came but faintly through the flooring, though the clamor of the general masculine chorus kept the pious *au courant* with their husbands. When weather or the whims of the more important ladies permitted, the window at the end was opened; it gave upon a little balcony, below which the men's chamber projected considerably, having been built out into the back yard. When this window was opened simultaneously with the skylight in the men's synagogue, the fervid roulades of the cantor were as audible to the women as to their masters.

Esther had always affected the balcony: there the air was comparatively fresh, and on fine days there was a glimpse of blue sky, and a perspective of sunny red tiles, where brown birds fluttered and cats lounged and little episodes arose to temper the tedium of endless invocation: and farther off there was a back view of a nunnery, with visions of placid black-hooded faces at windows; and from the distance came a pleasant drone of monosyllabic spelling from fresh young voices, to relieve the ear from the monotony of long stretches of meaningless mumbling.

Here, lost in a sweet melancholy, Esther dreamed away the long gray day, only vaguely conscious of the stages of the service—morning dovetailing into afternoon service, and afternoon into evening; of the heavy-jowled woman behind her reciting a jargon-version of the Atonement liturgy to a devout coterie; of the prostrations full-length on the floor, and the series of impassioned sermons; of the interminably rhyming poems, and the acrostics with their recurring burdens shouted in devotional frenzy, voice rising above voice as in emulation, with special staccato phrases flung heavenwards; of the wailing confessions of communal sin, with their accompaniment of sobs and tears and howls and grimaces and clenchings of palms and beatings of the breast. She was lapped in a great ocean of sound that broke upon her consciousness like the waves upon a beach, now with a cooing murmur, now with a majestic crash, followed by a long receding moan. She lost herself in the roar, in its barren sensuousness, while the leaden sky grew duskier and the twilight crept on, and the awful hour drew nigh when God would seal what He had written, and the annual scrolls of destiny would be closed, immutable. She saw them looming mystically through the skylight, the swaying forms below, in their white grave-clothes, oscillating weirdly backwards and forwards, bowed as by a mighty wind.

Suddenly there fell a vast silence; even from without no sound came to break the awful stillness. It was as if all creation paused to hear a pregnant word.

"Hear, O Israel, the Lord our God, the Lord is One!" sang the cantor frenziedly.

And all the ghostly congregation answered with a great cry, closing their eyes and rocking frantically to and fro:

"Hear, O Israel, the Lord our God, the Lord is One!"

They seemed like a great army of the sheeted dead risen to testify to the Unity. The magnetic tremor that ran through the synagogue thrilled the lonely girl to the core; once again her dead self woke, her dead ancestors that would not be shaken off lived and moved in her. She

ISRAEL ZANGWILL

was sucked up into the great wave of passionate faith, and from her lips came, in rapturous surrender to an overmastering impulse, the half-hysterical protestation:

"Hear, O Israel, the Lord our God, the Lord is One!"

And then in the brief instant while the congregation, with ever-ascending rhapsody, blessed God till the climax came with the sevenfold declaration, "the Lord, He is God," the whole history of her strange, unhappy race flashed through her mind in a whirl of resistless emotion. She was overwhelmed by the thought of its sons in every corner of the earth proclaiming to the sombre twilight sky the belief for which its generations had lived and died—the Jews of Russia sobbing it forth in their pale of enclosure, the Jews of Morocco in their *mellah*, and of South Africa in their tents by the diamond mines: the Jews of the New World in great free cities, in Canadian backwoods, in South American savannahs: the Australian Jews on the sheep-farms and the gold-fields and in the mushroom cities; the Jews of Asia in their reeking quarters begirt by barbarian populations. The shadow of a large mysterious destiny seemed to hang over these poor superstitious zealots, whose lives she knew so well in all their everyday prose, and to invest the unconscious shunning sons of the Ghetto with something of tragic grandeur. The gray dusk palpitated with floating shapes of prophets and martyrs, scholars and sages and poets, full of a yearning love and pity, lifting hands of benediction. By what great high-roads and queer by-ways of history had they travelled hither, these wandering Jews, "sated with contempt," these shrewd eager fanatics, these sensual ascetics, these human paradoxes, adaptive to every environment, energizing in every field of activity, omnipresent like sonic great natural force, indestructible and almost inconvertible, surviving—with the incurable optimism that overlay all their poetic sadness—Babylon and Carthage, Greece and Rome; involuntarily financing the Crusades, outliving the Inquisition, illusive of all baits, unshaken by all persecutions—at once the greatest and meanest of races? Had the Jew come so far only to break down at last, sinking in morasses of modern doubt, and irresistibly dragging down with him the Christian and the Moslem; or was he yet fated to outlast them both, in continuous testimony to a hand moulding incomprehensibly the life of humanity? Would Israel develop into the sacred phalanx, the nobler brotherhood that Raphael Leon had dreamed of, or would the race that had first proclaimed—through Moses for the ancient world, through Spinoza for the modern—

become, in the larger, wilder dream of the Russian *idealist*, the main factor in

"One far-off divine event
To which the whole Creation moves"?

The roar dwindled to a solemn silence, as though in answer to her questionings. Then the ram's horn shrilled—a stern long-drawn-out note, that rose at last into a mighty peal of sacred jubilation. The Atonement was complete.

The crowd bore Esther downstairs and into the blank indifferent street. But the long exhausting fast, the fetid atmosphere, the strain upon her emotions, had overtaxed her beyond endurance. Up to now the frenzy of the service had sustained her, but as she stepped across the threshold on to the pavement she staggered and fell. One of the men pouring out from the lower synagogue caught her in his arms. It was Strelitski.

A GROUP OF THREE STOOD on the saloon deck of an outward-bound steamer. Raphael Leon was bidding farewell to the man he reverenced without discipleship, and the woman he loved without blindness.

"Look!" he said, pointing compassionately to the wretched throng of Jewish emigrants huddling on the lower deck and scattered about the gangway amid jostling sailors and stevedores and bales and coils of rope; the men in peaked or fur caps, the women with shawls and babies, some gazing upwards with lacklustre eyes, the majority brooding, despondent, apathetic. "How could either of you have borne the sights and smells of the steerage? You are a pair of visionaries. You could not have breathed a day in that society. Look!"

Strelitski looked at Esther instead; perhaps he was thinking he could have breathed anywhere in her society—nay, breathed even more freely in the steerage than in the cabin if he had sailed away without telling Raphael that he had found her.

"You forget a common impulse took us into such society on the Day of Atonement," he answered after a moment. "You forget we are both Children of the Ghetto."

"I can never forget that," said Raphael fervently, "else Esther would at this moment be lost amid the human flotsam and jetsam below, sailing away without you to protect her, without me to look forward to her return, without Addie's bouquet to assure her of a sister's love."

He took Esther's little hand once more It lingered confidingly in his own. There was no ring of betrothal upon it, nor would be, till Rachel Ansell in America, and Addie Leon in England, should have passed under the wedding canopy, and Raphael, whose breast pocket was bulging with a new meerschaum too sacred to smoke, should startle the West End with his eccentric choice, and confirm its impression of his insanity. The trio had said and resaid all they had to tell one another, all the reminders and the recommendations. They stood without speaking now, wrapped in that loving silence which is sweeter than speech.

The sun, which, had been shining intermittently, flooded the serried shipping with a burst of golden light, that coaxed the turbid waves to brightness, and cheered the wan emigrants, and made little children leap joyously in their mothers' arms. The knell of parting sounded insistent.

"Your allegory seems turning in your favor, Raphael," said Esther, with a sudden memory.

The pensive smile that made her face beautiful lit up the dark eyes.

"What allegory is that of Raphael's?" said Strelitski, reflecting her smile on his graver visage. "The long one in his prize poem?"

"No," said Raphael, catching the contagious smile. "It is our little secret."

Strelitski turned suddenly to look at the emigrants. The smile faded from his quivering mouth.

The last moment had come. Raphael stooped down towards the gentle softly-flushing face, which was raised unhesitatingly to meet his, and their lips met in a first kiss, diviner than it is given most mortals to know—a kiss, sad and sweet, troth and parting in one: *Ave et vale*—hail and farewell."

"Goodbye, Strelitski," said Raphael huskily. "Success to your dreams."

The idealist turned round with a start. His face was bright and resolute; the black curl streamed buoyantly on the breeze.

"Goodbye," he responded, with a giant's grip of the hand. "Success to your hopes."

Raphael darted away with his long stride. The sun was still bright, but for a moment everything seemed chill and dim to Esther Ansell's vision. With a sudden fit of nervous foreboding she stretched out her arms towards the vanishing figure of her lover. But she saw him once again in the tender, waving his handkerchief towards the throbbing vessel that glided with its freight of hopes and dreams across the great waters towards the New World.

A Note About the Author

Israel Zangwill (1864–1926) was a British writer. Born in London, Zangwill was raised in a family of Jewish immigrants from the Russian Empire. Alongside his brother Louis, a novelist, Zangwill was educated at the Jews' Free School in Spitalfields, where he studied secular and religious subjects. He excelled early on and was made a teacher in his teens before studying for his BA at the University of London. After graduating in 1884, Zangwill began publishing under various pseudonyms, finding editing work with *Ariel* and *The London Puck* to support himself. His first novel, *Children of the Ghetto: A Study of Peculiar People* (1892), was published to popular and critical acclaim, earning praise from prominent Victorian novelist George Gissing. His play *The Melting Pot* (1908) was a resounding success in the United States and was regarded by Theodore Roosevelt as "among the very strong and real influences upon (his) thought and (his) life." He spent his life in dedication to various political and social causes. An early Zionist and follower of Theodor Herzl, he later withdrew his support in favor of territorialism after he discovered that "Palestine proper has already its inhabitants." Despite distancing himself from the Zionist community, he continued to advocate on behalf of the Jewish people and to promote the ideals of feminism alongside his wife Edith Ayrton, a prominent author and activist.

A Note from the Publisher

Spanning many genres, from non-fiction essays to literature classics to children's books and lyric poetry, Mint Edition books showcase the master works of our time in a modern new package. The text is freshly typeset, is clean and easy to read, and features a new note about the author in each volume. Many books also include exclusive new introductory material. Every book boasts a striking new cover, which makes it as appropriate for collecting as it is for gift giving. Mint Edition books are only printed when a reader orders them, so natural resources are not wasted. We're proud that our books are never manufactured in excess and exist only in the exact quantity they need to be read and enjoyed.

bookfinity™

Discover more of your favorite classics with Bookfinity™.

- Track your reading with custom book lists.
- Get great book recommendations for your personalized Reader Type.
- Add reviews for your favorite books.
- AND MUCH MORE!

Visit **bookfinity.com** and take the fun Reader Type quiz to get started.

Enjoy our classic and modern companion pairings!

Printed in the USA
CPSIA information can be obtained
at www.ICGtesting.com
JSHW022333140824
68134JS00019B/1449

9 781513 216461